What the critics are saying:

4 Stars! "*Happy Birthday, Baby* offers a potpourri of sizzling hot romances. Each uniquely crafted story radiates with its own special blend of exotic nectar." ~*Suzie Housley, RT Bookclub*

"This is one hot...hot...hot book that is a must read no matter which genre you like."~*Jennifer Ray, The Road to Romance*

"*Happy Birthday, Baby* is a delight to read. The author has a way of bringing out the characters' personalities with little effort and little space. Lynn LaFleur is a gifted author."~*Penny, Love Romances*

"I highly recommend this anthology and I eagerly await Ms. LaFleur's next masterpiece."~*Michelle Naumann, Just Erotic Romance Reviews*

"*Happy Birthday, Baby*, by newcomer Lynn LeFleur, is a great first offering. All four of these stories cater to different readers' tastes, but all four are well written. Don't miss this great new author, she's sure to be one to watch."~*Enya Adrian, Romance Reviews Today*

HAPPY BIRTHDAY, BABY
An Ellora's Cave Publication, July 2004

Ellora's Cave Publishing, Inc.
PO Box 787
Hudson, OH 44236-0787

ISBN #1-84360-891-X

ISBN MS Reader (LIT) ISBN #1-84360-759-X
Other available formats (no ISBNs are assigned):
Adobe (PDF), Rocketbook (RB), Mobipocket (PRC) & HTML

Edited by *Raelene Gorlinsky*.
Cover art by *Darrell King*.

HAPPY BIRTHDAY, BABY

THE BIRTHDAY GIFT

IT'S IN THE CARDS

ONE THING TO GIVE

UNEXPECTED

Lynn LaFleur

Dedication

To the Reporter Bunch. Thanks for your support, and your great ideas!

THE BIRTHDAY GIFT

Chapter 1

He'd been thinking about it for almost a week. Part of him wanted to do anything to please the woman he adored. Another part of him...

Jake picked up his mug of cooling coffee and took a sip. He'd come outside shortly after sunrise to sit at the round glass table beneath the huge oak tree in his backyard. It was the perfect place to think, especially before his wife awoke. He liked being alone in the early mornings. It gave him the chance to plan the day on his horse ranch, think about what he needed to do first, and rehash what he'd accomplished the previous day.

It also gave him the chance to formulate his plan.

If he went through with this, he'd have to do it soon. Patrick had been here a week and would be leaving on Sunday. He was the only man Jake could ask to do this. They shared the same blood, and a closeness that Jake doubted many men experienced.

But would his cousin be willing?

He and Patrick had experienced some wild times together. Jake smiled to himself as he remembered one of the wildest—a four-couple orgy during their sophomore year in college. While they'd each had sex with different women that night, they hadn't shared a woman at the same time. Jake didn't know if Patrick would even *want* to do something like that.

He couldn't imagine Patrick *not* wanting to make love with a woman as beautiful and sexy as Amanda. With her curly blonde hair, huge blue eyes, and incredible body, he couldn't imagine *any* man not wanting to make love to Amanda.

The sound of the sliding glass door opening made Jake glance over his shoulder. He watched his cousin walk toward the table. Looking at Patrick made Jake feel as if he were looking in a mirror. Jake possessed the same dark brown hair, chocolate eyes, and muscular build as his cousin. Jake's and Patrick's fathers were identical twins, and they'd passed their looks down to their sons. Jake kept his hair shoulder-length while Patrick's hung halfway down his back; Jake had a mustache, while a mustache and neatly trimmed beard covered Patrick's lower face. Other than those two differences, someone who didn't know them well would have a hard time telling them apart.

"Morning," Patrick said as he sat across from Jake.

"Mornin'."

"You're up early."

"I like early."

"Early's the only time around here when a person can stand to be outside."

Jake chuckled. Patrick lived outside of Aspen and preferred the cool weather of Colorado to the hot North Texas summer. "The heat keeps the blood flowing smooth."

"The heat makes a person crazy. You and Amanda will never give me a second cousin 'cause you can't stand to get close to each other."

"Hey, don't push for a second cousin yet. We've only been married two years and we aren't ready to start a family. But getting close to Amanda is no problem. Air conditioning is a wonderful invention." He grinned. "And we have a big ceiling fan over our bed."

"I've noticed you have a ceiling fan in every room of the house."

"Sex isn't just for the bedroom."

"True." Patrick took a mug from the tray in the middle of the table and poured coffee from the thermos-style carafe. "You're a lucky man, cuz. Amanda's really gorgeous, as well as sweet. I'm sorry I haven't had the chance to meet her before now."

"Me too. I wish you could've been at our wedding. You were supposed to be my best man."

"My lungs had other ideas. It was a lousy time for a bout of bronchitis. But I'm here now, and I'm glad I finally got to meet Amanda. It's obvious by the way she looks at you how much she loves you. Although why, I'll never understand."

"She has good taste."

"Shit. Don't make me sick so early in the morning."

"You're just jealous."

"You're damn right I am. I'm a year older than you. I was supposed to find someone like Amanda first."

"No prospects?"

Patrick shook his head.

"Man, you own a ski resort. You have beautiful women around you all the time."

"Getting laid and having someone to love are two very different things."

"Yeah, they are. But don't ever give up on finding that special woman, Pat."

"Oh, I won't." He grinned. "If *you* conned a woman into falling for you, it'll be a cinch for *me* to do that." Patrick sipped his coffee. "Seriously, cuz, you're a lucky man. You have a wife who loves you. You're building a business doing something you love. You have a great place to live, even if it is too hot."

"It's only hot in the summer. The weather is great the rest of the year."

"But no snow."

"We have snow…every three or four years."

Leaning back in his chair, Patrick propped one ankle on the opposite knee. "We didn't have any snow when we were growing up in San Diego either, but I love it. I don't ever want to live any place that doesn't have snow."

"What if Ms. Right shows up at your lodge and lives in Florida?"

Patrick rubbed his chin. "Florida, huh? And she's definitely Ms. Right?"

"Definitely," Jake said with a grin.

"No problem. I'll just use all my considerable charm and convince her to stay in Colorado." He returned Jake's grin and took another sip of coffee. "So, what's on your agenda today?"

"I have to pick up some supplies in town and run a couple of errands this afternoon. There's a guy coming over about ten who's interested in Texas Thunder. Hopefully, he'll bring his checkbook."

"First sale?"

Jake nodded. "The first of many, I hope."

Patrick set his mug on the table. "Are things tight for you? I can lend you some money if you—"

"No," Jake said firmly.

Patrick frowned. "Don't pull that macho shit on me, cuz. It doesn't mean you're a failure just because you need some help until things get better."

"I don't..." Jake stopped and ran his hand through his hair. He didn't want to hurt Patrick's feelings, but his pride wouldn't let his cousin bail him out of a jam. His ego already suffered from having to live off Amanda's commissions instead of being the major breadwinner. "Thanks for the offer, but we're okay. Amanda's done pretty good with commissions. In fact, she's showing a house today that should be a sure thing, according to her. Her commission on it will be close to thirty thousand."

Patrick released a long whistle. "For one house? Not bad."

"Nope, not bad at all."

"If it falls through or you change your mind—"

"You'll be the first to know, I promise."

Patrick refilled his mug and took a sip of the steaming coffee. "Will any of your errands take you close to a store where I can buy a birthday gift for Amanda?"

Jake stopped in the act of picking up his mug. "Birthday gift?"

"I know Friday's her birthday. She's been great to me and I'd like to get her a gift." He snapped his fingers. "I know. I could get her something to add to her Garfield collection. Or is that collection special to the two of you?"

"It's special, but not exclusively ours. Her friends add to it all the time, and her mom always sends her something at Christmas." Jake cleared his throat. "Actually, I do have a gift in mind that you can give her."

"What is it?"

Beating around the bush had never been Jake's way, especially with Patrick. He figured the best way to tell his cousin would be to simply say it. "Sex."

Patrick almost choked on the coffee he'd just sipped. He stared at Jake for a moment, his eyes wide. Slowly, he lowered his mug back to the table. "You want to run that by me again?"

"I want you to be part of a threesome."

"You're joking, right?" He shifted in his chair and laughed without the least bit of humor. "Tell me you're joking."

12

"I'm absolutely serious." Jake leaned forward and rested his folded arms on the table. "A couple of months ago, Amanda and I were talking about sexual fantasies...you know, just kidding around with each other after sex. She told me her fantasy is to be with two guys at once. I want to give her that for her birthday."

"Wait a minute, wait a minute." Patrick held up one hand. "You want me to fuck your *wife*?"

"Honestly? No. I don't want another man to ever touch her. She's the love of my life, my *whole* life. I like knowing I'm the only man in her bed. But this is something she wants, so I want to give it to her." He looked down at the table for a moment before gazing at his cousin. "You're the only guy I could ask to do this, Pat, the only guy I would *trust* to do this. We may only be cousins, but we're as close as brothers, even if we don't get the chance anymore to see each other but every few years. I'd never let another man touch my wife."

"Shit." Patrick closed his eyes and rubbed his forehead. "You've blown me away, Jake. I never expected anything like this."

"We've done some pretty wild things, Pat."

Patrick looked at Jake again. "Yeah, we have, but that was a long time ago, and we've never done a threesome. And you've never been married. Plus I just met her a week ago. Hell, man, she may not want me anywhere near her."

"She likes you, Pat, and she feels comfortable with you. I couldn't even suggest this if I didn't believe Amanda would be okay with it." A sudden thought occurred to Jake, something that he hadn't previously considered. "Do you have some kind of moral hang-up about having sex with a married woman?"

"No, nothing like that. I'm certainly no saint when it comes to sex. I just never expected something like this from *you*. You're crazy about Amanda."

"Yes, I am, which is why I'm asking you to help me fulfill her fantasy. I want to make her happy."

Jake waited while Patrick once again picked up his coffee mug and took a sip. He knew that look in his cousin's eyes...that look that said Patrick was thinking, studying the situation from every angle. It was a trait that had helped make Patrick's ski lodge a huge success.

"Let me get all this straight," Patrick said. "I've been here a week now. You haven't bothered to introduce me to any women, so you know I haven't been laid since I've been here. With all the expansion work on the lodge and the crazy hours I've been keeping, I haven't exactly been burning up the sheets at home lately either. Now you're asking me if I want to have sex with a beautiful, sexy, willing woman." He paused. "She *is* willing, isn't she?"

"She will be once we start on her."

"Damn, man," Patrick said with a groan, "I'm getting a hard-on."

Jake grinned. "So, you'll do it?"

Patrick leaned forward in his chair. "Is this wild, uninhibited, anything-we-want-to-do sex?"

"It's anything-*she*-wants-to-do sex, which will probably be pretty wild and uninhibited."

"Is anything taboo? Is there something she doesn't like?"

"If there is, I haven't found it yet."

Patrick once more leaned back in his chair. "When do we do this?"

"Friday evening. I have everything planned…"

Chapter 2

Amanda decided closing a deal that would net her a large commission was a wonderful way to spend her birthday.

The house and thirty acres had been on the market for three years. It had been vacant as long as she could remember. Amanda had shown it to several clients, but no one had wanted to buy it. The grounds were an overgrown jungle and the house in need of major repairs. Despite the outward appearance, the Hudsons had taken one look and fallen in love with the place. They believed they could turn it into a beautiful and profitable bed and breakfast.

Stepping inside her front door, Amanda slipped off her high heels and sighed from relief. She believed she should look professional when showing a house, which meant a business suit and heels. The summer heat let her replace her usual business suit with a sleeveless shift, but she hadn't been able to talk herself into replacing the heels with sandals.

A drink topped her list right now before she did anything else. Iced tea would hit the spot after being outside for the last two hours. Showing a house in the 96-degree heat wasn't her favorite thing to do, but the commission on the sale to the Hudsons would make every drop of sweat and discomfort worth it.

She really needed that commission.

Amanda hadn't realized how expensive running a ranch would be when Jake told her he wanted to raise horses. He'd had a tidy sum in the bank from an inheritance when they married, but that had quickly diminished to a few thousand dollars. Even with Jake doing as much of the work as he possibly could, he still had to pay for help along with the feed, vet bills, and other expenses. Their only income came from Amanda's real estate commissions. While those had been steady enough so she and Jake lived comfortably, the commission from the Winslow mansion sale meant their household expenses would be covered for several months.

Hopefully, Jake would sell a horse sometime during those months.

She'd talked to Jake about buying a new computer when she closed the sale on the Winslow mansion. She felt guilty for even considering such an expense when she should save every dollar possible, yet she wanted to log on to the computer sites right now and start comparing prices. Jake had told her to go for it, that she deserved a new one after having her old computer for almost five years. He'd said to buy the best, with whatever options she wanted.

She knew Jake would agree to whatever she wanted to buy. They'd been married for two years and together as a couple for four. In those four years, he'd shown his generosity in so many ways. A single pink rose appeared on her pillow several times a month. Whenever a book by one of her favorite authors was released, she would find it on her nightstand. Her favorite candy would show up in her briefcase. She'd open her desk drawer and find a figurine of Garfield to add to her collection.

So many little things, but they meant more to her than diamonds.

He didn't buy her a birthday present for they'd agreed not to exchange gifts on their birthdays, but he knew he'd be dead meat if he didn't give her a card.

This year, he'd given her more than a card. He'd woken her this morning with his tongue between her thighs.

Amanda laid her briefcase and car keys on the kitchen counter. Remembering the way Jake had loved her with his mouth made her shiver, despite the hot summer day. After four years together, Jake knew exactly where to touch her, and how, to give her the ultimate pleasure. She loved the way he used long, gentle licks from her anus to her clitoris to arouse her. Once her desire started to build, he'd concentrate more on her clitoris—licking it, sucking it, pulling it between his lips. He'd dip his tongue inside her pussy, over and over, then move back to her clitoris for more of his expert attention. It would take only moments for a heart-pounding, breath-stealing orgasm to race through her body.

What he did with his tongue was probably illegal in fourteen states.

This morning had been no exception. Jake had raised her desire to fever-pitch with his tongue until her body shook from her climax. She'd barely had the chance to catch her breath before Jake turned her to her side. He'd snuggled up behind her, lifted her leg, and pushed his cock deep inside her. He'd moved slowly while caressing her breasts.

"Touch yourself," he'd whispered in her ear.

His warm breath sent goose bumps scattering across her skin. Jake loved to watch her pleasure herself. Wanting to please him, as well as herself again, she began rubbing her clitoris in time to his thrusts. Jake's breathing became harsher, his thrusts harder. Another orgasm built and Amanda surrendered to it as she felt Jake shudder with his own release.

How she adored making love with her husband.

Amanda sighed happily. *I'm married to a generous, sensitive, sexy, handsome hunk who loves me as much as I love him. How did I get to be so lucky?*

She glanced out the kitchen window as she reached to open the cabinet door to get a glass. She stopped with her hand in mid-air when she saw Jake and Patrick huddled together beneath an oak tree in the backyard.

Amanda smiled. Jake was enjoying Patrick's visit so much. Even though she and Jake had been together several years, she'd never had the opportunity to meet Patrick. Starting a horse ranch had consumed Jake for the last two years. Before that, Patrick had been busy building his ski lodge. He'd been recuperating from bronchitis when they got married, so he missed their wedding ceremony. The cousins had stayed in contact by telephone and e-mail, but since they lived in different states, this was the first time they'd seen each other in five years.

She continued to watch them. Her smile faded and she frowned slightly. They were up to something besides catching up on each other's lives. They'd been conspiring with each other for the last two days. Amanda would catch them whispering, which would stop immediately as soon as she got close enough to hear them. Sneaking up on them hadn't been possible, and she'd tried it several times. Jake had incredible hearing, the bum.

She wondered if their plotting had something to do with her birthday. Maybe they planned to surprise her with a special dinner. Not having to cook on her birthday would be a very nice gift.

Watching them, she looked for any kind of clue that would tell her what they were saying. Even if she couldn't figure out what they were up to, she enjoyed simply looking at them. Her husband was so handsome, and Patrick could pass for his brother. They had the same build, the same hair color, the same eyes, the same way of moving...

She wondered if they were the same in bed.

Embarrassed by her thoughts, Amanda looked away from the tempting vision out the window. She had no right to fantasize in any way about Patrick. She'd known him for only a few days, and Jake kept her completely satisfied sexually. If she could personally pick out every trait a lover should have, Jake would be the end result.

Still…

Thoughts of having both of them at the same time had occupied her mind since Patrick's arrival. The only explanation Amanda had was the fact that Patrick looked so much like Jake. He was an inch or two taller and a bit huskier, but the two favored each other so much, it was almost scary.

She felt guilty fantasizing about a man other than her husband, yet she couldn't help letting those fantasies run rampant through her mind. She imagined having two Jakes who would do whatever she wanted, however she wanted it. Two Jakes could lick and suck her nipples at the same time. Or one could suck on her nipples while the other one licked her clitoris. Or maybe one could slide his cock inside her while the other one circled her anus with his tongue. She loved it when Jake licked her there. It seemed almost…taboo, but felt so good.

Jake's mustache felt wonderful on her skin. Patrick's full beard would probably feel even better…

Desire coursed through her body and Amanda closed her eyes as she shivered again. *Get your mind off of sex and back to business. You have to finish the Hudsons' contract before they call.*

She took one more glance outside, but Jake and Patrick were gone. She heard Jake's pickup start, then the door to the mud room open and close. A moment later, her husband came in the back door.

"Hi," he said with a smile.

"Hi."

He walked over to her, tilted up her chin, and dropped a soft kiss on her lips. "How did it go with the Hudsons?"

"I'm going to start computer shopping tomorrow."

Jake looped his arms around her waist. "That's great. Congratulations."

"Thanks. I tried not to get my hopes up too much, but I really wanted this sale. That monstrosity of a house has been on the market for three years."

"And you love that huge commission."

Amanda grinned. "And I love that huge commission."

"Do you know what they plan to do with the place?"

"They want to turn it into a bed and breakfast-slash-resort, complete with fishing, swimming, tennis, golf course…the works. That's going to take a lot of time and a lot of money, but they apparently have plenty of both. And we could use something like that in our area. It'll bring in more tourists, which will lead to more people settling here, which will lead to—"

"More commissions for you," Jake said with a grin.

She smiled. "Yeah. Do I sound money hungry?"

"Not a bit. You sound like a successful businesswoman and I'm very proud of you."

His words warmed her heart. Jake's approval was so important to her. As long as she had him, nothing else mattered.

Wanting to be closer to him, she touched his chest. She let her palms glide over the soft cotton of his T-shirt, liking the contrast of the smooth material over his solid muscles. Working with horses had definitely given him a killer body. "I was about to fix me a glass of iced tea. Want one?"

"In a minute." He tightened his arms around her waist. "You aren't the only one around here with good news today. George Mayo bought Texas Thunder."

With a squeal of delight, Amanda threw her arms around Jake's neck and hugged him tightly. "That's wonderful!"

"Yeah, I think so too."

The feel of Jake's firm chest against her breasts brought back all her desire from a few moments ago. Trying to be a good girl and listen to what her husband had to say instead of jerking his clothes off, Amanda pulled back and looked at Jake's face. "Did he agree to your price?"

"He didn't even bat an eyelash when I told him what I wanted, which tells me my price was probably too low. But that's okay. I'm happy to finally bring some money into the house."

Amanda had suspected Jake wasn't happy about not selling any horses, but this was the first time he'd actually said anything to her. "We've done fine, Jake."

"No thanks to me."

"It takes time to build up a clientele for the horses. You expected that."

"Yeah, but I didn't think it'd take *this* long. I've practically wiped out our savings."

"*You've* done no such thing. We're a partnership, remember?"

"Yeah, but—"

Amanda touched his lips to stop his argument before he could start it. She refused to let him feel guilty about his business getting a slow start. "No 'buts' allowed. Whatever we do, we do together."

Jake moved her hand and held it tightly in his own. "You've brought in a steady income, Amanda. I haven't."

"Do you think I love you any less for it?"

"No, of course not."

"Then what's the problem? We both knew it would take time to build your business. Things have been tight sometimes, but we've done fine." She raised his hand to her mouth and kissed his palm. "I wouldn't change one thing about our time together, Jake. *Not one.* It's been more wonderful than I ever imagined."

Jake softly caressed her lips with his thumb. "I'm so lucky to have you." Leaning back against the counter, he pulled Amanda between his spread legs. His groin nestled snugly between her hips. "How did a plain, ordinary guy like me get you to fall in love with me?"

"Oh, I don't know," Amanda said as she wrapped her arms around his neck. "I guess you were just blessed."

"That must be it." He slid his hands from her underarms to her hips and back again. "So, do you have any ideas how I could keep on being blessed?"

A devilish gleam lit his eyes. Amanda knew from that gleam and the feel of his cock hardening against her exactly how "blessed" he wanted to get. That was fine with her. She would take any chance possible to make love with her husband. "I might. Do *you* have any ideas?"

"Oh, I'm sure I could think of something we'd both enjoy."

She had no doubt of that. Jake's imagination and spontaneity kept their sex life hot and spicy. He often surprised her in the kitchen, or the laundry room, or the barn, with passionate kisses and lusty lovemaking. Just the thought of it made her clitoris throb. "Where's Patrick?"

"I sent him to the store for steaks. I'm going to barbecue tonight."

"So he'll be gone...how long?"

Jake moved his hands from her hips to her buttocks. "Long enough," he said before covering her lips with his own.

Amanda groaned deep in her throat when Jake's tongue slipped past her lips. One kiss from this man was all it took for dampness to form between her thighs. While she hadn't had a vast number of lovers before her marriage, none of them had affected her as strongly as Jake. Never had she wanted a man as much as she wanted Jake. She arched into him, moving her hips from side to side, getting as close as possible while still wearing clothes. His hands kneaded her buttocks while his tongue stroked, caressed, tempted her.

She was more than willing to do whatever he wanted.

Her willingness had to be apparent to Jake, so it surprised her when he stopped their kiss. Still in the throes of passion, she struggled to open her eyes as he cupped her face in his hands. "Do you have any idea how much I love you?" he whispered.

His expression was so fierce and serious, Amanda didn't know what to say for a moment. "Of course I know you love me. I love you, too."

"I'd do anything for you, do you know that?"

"Yes, I know that. I'd do anything for you, too. Jake, what—"

"I just want you to know exactly how I feel about you, how much you mean to me."

"I have no doubts about how much I mean to you. Now cut out all this talk and kiss me again."

He obeyed her immediately. Amanda moaned softly when Jake's tongue slipped past her lips again. Parting her lips wider, she drew his tongue deeply into her mouth and sucked on it. Her action drew a groan from Jake.

"God, I love kissing you," he whispered.

She didn't get the chance to respond for he kissed her again before moving his mouth to her throat. Amanda tilted her head when Jake lightly bit her neck. A single lick of his tongue soothed the tender nip, then he covered her lips with his again.

Cool air brushed against the back of her legs and slowly climbed upward. Amanda felt Jake's warm, calloused palms cup her buttocks. Through the fog of desire clouding her brain, she realized he had pulled her dress up to her waist.

"Mmm, I love it when you wear these tiny little thongs."

"I know you do. That's why I wear them."

His fingers slid into the cleft between her buttocks. "Are you wet?"

"You know I am."

"Maybe I'd better find out for sure. Maybe I should bend you over the table and — "

The back door opened. Amanda glanced to her left as Patrick stepped inside.

Her first instinct was to pull away from Jake and jerk down her dress. The hot look in Patrick's eyes stopped her. She watched his gaze travel to her buttocks and linger there for a long moment before he looked at her face.

"Sorry," Patrick said. "I forgot my wallet."

The sound of his voice shattered Amanda's trance. She tugged down her dress while warmth climbed into her cheeks...partly from embarrassment, and partly from the heat still in Patrick's eyes.

"No problem," Jake said. "I was just telling Amanda about the horse sale."

Amanda whipped her head toward Jake. He didn't sound the least bit concerned that Patrick had seen her bare bottom. In fact, with the way he was pressing his still-hard cock against her, it appeared he'd actually *liked* it.

"Horse sale, huh?" Patrick asked with a grin. "Looks to me like you two were making out."

"That too. I love making out with my wife."

"If I had a wife like Amanda, I'd love making out with her, too."

She didn't understand this conversation, but she'd had enough. She was embarrassed...and still incredibly aroused. "Patrick, go get your wallet."

He nodded once, then turned and left the room. Jake took Amanda in his arms again. "Now, where were we?" he asked before kissing her neck.

"Do you want to explain that?"

"Explain what?"

"What just happened here. Patrick walked in on us with my butt hanging out, and you did nothing."

Jake looked at her. "What was I supposed to do?"

"Cover me up!"

"Amanda, he got a two-second glimpse of your butt. Why are you so upset about it?"

"Doesn't it bother you that your cousin *saw* me?"

"Does it bother *you* that my cousin saw you? You told me not two months ago that your fantasy is to be with two guys at once."

Amanda knew that little bare-all session would come back to haunt her. "Well, yeah, I said that, but it's just a fantasy. I don't expect it to ever happen. We have a wonderful sex life."

He cupped her face in his hands. "We have an *amazing* sex life, but is there anything else you want?"

Amanda didn't answer his question for her cellular phone rang from her purse. She did all her real estate business on her cellular phone, so she couldn't ignore it. "I have to get that."

"I know you do." He tilted her face up and kissed her lips softly. "I'll go to the store with Pat and make sure he buys sirloin and not chuck."

Amanda watched him leave the room. His previous actions confused her. He hadn't been the least bit concerned that Patrick had walked in on them. And she didn't understand him bringing up their conversation about her fantasy. They'd had that discussion two months ago.

Unless he planned to...

No, of course not. Jake would never share her with another man, despite her silly fantasy. Not even his cousin.

The phone's third ring made her scramble for her purse. *Business now, sex later, Amanda.*

Chapter 3

"You did a great job on those steaks, cuz," Patrick said as he wiped his mouth with a napkin.

"Thanks. Cooking on the grill I can do, but I'm not so good with a regular stove."

"I don't mind that you aren't a great cook," Amanda said, "since you do other things *so* well." She bobbled her eyebrows twice before dropping a kiss on his lips.

Patrick chuckled. "I think we're getting into that T.M.I. territory."

"Sorry." Amanda grinned, then stood and began gathering up their plates. "Since you cooked, I get to clean."

"You do not." Jake also stood and took the stack of plates from Amanda. "It's still your birthday and you aren't allowed to do anything that might be considered housework. Pat and I will clean up. Why don't you go ahead and take your bath?"

"I'd like that." She touched his face, letting her fingers glide over his cheek. "Will you come up and wash my back?"

The invitation in that simple question made his cock swell and almost tempted him to say yes. Jake frequently joined Amanda in their garden tub. He loved to wash her back...and whatever else she wanted washed. But not tonight. Tonight, he had other plans for her. "I'm going to clean up the kitchen while you bathe. Take a nice long one and enjoy yourself. When you're through, come back down and we'll have your birthday cake."

Her eyes lit up like a child's at Christmas, erasing all traces of the desire he'd seen there a moment ago. "Birthday cake? What kind?"

"Now, what kind do you think?"

"Chocolate?"

"Of course."

Amanda grinned. "I'll hurry."

Jake watched Amanda leave the dining room. She was such a delight to be with, and not just sexually, although he had no complaints in that department. Simply being with her made him happy.

Patrick picked up the glasses and silverware from the table. "Need some help with this stuff?" he asked, following Jake into the kitchen.

"Nah. I'm just gonna rinse them off and stick them in the dishwasher. Amanda doesn't run it until there's a full load, but she hates to see dirty dishes in the sink." He set the plates on the counter next to the sink. "Is everything ready?"

"Everything you asked for. It's all in the closet under the stairs." Patrick placed the glasses next to the plates on the counter. "I'll bring the rest of the stuff from the dining room, then I'm gonna take a quick shower."

"Go ahead. I'll grab one after I finish here."

Patrick turned as if to leave the kitchen, then stopped and faced Jake again. "Do you think she suspects anything? I mean, I almost blew it today when I came in and caught you two." He grinned. "By the way, she has a great ass."

Jake chuckled. "Yes, she does."

Patrick quickly sobered again. "You know, we haven't seen each other in a long time since we've both been busy building our careers. Even though I haven't seen you in five years, I still consider you my best friend. I don't want anything to mess that up, Jake. If you think Amanda and me having sex will mess up you and me, maybe you should find someone else to do this."

"I feel the same way, man. I'm sorry we let so much time pass without getting together, but we're still solid. That isn't going to change. And it's you or no one as far as Amanda is concerned. I won't let another man touch my wife, no matter how much I want to please her."

"So you're really okay with this? As long as *you're* sure, *I'm* certainly willing. Celibacy sucks."

"Yeah, I'm really okay with this." He motioned toward the door. "Go take your shower so I can take mine."

After Patrick left the room, Jake returned to his clean-up duty. As he rinsed the dishes and loaded the dishwasher, he went over the conversation he'd just had with his cousin. Yes, he was okay with this, more than he thought he would be. Ever since Patrick had walked in on them this afternoon, Jake had been fantasizing about this evening. He imagined all the things the two of them would do to Amanda…and he imagined the things he'd watch Patrick do to her.

He never thought this would happen. He loved the fact that he and Amanda were so wrapped up in each other, no one else could ever come between them. But he wanted to see how she'd react to another man touching her, kissing her, sliding his cock inside that beautiful, wet pussy…

He had to be honest with himself and admit the idea of watching another man fuck his wife was arousing as hell.

Jake wiped off the cabinet and draped the dishcloth over the faucet. Amanda would be surprised at first, perhaps embarrassed, but also very turned on. That's exactly what he wanted. This birthday would be one she wouldn't soon forget.

He heard the water in the main bathroom stop, so Patrick must be through with his shower. Glancing at the clock on the stove, he saw that Amanda had been in the bathtub for about fifteen minutes. She loved to soak until the water started to cool, so he figured he had at least ten more minutes to grab his shower before she came downstairs.

* * * * *

Amanda tugged down her T-shirt over the waistband of her shorts as she descended the back stairs into the kitchen. She expected to find Jake and Patrick there, getting her cake ready to serve. The kitchen was empty.

"Jake?"

No answer. Amanda saw no sign of a cake anywhere. Maybe Jake had decided to serve it in the dining room.

Masculine laughter greeted her as she stepped through the kitchen doorway. She followed the laughter to the living room. She was about to ask about her cake, but stopped in her tracks when she saw the two men sitting on the couch. Both Jake and Patrick wore denim cut-offs…nothing else.

Amanda had never seen Patrick in only cut-offs. She'd caught a glimpse of him without a shirt when he was going into the bathroom, but only once. This was the first time she'd seen him wearing so little.

Her heart began to thud in her chest.

Stop it, Amanda! Patrick is gorgeous, but he's not your husband.

She took another step into the room. The soft light from the lamps on either end of the couch reflected off their hair. It was damp, as if they'd both recently showered. That surprised her, since Jake hadn't used their bathroom to shower.

They were obviously up to something.

"Hey, babe," Jake said with a smile. "C'mere and we'll have some cake."

Amanda glanced at the coffee table. A large chocolate cake sat in the center, with a large knife, saucers, and forks next to it. She returned her gaze to the two barely clothed men. Both had tan chests and legs sprinkled with dark hair. Both had broad shoulders and muscled arms. She let her gaze wander farther south. Both filled out the crotch of those cut-offs very nicely.

Amanda could sit either on the couch between them and be surrounded by all that testosterone, or on the floor across the coffee table from them.

She chose the couch.

Once she was seated, Jake picked up the knife and held it over the cake. "How much?" he asked.

Amanda arched one eyebrow. "It's chocolate and you have to ask?"

"Sorry. I lost my head there for a moment." He proceeded to cut a generous slice for her. "How's that?"

"Perfect."

After serving Amanda, Jake looked at his cousin. "How much, Pat?"

"I can't let Amanda eat more than me."

Jake's damp hair still puzzled her. She touched it as he cut Patrick's cake. "Did you take a shower?"

He glanced at her before returning to his task. "Yeah."

She ran her fingers through the damp strands, releasing the scent of shampoo and man. "You didn't shower in our bathroom."

"I didn't want to bother you." Jake placed the cake slice on a saucer and handed it to Patrick.

It sounded like the type of considerate thing Jake would do, but Amanda was still suspicious. Jake usually took his shower right before they went to bed. "You wouldn't have bothered me."

"Great cake," Patrick said.

"Yeah, it is," Jake said after taking a bite of his own slice. "Mrs. Scheerer is a great cook."

Well, that's an obvious change of subject. Amanda thought about questioning Jake further, then mentally shrugged and took a bite of cake instead. So he'd showered early. It wasn't the first time he'd done that, and it certainly didn't mean anything.

Amanda settled back on the couch to have her cake while she listened to the two cousins talk about Patrick's ski resort. She'd often thought about learning to ski. She loved the snow, and she imagined the Colorado mountains would be breathtaking. She and Jake had taken several weekend trips to different places in Texas and states to the east, but never to the west. Jake had mentioned taking her to San Diego to show her where he'd grown up, yet they'd never managed to fit it into their schedules.

Having Patrick for a ski instructor would be fun. And she'd love to have Jake all to herself in a hot tub after a day outside in the cold. She glanced at Patrick. Maybe she could have *both* of them in the hot tub...

She jumped slightly when Jake touched her knee. "You're awfully quiet," he said.

Warmth spread into her cheeks when she realized where her thoughts had been. Having such a lusty lover for a husband meant sex was a big part of her life, but she couldn't remember a time when it had been on her mind so much. She'd never had another handsome man living in her house for several days, either. She glanced at Patrick again. It was all his fault. He was so good-looking, and so close, and her fantasy kept popping into her head...

Clearing her throat, Amanda nodded toward her empty saucer. "I was busy."

"I see that. Would you like another piece?"

"I don't have room for it." She leaned forward to set her saucer on the table next to Jake's empty one. "But there's always tomorrow."

"True." She felt his hand encircle her nape. "You've had your bath and chocolate. The only thing that's left is a massage."

Amanda loved getting a massage from Jake, but it would have to wait until they were alone in their bedroom. What started out as therapeutic usually ended up as a prelude to lovemaking. "That sounds...mmm." She moaned when Jake pressed his thumb into her shoulder. "Oh, that's nice."

"Lean back."

Not able to resist, Amanda did as Jake suggested. Her eyes drifted closed when his fingers began rubbing her shoulders and neck. "Oh, that's nice."

"You said that already."

"It's worth repeating."

"Too bad I can't do a foot massage at the same time, huh?" Jake said next to her ear.

The only thing better than Jake's back massage was his foot massage. "Yeah, having both at once would be wonderful."

"Hey, I can help with that," Patrick said.

Amanda's eyes popped open.

"I give a great foot massage." Patrick patted his thigh. "Put your feet right here."

She couldn't do that, not with the sexy fantasies she'd been having lately. Besides, a foot massage seemed…personal.

Patrick made the decision for her. Slipping his arm underneath her calves, he lifted her legs until her heels rested on his thigh. Caught off-balance, the sudden move made her lean farther back so she was practically in Jake's lap. She chuckled nervously from the awkward position. "Hey, guys, I don't think this will…" She stopped when Patrick pressed his thumb into the arch of her right foot. It felt so good, she almost groaned aloud.

"You don't think this will what?" Jake asked.

"Never mind."

She could feel Jake's rumble of laughter against her back. "So, you like all this attention, huh?"

"What's not to like?" She drew in a sharp breath when Patrick touched a sore spot on her instep.

"Sorry," he said. "Did I hurt you?"

"No. It's just a little sore. Too much time in high heels."

"It would be easier with some lotion or oil."

"And if you were lying down," Jake said.

Lying down was not an option…not when two gorgeous, practically naked men were talking about using oil on her skin. Amanda had willpower, but she was only human. "I'm fine."

"This position can't be comfortable for you, babe. Pat, go get a quilt and we'll move this to the floor."

The floor. Okay, she could handle the floor. If Jake had said "bedroom," she would've put an end to this right now.

But having her back and feet massaged at the same time sounded so tempting...

Patrick came back a moment later carrying one of her older quilts and a white plastic bottle. He set the bottle on the coffee table before spreading out the quilt on the floor. Amanda wondered how he'd found the quilt so quickly in the upstairs linen closet, and where he'd gotten that bottle.

A tiny bit of suspicion began to grow inside her head.

Jake squeezed her shoulders. "Lie down, babe."

Amanda watched Patrick drop to his knees at one end of the quilt before she rose from the couch and walked the short distance around the coffee table. She wasn't sure if she should do this. A massage on her back and feet would feel wonderful, but she knew her own body...and how she reacted when Jake touched her. She loved her husband and desired him fiercely. It wouldn't take but a few moments of his hands on her before she'd be breathing heavy and trying not to moan. If she embarrassed herself in front of Patrick, she'd never be able to face him again.

Jake circled the coffee table and also dropped to his knees at the opposite end of the quilt from Patrick. He patted the floor in front of him. "C'mere."

Get your mind out of the gutter. This is your husband and his cousin doing something nice for your birthday. This has absolutely nothing to do with sex and you have no reason to be suspicious.

The pep talk she gave herself helped Amanda relax. She stretched out on the quilt, resting her head on her folded arms.

"Hey, Pat, grab one of those thick pillows off the couch. Amanda needs one under her stomach since her tits are so big."

Amanda raised her head and glared at her husband. "Jake!"

"Well, it's true. You always put a pillow under your stomach."

"You don't have to broadcast that fact to Patrick."

"You don't think he knows you have big tits? He isn't blind."

The teasing gleam in Jake's eyes made Amanda shake her head. "Good grief," she muttered. She pulled the pillow that Patrick tossed on the floor under her stomach and rearranged herself to a comfortable position. "After a comment like that, I'd better get a damned good massage."

"Yes, ma'am."

Jake touched her shoulders again. A moment later, she felt Patrick's hands on her left foot. His fingers slid easily over her skin, so he must be using the liquid in that white bottle. Amanda sighed contentedly and closed her eyes. Heaven couldn't possibly be any better than this.

Jake pressed the heels of his hands into her shoulders, her upper back, her middle back. Amanda relaxed more with every stroke...until she felt his hands on her bare back, above the waistband of her shorts. She opened her eyes a crack. She had a perfect close-up view of Jake's crotch...and the large bulge there.

Obviously, she wasn't the only one affected by her massage.

Amanda's mouth watered with the desire to unzip Jake's shorts and lick him from the head of his cock to his balls. She loved taking him in her mouth, feeling him swell as his desire grew. If Patrick wasn't here...

Realizing Patrick *was* here made her concentrate again on his touch. His hands were no longer massaging her feet, but were sliding up and down the backs of her legs in a slow caress.

Heat began to build low in Amanda's tummy.

"Raise up a little, babe."

Not thinking anything of his request, Amanda raised her torso a few inches off the floor. Jake pulled her T-shirt up to her shoulder blades. When she felt her bra strap tighten as if he planned to unsnap it, she quickly scrambled up to her knees.

"Okay, what's going on here?"

Jake glanced at his cousin. Amanda quickly swung her gaze to Patrick and back to Jake. The two men exchanged a look...a look of conspiracy. "We're giving you a massage," Jake said. "Isn't that what you wanted?"

"This is more than just a massage, Jake. Patrick was nowhere near my feet and you were about to unsnap my bra. I want to know what you're doing."

Jake remained quiet a moment, then he cradled her face in his hands and kissed her tenderly. "Fulfilling your fantasy."

Chapter 4

Jake watched Amanda's eyes widen. She bit her bottom lip, and glanced over her shoulder at Patrick. A pink blush spread across her cheeks. He saw her throat work as she swallowed.

She looked back at him. Her voice was soft and breathless when she spoke. "You're... I mean, I didn't... Jake, I never asked you to do this."

"I know you didn't. It's your birthday gift."

"You want Patrick to...him and me...together?"

"*All* of us together."

Amanda sat back on her heels. "This is what you two have been whispering about for the past two days?"

Jake nodded.

"So this was all planned? You took your shower early because this was all planned?"

"It was all planned."

"You... I..." Amanda pushed her hair behind her ears...another sign of her nervousness he recognized. "I don't know what to say. Or do."

"You don't have to do anything. We'll do it all." He spoke to his cousin without looking away from his wife. "Pat, why don't you take care of the lights and music?"

"Will do."

Tears filled Amanda's eyes. Cradling her face in his hand, he gently caressed her cheek with his thumb. "Why are you crying?"

"I'm not."

"That wet stuff in your eyes looks like tears."

"I can't believe you're doing this for me."

"Why not? You know how much I love you. You said your fantasy was to be with two men at once. I want to make your fantasy come true."

Soft instrumental music began playing. Amanda smiled. "My favorite CD."

"Five of your favorites are loaded. I know how much you like music when I give you a massage."

"And candlelight."

"That's next on Pat's list."

Jake had already instructed Patrick to light several candles and play soft music while they gave Amanda her massage. Amanda was a candle nut, so there were always plenty of them set around the living room during every season of the year. Patrick lit all of them, then turned off the lamps and returned to his spot on the quilt.

The candlelight turned Amanda's blonde hair golden and illuminated her skin. Her eyes still shimmered with tears, her face was still flushed from embarrassment...and, Jake suspected, from the beginning of arousal. She was an incredibly lovely woman, but he didn't think she'd ever been more beautiful than right now. "Ready for your massage?"

"I think so."

Jake touched the hem of her T-shirt. "Off with this, okay?"

She bit her lower lip again, then lifted her arms. Jake drew the shirt over her head and tossed it to the floor. His gaze dropped to her breasts. She wore a lacy white bra, one he'd never seen. The cups barely covered half her breasts. "New bra?"

She nodded. "And a thong to match."

"You're wearing it now?"

"Yes."

Heat pooled in Jake's groin. He almost groaned aloud as all the blood in his body rushed to his cock. "You'd better lie down before I forget all my good intentions and ravage you."

Amanda kissed him softly, then lay on her stomach, resting her cheek on her folded arms. Jake picked up the bottle of oil and poured a generous amount into his palm. He passed the bottle to Patrick, then rubbed his hands together before touching Amanda's shoulders. Using a gentle gliding motion, he spread the oil over her skin, from shoulders to waist. He passed over her bra strap, deciding not to unhook it until she was more comfortable with him and Patrick both touching her.

"Mmm, coconut," Amanda murmured. "Smells nice."

"I'm glad you approve." He bent over so he could whisper in her ear. "It's the edible kind too."

Jake would swear he heard her swallow.

Straightening again, Jake watched his cousin pour oil into his palm and lift Amanda's right foot. Using his thumbs, he slowly smeared the oil all over her foot and ankle. Jake heard Amanda breathe in and out slowly. Next to a back rub, Amanda loved nothing more than having her feet massaged. It wasn't unusual for her to fall asleep while he still stroked her feet.

He doubted if she'd fall asleep any time soon.

Patrick concentrated on Amanda's left foot while Jake moved down to her low back. He let his fingers dip beneath the elastic waistband of her shorts, until he felt the thin strip around her hips. She looked so sexy in those tiny thongs. Not able to resist, he let his hands drift lower until he could cup that luscious ass. He spread his oiled fingers wide over her buttocks, letting them travel over her skin. Whatever she used in her bath water made her skin so soft, like silk.

The throbbing in his cock dictated Jake go lower still, but it wasn't the right time yet. This evening was for Amanda and what *she* wanted, not his randy anatomy. He moved his hands back to the neutral territory of her low back.

His cousin had stopped caressing her feet; instead, his hands journeyed up and down her legs from her ankles to her thighs, leaving a slick path of oil with each trip. Jake followed the movement of Patrick's hands over his wife's skin. Each slow pass up her legs brought his fingers a bit closer to the hem of Amanda's shorts. Since Amanda liked her shorts to hit at the top of her thighs, it wouldn't take long before Patrick reached her ass.

Jake stilled a moment while he waited for Patrick to touch his wife intimately for the first time.

Patrick's thumbs disappeared beneath the hem of Amanda's shorts on his next trek up her legs. He slid them to the inside of her thighs, at the crease of her leg. Jake heard Amanda's breath catch sharply.

Jake bent down so he could whisper into her ear again. "Do you like what Pat's doing?"

"Mmm-hmm."

"Do you want more?"

Amanda nodded her head, then turned her face down. Deciding she was getting used to this threesome idea, Jake unhooked her bra. Without that barrier, he had the freedom to caress her entire back and shoulders while he watched Patrick's fingers dip beneath the hem of her shorts again.

Jake moved his hands around to Amanda's sides, until he could touch the outer curves of her breasts. Wanting his hands more slippery for what he planned next, Jake picked up the plastic bottle and poured additional oil into his palm. Once his hands were slick, he slid them beneath Amanda. She lifted her torso slightly, enough so he could cup both breasts and feel her hard nipples in the center of his palms.

Jake loved everything about his wife's body, but especially her breasts. He loved the satiny feel of the skin, the way the areolas puckered when she began to get aroused, the dark pink color of her nipples. He loved that they were so full and firm, and so responsive. He only had to touch Amanda with a fingertip for her breathing to deepen, and she became aroused quickly when he licked and sucked on her nipples.

So did he. He wished he had one in his mouth right now.

Shifting his attention back to his cousin, he watched Patrick tug on the waistband of Amanda's shorts. "Lift your hips, Amanda," Patrick said softly. She obeyed. He slid her shorts down her legs and tossed them on top of her T-shirt. For a moment, he sat back on his heels and stared at her. Jake couldn't blame him. Amanda had an incredible ass...firm and toned from faithful walking, and tan from lying outside in the nude. She took full advantage of their private backyard whenever possible to sunbathe. The result left her entire body golden.

Patrick looked at Jake and mouthed the word, "Wow."

Jake grinned.

Picking up the bottle of oil, Patrick also poured more into his palm. He began a slow, circular motion over her ass, liberally applying the oil to her skin. Amanda shifted and spread her legs a bit more. Patrick slid his thumbs in the cleft between her buttocks. Jake couldn't see exactly where Patrick was touching her, although the pounding of her heart beneath his palm gave him a good idea. Her back rose and fell with her deep breathing, evidence that she was becoming very aroused.

That's exactly what he wanted.

A whimper came from deep in her throat. She rose up to her elbows, giving him more room to caress her breasts. He increased the pressure, adding a gentle tug on her nipples with thumbs and forefingers when she arched her back. Patrick slipped his left hand underneath the elastic of her thong, then moved forward to between her thighs. Jake could see his hand moving, increasing in speed little by little. Amanda's hips began to undulate, her breathing became more choppy. A moment later, her body shuddered from her climax.

Chapter 5

Amanda lay still as the final tremors shook her body. The orgasm had taken her completely by surprise, galloping through her before she even realized it was building.

Jake hadn't been her first lover, but Amanda hadn't learned how to relax and truly enjoy lovemaking until she became involved with her husband. He'd helped her learn her own body, touched her in ways no one else ever had, until she always found satisfaction in his arms.

Waiting for her heart to stop pounding gave Amanda time to reflect on what had just happened with Patrick. Reaching an orgasm so quickly surprised her, until she realized Patrick had known exactly how to touch her to give her that staggering climax. The teasing glance of his fingertips, the slow build-up of that contact until she was writhing to get closer to it, was exactly what Jake did.

Apparently, setting up this whole scenario wasn't the only thing the two cousins had discussed.

Once her blood stopped rushing through her veins, she realized that Jake's hands were back on her shoulders and Patrick was massaging her feet again. A gal could get spoiled by all this pampering. Not having any idea what else these two had planned, Amanda decided to lie still and wait for what happened next.

"How do you feel?" Jake whispered in her ear.

"Weak. Limp. Spoiled."

"You aren't going to fall asleep, are you?"

"Sleep isn't even an option right now." She raised up on one elbow and looked at Jake's crotch. His zipper looked as if it would pop open at any moment. "You certainly don't look the least bit sleepy."

Jake chuckled. "No, I'm definitely not sleepy."

Amanda rolled to her side and glanced at the large bulge in Patrick's cut-offs. "I assume you're not sleepy either."

"Not hardly."

"So, what's next, guys?"

"What do you *want* to be next?" Patrick asked.

She looked from Patrick to her husband and back to Patrick. She wanted everything...kisses, caresses, licking, sucking, and hard cocks inside her. Since they had gone to the trouble of planning all this as a birthday gift to her, it would be terribly rude if she didn't enjoy it to the fullest. "I want to see more skin. Y'all are wearing *way* too many clothes."

Jake rose first. He unfastened his cut-offs and pushed them to the floor. She'd suspected he wasn't wearing any underwear.

She was right.

Amanda stared at the perfect form of her husband. He had the most incredible body: broad shoulders, muscled arms, a flat, firm stomach, strong legs, and a cock so hard and erect, it practically lay against his belly.

A movement from her left drew her attention to Patrick. He, too, rose and let his cut-offs fall to the floor.

"Damn," she muttered.

Amanda sat up and removed her bra. Rising to her knees, she watched Patrick move to stand next to his cousin. Not sure what to do first, she simply looked. The two men favored each other so much, but them being nude let her see the subtle differences in their bodies. Patrick was huskier than Jake, his shoulders, chest and hips broader, his thighs heavier. Jake had more hair on his chest, but less on his stomach. Jake's cock was thicker, Patrick's longer.

One thing they had in common — they both had lust in their eyes, as if they would pounce on her at any moment.

That worked for her.

Enjoying the sight of two handsome, aroused men was definitely fun, but she wanted more, a lot more. Glancing over her shoulder, she located the bottle of oil on the coffee table. That would do for a start.

She picked up the bottle and poured a generous amount in her palm. She replaced the bottle on the table, then rubbed her palms together to distribute the oil to her hands. After looking directly into both men's eyes, she wrapped her hands around their cocks.

Her oiled hands slid easily over satiny skin. Amanda caressed the plum-shaped heads, the hard shafts, the tight scrotums. When she reached their groins, she started over again...slowly, so slowly, enjoying every impressive inch of their cocks. She'd always loved touching Jake like this, especially rubbing her thumb over the head because she knew it made him crazy. She did so now, and heard him moan.

Wondering if Patrick was as responsive as Jake, she rubbed her thumb all over the head of his cock. He thrust his hips forward and a similar moan passed his lips.

Apparently Patrick was just as sensitive as his cousin.

The sound of their breathing grew heavier, deeper. Amanda looked up into Patrick's face. His gaze was focused on her breasts. A delicious thrill zipped through her body at the thought of his mouth on her nipples. His gaze shifted to her hand on him, then to her face. He ran his tongue over his bottom lip. Amanda took that as his silent assurance that his thoughts mirrored hers.

She looked at her husband's face. His eyes were dark, his cheeks flushed, his neck and chest shiny from perspiration. She could tell by the subtle shifting of his hips that he was close to a climax. Squeezing him tighter, she increased the speed of her caress.

Jake grabbed her wrist. "Mandy, stop."

"Why?"

"You know why. I'm about to come."

"That makes two of us," Patrick said.

"This evening is supposed to be what *you* want, not us."

"I *do* want this." She let her fingers glide up and down the length of their cocks while she gripped them tightly. "I've had an orgasm. It's only fair that y'all do too."

"Mandy... Aw, shit."

Jake widened his stance and bent his knees. Amanda felt his cock jerk in her hand and pulled it lower. Warm semen hit her right breast. She heard him growl deep in his throat as he ejaculated again. Wanting to extend his pleasure as long as possible, she kept caressing him, running her hand up and down his shaft until every drop had been expended.

No sooner had Jake's orgasm ended than Patrick's began. Amanda watched as his semen splashed on her left breast. She milked his cock the same way she had Jake's until she was sure his climax had ended.

Both men wilted to the floor. Amanda chuckled when Patrick sat down with a hard thump. Jake dropped to his knees, his breathing hard and erratic. He closed his eyes for a moment before gazing at her breasts.

"You're pretty messy, Mandy."

Amanda touched one of the spots on her skin. "Yeah, I am." Scooting across the floor, she drew two tissues out of the box on the end table and began to wipe off her breasts.

"Want some help with that, Amanda?" Patrick asked, his voice husky.

Amanda stilled and looked at Patrick. He sat with one leg straight, the other bent so his foot rested on the floor, watching the movements of her hands. His position let her clearly see his relaxed-but-nowhere-near-soft cock. Jake had amazing recuperative powers. Patrick must possess the same trait.

Amanda loved that trait.

She had already cleaned most of the semen from her breasts, but if the guys wanted to help her, she wouldn't turn them down. Dropping the soiled tissues on the table, she took two more out of the box and scooted back across the floor. She held up one tissue to each man. "Please."

Jake took a tissue and began gently wiping her right breast. Patrick took a tissue also. He glanced at it, then let it fall to the floor without using it. Leaning forward, he fastened his mouth over her left nipple.

"Oh, God." Amanda rested her hands on the floor behind her and arched her back. Patrick opened his lips wider, enveloping the entire areola in his warm mouth. He suckled gently while swiping his tongue across the nipple. Amanda moaned, then gasped softly when Jake licked her right nipple. She looked at her husband. A devilish gleam lit his eyes.

"I can't let Pat have all the fun."

"No, you certainly can't," she said as she pulled Jake's mouth closer to her breast.

Amanda closed her eyes, tilted her head back, and enjoyed the sensations zinging from her breasts to her womb. Each tug on her nipples made her clitoris throb. Each lick made her breath catch. The feeling was so intense, she wondered if it were possible for a woman to climax from having her nipples sucked.

Jake lifted his mouth from her breast and kissed her deeply. His tongue dove into her mouth over and over, making her head spin and leaving her weak with desire. "Lie back, Mandy."

Gladly doing as Jake instructed, Amanda lay back on the quilt. Patrick followed her. She didn't have the chance to react before he covered her mouth with his own in a drugging kiss.

She'd kissed no other man in over four years. The kiss seemed more personal, more private, than his mouth on her breast or his hand between her thighs. She tensed at first, then relaxed as his tongue swept across her lower lip. His lips tantalized, then coaxed a response from her. Amanda loved kissing, and Patrick definitely knew how to kiss. His technique was different from Jake's, but no less arousing. Wrapping her arms around his neck, she returned his kiss with all the passion he gave her.

Amanda ran her fingers over Patrick's head and touched the elastic band holding his hair in a ponytail. She tugged it loose. His long hair fell around her head, enclosing them in a private cocoon.

The feel of her husband's lips against her mound made Amanda moan into Patrick's mouth. Jake kissed her there again before peeling off her thong. He spread her legs and kissed the inside of each knee. His kisses traveled up her legs at an unhurried pace, one and then the other, until he touched her clitoris with the tip of his tongue.

Amanda pushed Patrick away so she could gulp oxygen into her lungs. She'd forgotten to breathe while concentrating on what Jake was doing. She inhaled sharply when he spread the feminine lips with his fingers and slowly licked her. Propping her feet on the floor, she opened her legs wide, silently encouraging him to continue.

Jake blew on her clitoris at the same time that Patrick fastened his mouth over the tip of her left breast again. The dual stimulation made her whimper. Patrick laid his hand on her right breast, his fingertips lightly brushing the nipple. Jake's mouth became bolder. Closing her eyes, Amanda lifted her hips in time to her husband's licks. When he took her clitoris between his lips and suckled gently, she came apart. She stretched her arms over her head and gave herself up to the sensations zipping through her body.

When Amanda opened her eyes, she saw a very large, very hard cock inches from her mouth.

"Suck me, Mandy," Jake growled.

She was only too happy to comply.

Jake knelt on the floor, his legs spread. Amanda rolled to her stomach and took his cock in her mouth. Sliding her hand between his legs, she caressed his scrotum and perineum while she sucked him. She loved the intimacy of oral sex, both giving and receiving. Knowing how much Jake enjoyed the giving and receiving too made it even more special to her.

She jerked when Patrick lightly bit her bottom. She sighed when he caressed that bite with his tongue, and moaned when he slid his tongue between her buttocks. He licked her from anus to clitoris and back again...once, twice, three times.

Two intense orgasms should've been enough for Amanda. Rarely did she have three when she and Jake made love. This was different. Her body was so hot, her hormones in a frenzy. She had two men wanting to pleasure her, so she saw no reason why she shouldn't be greedy and take everything they had to offer.

She spread her legs and lifted her hips.

Jake's cock seemed to grow in her mouth. She knew he couldn't see exactly what Patrick was doing to her, but he must have a good idea. It had to be affecting him almost as much as her. He began moving his hips, pumping his cock in and out of her mouth. Amanda opened her mouth wider and relaxed her throat so she could take all of him.

"Oh, yeah," Jake muttered. "God, that feels good, babe."

"Good" didn't even come close to describing how Amanda felt. "Frenzied" was more like it...especially when Patrick's tongue circled around her anus, then darted inside. His murmur of pleasure vibrated against the sensitive tissue. His tongue became more frantic, the thrusts deeper inside her ass as his thumb circled her clitoris.

It couldn't happen. Another orgasm couldn't possibly build so quickly.

She was wrong. The climax washed over her in waves, making her heart pound and leaving her as weak as a newborn kitten.

Jake's cock popped out of her mouth as Amanda lowered her head to the floor and panted for breath. She only had a second to think about her need for air before Patrick jammed his cock into her pussy. He held her hips tightly while he thrust hard and fast, his groin slapping against her buttocks. It felt so good, but she needed more. Raising her head, she found Jake's glistening cock close to her lips. She latched onto it and sucked it as far into her mouth as she could.

"God, babe." Jake cupped her head and started pumping his hips again. "Yeah, just like that. Take it all."

Jake's semen hit the back of her throat. Patrick dug his fingers into her hips and cursed softly. Knowing both men were coming at the same time sent Amanda over the top again. She greedily swallowed Jake's semen as another orgasm rushed through her body.

Chapter 6

It should've been enough. Jake knew it should've been enough.

It wasn't.

Watching his cousin touch his wife, lick her, fuck her, did something to him that he'd never experienced…something almost animalistic. Thinking about Patrick being with Amanda had been exciting, a taste of the forbidden, a fantasy. The real thing had been raw, earthy, beyond anything sexual he'd ever experienced.

Earth-shattering.

He loved sex with his wife. Making love with Amanda was always amazing. Tonight, it went beyond amazing.

Jake looked down at his wife. She lay on her stomach, her cheek resting on his thigh, her eyes closed. The candlelight reflected off her sweat-glazed skin. She had to be exhausted. So should he, yet he wasn't. He wanted her again.

He looked at his cousin. Patrick was still on his knees between Amanda's spread legs. His chest rose and fell rapidly from his heavy breathing, his skin was bathed in sweat. He stared at her pussy as if he was starving and it was a steak dinner.

Patrick raised his head and gazed at Jake. The wild look in Patrick's eyes told Jake that his cousin wasn't finished either.

Jake and Patrick had already discussed in detail everything they planned to do tonight, so Jake knew what came next. He reached for the pillow on the floor behind him and slipped it under Amanda's cheek. Picking up the bottle of massage oil, he moved over next to Patrick. "Want this?" he asked.

"Yeah." Patrick took the bottle and tipped it upside down, allowing a thin stream of oil to flow between her buttocks.

Amanda shifted when the oil touched her. "No way, guys. I'm pooped."

Jake scooped some of the oil on his fingertips and spread it over her buttocks. "It's still your birthday. Pat and I want to draw out your present for awhile longer."

"Jake—"

"Just lie still, Mandy, and let us play a little."

Jake slid his fingers between her legs. The oil, mixed with her own body's wetness and Patrick's semen, let him easily glide two fingers inside her pussy. He slowly pumped them in and out as he watched his cousin slide his thumb through the oil and press it against her anus.

Amanda tightened her buttocks, but Patrick didn't stop. He held his thumb against her until she relaxed again and allowed his touch. Patrick pressed his thumb a bit farther inside her, withdrew, and pressed again. Anal sex wasn't Amanda's favorite thing, but she did enjoy being touched and licked there. Jake had fucked her there only a few times in their four years together, and only when she was very aroused.

He had a feeling the "very aroused" bit wouldn't be a problem tonight.

Patrick pushed his thumb all the way inside her. Amanda bucked once, and Jake heard her sharply indrawn breath.

"You okay, Mandy?"

"Yes."

"Does this feel good, Amanda?" Patrick asked as he began moving his thumb faster inside her.

"Mmm, yesssssss…"

Jake increased the motion of his fingers. He withdrew them every few moments and dipped down to touch her clitoris, then plunged back inside her. Amanda began to lift her hips in time to their movements. When she raised up to her knees and spread her legs farther, Jake knew she wanted more. He looked at Patrick and nodded.

Patrick removed his thumb and picked up the bottle of oil. He poured a generous amount on the fingers of his left hand, and more between Amanda's buttocks. She moaned when Patrick pushed his index finger inside her ass. Jake increased the pumping of his own fingers as he watched Patrick add his middle finger to the first.

"God, she's tight," Patrick said, his voice husky.

Twisting his wrist, Patrick drilled his fingers farther inside her. Amanda pushed her hips back at them. Seeing his wife so open, so hot, made the animal rear up inside Jake again. He pulled his hand from her and crawled to her side. Lying next to Amanda, he brushed her hair from her face. Her eyes were half-closed and burned with hunger.

Leaning over her, Jake kissed her jaw, her cheek, her temple. "Ride me, Mandy," he breathed in her ear.

* * * * *

Jake's whispered request penetrated Amanda's lust-fogged brain. He couldn't mean... They couldn't be thinking of her taking both of them at the same time. She'd read books with double penetration and had seen it in an X-rated movie Jake talked her into watching, but she didn't think it was even physically possible for her to do that.

The thought intrigued her...and excited her.

Tonight, she wanted to try everything.

Jake lay on his back. "C'mere, Mandy."

Amanda swung one leg over him and straddled his hips. Grasping his cock in her hand, she slowly slid down until he was all the way inside her.

Jake cradled her face and pulled her head down to his. She lay sprawled on his chest, her buttocks in the air, while he kissed her over and over. Patrick kept moving his fingers in and out, in and out, getting her ass ready for him.

When Patrick removed his fingers, Amanda tensed. Jake must have felt her reaction for he kissed her again and nuzzled her neck. "Relax, Mandy," he whispered. "Let us love you."

Amanda stared down into her husband's handsome face. He would never hurt her, and he would never let anyone else hurt her. She trusted him, and she trusted Patrick.

Patrick's cock brushed her anus. Concentrating on total relaxation, Amanda took a deep breath and let it out slowly. He pressed a bit harder, and the head slipped inside her.

"Ohhh..."

"Okay, babe?" Jake asked.

Amanda nodded. She laid her head on Jake's shoulder. He grasped her behind her knees and pulled them closer to his waist. The new position raised her buttocks higher in the air.

The oil on her skin made it easier for Patrick to move. He withdrew and advanced several times, entering her a bit farther with each stroke. Amanda bit her bottom lip when his thighs touched the back of hers and she knew he was all the way inside her.

Both men remained still for long moments. Jake was the first to shift beneath her. He lifted his hips, driving his cock deeper. He lowered his hips at the same time that Patrick moved forward. They repeated the action until they developed a rhythm with her. Slowly, so slowly, they moved inside her. As one withdrew, the other one drove in.

Amanda practically purred. It felt incredible.

Their thrusts picked up speed, and so did Amanda's heartbeat. She listened to their breathing become more ragged, watched as sweat pooled in Jake's hairline and neck. Reaching for the pinnacle of pleasure, she joined in their rhythm, slamming her hips down on her husband, then back up at his cousin.

It must have been the signal Patrick needed. He gripped her hips and began fucking her hard and fast.

Jake came first, bucking beneath her as he growled low in his throat. Patrick soon followed, pressing his groin tightly against her buttocks and groaning loudly. His last thrust sent Amanda over the edge into oblivion.

* * * * *

Amanda drained her glass and held it out for Patrick to refill. The cold white wine tasted wonderful. She didn't think she'd ever been so thirsty.

"Better be careful with the wine, Amanda," Patrick said as he poured the last of the bottle into her glass. "Too much wine will loosen your inhibitions."

"*What* inhibitions? I don't have any of those."

"Especially after tonight," Jake said.

"That's true." Amanda sipped her wine. She felt deliciously light-headed and weak after two glasses of wine and three hours of astonishing sex. Five orgasms. She'd *never* had five orgasms, not even when she and Jake had first gotten together and couldn't keep their hands off each other.

Patrick lay stretched out on his side on the quilt. Jake sat propped against the recliner, his legs out in front of him and crossed at the ankles. Amanda sat so she could see both of them with her legs drawn up to her chest. No one had bothered to put on any clothes. Looking at two gorgeous nude men was almost as good as having sex with two gorgeous nude men.

Almost.

"I have some questions."

"I figured you would," Jake muttered. He drained his own glass of wine and set it on the floor. "Shoot."

"When did y'all plan this?"

"I am completely innocent," Patrick said. "This was all Jake's idea."

"Innocent, my ass. You thought the idea was great when I told you about it."

"I didn't say I didn't think it was a great idea. I said it was *your* idea."

"Okay, guys, I get the picture. It was Jake's idea." She looked at her husband. "Did you plan this before Patrick got here?"

"No. Pat had been here several days before I approached him about doing this for you. I wasn't sure if he'd want to, and I wasn't sure I'd be able to share you."

"But you decided to."

"Yeah, because you said it was your fantasy. I wanted to give you what you wanted."

His words warmed her heart. How she loved this man. Her gaze flickered from Jake to Patrick and back again. "You've never done anything like this?"

She saw Patrick glance at Jake before he turned back to her and said, "No."

"Wait a minute. I saw that look you gave Jake, Patrick. You're lying to me."

"No, I'm not. Jake and I have never been in a threesome before tonight."

"I hear a 'but' after that sentence."

When he didn't say anything else, Amanda faced her husband. "Jake?"

He rubbed his chin. Amanda recognized that stalling tactic and waited for him to speak.

"Patrick and I have been close all our lives, Amanda. We're both only children and there's less than a year between us. We grew up like brothers. Brothers...share things."

"Explain."

Jake ran his hand through his hair, another stalling tactic Amanda recognized. "We went through school together in San Diego. We went to college there for two years before Patrick moved to Colorado. College can be..." He stopped.

"Entertaining?" Amanda supplied.

"Very," Patrick said with a wicked grin.

"So y'all had sex with the same women?"

"Maybe once," Jake said. Amanda arched one eyebrow at him. "Okay, maybe more than once. We were young and healthy with raging hormones, Amanda."

She looked from one man to the other again. They were both incredible lovers. In her opinion, they still had raging hormones. "Are you talking orgies, Jake?"

"We...did that a time or two, yeah."

Amanda thought about that a moment. They'd grown up together. They'd had orgies together. She'd wondered why they were so at ease with each other. She doubted if many men sat around naked on the living room floor. "That explains it then."

Jake frowned. "Explains what?"

"Why y'all are so comfortable together naked. I'm not speaking from experience, but I would imagine two guys in a situation like this would be uneasy to be so close to each other. They'd be afraid if they touched each other, it meant they were gay or something."

"Shit, Pat and I practically grew up naked. I've seen his wanger as often as I've seen mine. It's no big deal."

"I beg your pardon," Patrick said. "It is too a big deal."

Amanda lifted her glass towards him and grinned. "I'll drink to that." She took another sip of wine and set her glass on the coffee table behind her. "So, how detailed did you get with Patrick about me?"

A guilty look flashed through Jake's eyes. "What do you mean?"

"I mean, he knew exactly how and where to touch me."

"Amanda, every woman has tits, an ass, and a pussy."

She scowled at him. "Don't be crude, and don't act dumb. Different women need different things sexually. Patrick couldn't have touched me the way he did to make me come so quickly if he hadn't known some details."

Jake quickly glanced at his cousin before looking back at Amanda. She could still see the guilt in his eyes. "I may have...coached him a bit."

Patrick sat up. "Amanda, don't be angry at Jake. You're right. Women are different. Jake told me some things about your body and how you like to be touched, but only because he wanted to be sure you were completely satisfied tonight."

"I'm not angry, Patrick," Amanda said softly before smiling at her husband. "I love Jake for being so unselfish and so caring. And I was most definitely completely satisfied. You were both amazing. It was a wonderful birthday present."

"So you're happy?" Jake asked.

"Happy and exhausted."

"I'll second that exhausted part," Patrick said. "I think I'll hit the sack."

"That's a good idea." Amanda straightened her legs and stretched her arms over her head. "I'll probably sleep 'til noon tomorrow."

"Not if you keep flashing those gorgeous breasts at us, you won't," Jake said with a wicked leer.

"You can't *possibly* be thinking of more sex."

"I can *think*. I'm not promising I can *do* anything."

Patrick chuckled. "That goes for me too." He picked up his empty wineglass. "Before I go to bed, cuz, I have a request."

"Shoot."

"I want you and Amanda to come to the lodge this winter. I'm really proud of all I've accomplished and I want you to see it. We've talked about it a lot of times, but you've never made the trip. This time I want your promise you'll be there."

"You got it."

Patrick shifted his gaze to Amanda. "Maybe we can fulfill a fantasy of mine next time."

"Which is?" she asked.

He gave her a devilish grin. "You'll just have to wait and see."

A threesome was supposed to be a one-time thing, a fantasy only. She loved her husband fiercely and didn't need another man in her life, or her bed.

A ski lodge, a hot tub, a fireplace...the possibilities were endless.

Amanda smiled. "Well, I have always wanted to learn to snow ski..."

The End

IT'S IN THE CARDS

Chapter 1

It had to be the right one. If she had to stand here all day and look at every one of them, she'd do it until she found "the one."

Catherine Ryan returned the birthday card to the display rack and chose another. Picking the right birthday card for her sister Anita always took time. Actually, picking the right *cards* took time because Catherine always bought two—a serious one and a funny one. She treasured her relationship with her sister, and it was important to her that the cards express how much Anita meant to her.

Ten cards later, Catherine found it. The picture on the front—a crystal vase filled with pink roses—was exactly the type of picture Anita would love. The caption said a simple, "Happy Birthday to My Sister". Hopefully, it didn't have one of those long, sappy verses inside the card. Catherine preferred something short and to the point, but she still wanted it to convey how she felt.

The sentiment inside the card brought a lump to Catherine's throat and tears to her eyes.

I wish I had the words to tell you how special you are to me. If I could choose anyone in the world to be my sister, it would be you. Happy birthday to my sister, and my best friend.

"Perfect," Catherine whispered.

Now, to find a funny one...and maybe just a bit naughty.

Finding a funny one didn't take nearly as long as finding a serious one. The picture of a sweet kitten on the front, combined with a raunchy verse inside, would make Anita laugh out loud. Smiling, Catherine clutched both cards in her hand and turned to make her way to the register.

A flash of purple caught her eye. A flash of purple *always* caught her eye; it was her favorite color. She could see just the top of a card on the lowest shelf of the display rack, hidden behind several other cards. Catherine frowned. She'd already looked at that row and she hadn't seen this card. There was *no way* she would've missed a purple card.

Unable to resist, she touched the part of the card that she could see. She felt...something. She didn't know how to describe it, but something electric, almost shocking, passed through her fingers.

Taking the card between her thumb and forefinger, Catherine slowly drew it out of the slot. The front was a deep, solid eggplant color with the words "Happy Birthday" in a flowing silver script scrawled across the front. There was nothing special about the card—no beautiful picture, no romantic saying, nothing that should draw her so intently to it, yet she felt compelled to look at it. Her fingers trembling, she opened the card, peered inside...and gasped.

It was him. *Him.* Her fantasy man. The man who filled her dreams at night, and her mind by day. The man she imagined in her life, in her bed, in her body.

She stared at the picture, which took up the entire inside of the card. He reclined among rumpled white satin sheets, his torso propped up on several pillows. His handsome face was tan, with the beginning of a five-o'clock shadow covering his cheeks and chin. His deep brown eyes were half-closed, a hint of a grin turned up the corners of his mouth. A corner of a sheet draped over his groin, but she could still see his bare hip. One arm was folded under his head, showing her his impressive biceps. Long, dark brown hair spread over the pillow. That same dark hair generously spread over his chest and tapered down his stomach until it disappeared beneath the sheet. Tanned legs, lightly sprinkled with dark hair, peeked out the other end of the sheet. His body was muscled in all the right places...not the muscles of a bodybuilder, but of a strong, healthy man.

The bulge in the sheet indicated that he didn't lack anything in *that* department.

"Do you need some help?" a feminine voice asked.

Catherine jumped and quickly closed the card. Her cheeks heated and her palms began to sweat as she turned to face the clerk. "Uh, no, I'm fine."

"Did you find everything you need?"

"Yes, yes, I did. I found the perfect cards for my sister. Her birthday is next week. She's turning thirty-five and I'm having a wonderful time teasing her about it." Catherine knew she was rambling, but she couldn't seem to stop. She didn't think she'd ever been so embarrassed in her life. Getting caught drooling at a picture on a card was mortifying.

The clerk tilted her head and peered at the cards in Catherine's hands. "Oh, that's a pretty one," she said, tapping the card with the roses on it. "Does your sister like roses?"

"Yes, she does, very much."

"We have some heavenly rose-scented potpourri and candles that would go wonderful with that card."

Catherine realized the clerk was simply doing her job, but she wished the girl would just leave so she could look at her fantasy man again.

The clerk glanced down at Catherine's hands, and frowned slightly. "What's that?"

Catherine clutched the cards a bit tighter. "What's what?"

"That purple card. I don't remember that one."

"I, uh, I found it on the bottom row."

Without asking, the clerk slipped the card from Catherine's grasp. Losing the card made Catherine feel as if she'd just lost a friend. Her chest actually hurt.

"I restocked that row this morning. I've never seen this card." She turned it over and looked at the back. "It has our imprint, but I swear I've never seen it. How strange."

Trying not to seem rude, Catherine plucked the card out of the clerk's hand. "Well, you have so many, you probably just forgot this one."

"I guess."

The clerk didn't look convinced, but Catherine wasn't about to let go of her prize again. She put her hand with the cards behind her back. "I'm ready to check out please. And I'll take a bag of the rose potpourri and a dozen votives too."

The clerk smiled, obviously forgetting about the card with a larger sale on the horizon. "Wonderful. I'll get them for you and meet you at the register."

* * * * *

Catherine opened the card, laid it on the kitchen table, and stared at the picture one more time. She'd been looking at it most of the evening. She couldn't get over how much this man looked like the man of her dreams. It was as if someone had gone inside her head, taken the mental picture she carried, and copied it on this card. Even the sentiment written in small letters at the bottom gave her goose bumps: *May all your dreams come true.*

This was just too weird.

She touched his hair with one fingertip. She loved long hair on a man, especially dark brown hair like this. So much of it lay across the pillow, it had to be past his shoulders in length. Her fingertip traveled farther...over his arms, across his chest, down his stomach, stopping at the top of the sheet. She skipped over the enticing bulge at his groin and let her fingertip glide down his legs. The picture stopped at his knees, but she imagined his calves and feet were every bit as gorgeous as the rest of him.

The bulge beneath the sheet drew her attention once more. Peering around her kitchen first to make sure no one could see her, she touched that bulge with the barest tip of her finger. She drew a circle on it, over and over, wishing it could really be *him* she was touching. It had been so long since she'd touched a man, or had a man touch her...

Catherine snatched her hand away from the card as if it had suddenly turned into a hungry rattlesnake. *Get a grip, Cat. It's just a picture. He isn't real. He'll never be real.*

Disgusted with herself for her foolish action, Catherine rose and crossed the room to the refrigerator for something to drink. She took out a Pepsi, popped the top, and took a large drink. Despite her central air conditioning, she still felt warm and sticky. The weather had been so hot already, and it wasn't even the end of April. Summers in North Texas could be brutal, and it looked like this one would be every bit as hot as usual.

Her gaze wandered around the kitchen as she took another drink. She loved her house, and had worked so hard to make it truly *hers*. After her bum of a husband walked out on her, Catherine poured her heartache and anger into redecorating the small, two-bedroom house in the suburbs of Fort Worth. She'd done most of the work herself, hiring only for those services that she did not know how to do. She'd mixed cool pastels with deep jewel tones, creating a color scheme that made her feel proud of her accomplishments.

If only it would help her feel less lonely.

The card drew her attention once again. Catherine put her half-empty soda can in the refrigerator before wandering back to the table.

She touched the face in the picture, rubbing her thumb across the handsome man's cheek.

"I wish you were real," she whispered.

With a final sigh, Catherine turned off the light and left the kitchen.

* * * * *

He rose through a thick fog until he stood on shaky legs. Finally, the woman he was destined to be with had found him. He'd lost all track of time during his imprisonment, so didn't know how long he'd waited…months, years, decades, centuries?

Stretching to loosen tight muscles, he looked around the room. He didn't recognize many of the items surrounding him, yet that didn't surprise him. Things had to have changed in the time while he waited for her. He'd catch up on everything, learn everything he had to know, with her.

Thinking of the things he wanted to do first with her caused the blood to rush to his cock. She'd dreamed of him for a long, long time. It was time he made those dreams come true.

Chapter 2

He walked quietly through the dark house, seeing easily despite the absence of light. She had found and released him from his prison. That meant she was his mate, the woman created just for him. He'd be able to find her anytime, anywhere.

He knew exactly which door to open in the strange dwelling. She lay on the bed beneath a pale sheet. Moonlight shone through the open curtains and spilled across her skin, giving him enough illumination to make out her features. He could see her small, turned-up nose, her full lips, her high cheekbones. Her chin-length, light-colored hair reflected the moonlight and practically glowed.

She was incredibly lovely.

He stepped closer to the bed. She shifted and rolled to her back, throwing one arm over her head. The new position lifted her breasts. They weren't large, but the perfect size to fit in his palms. The hard nipples pebbled beneath the thin nightshirt she wore would taste wonderful. He wanted to lick them, suck them, until they became even harder.

His gaze traveled down her body. One leg had come uncovered when she turned. All that skin was too much for him to resist. He touched her knee. Her skin was as smooth and soft as he knew it would be. He let his hand linger on her knee for a long moment before leisurely moving it up her thigh.

Silk...warm silk.

One spot on her would be even warmer.

Placing one knee on the bed, he leaned closer until his nose almost touched her mound. Her scent...ah, her scent was incredible. If he could do nothing but absorb that wonderful fragrance, he'd be happy.

His cock throbbed. *It* wouldn't be happy with simply absorbing her fragrance.

He wanted to touch every part of her body with both his hands and his mouth. He wanted to take her to heights where she'd never been.

His hand drifted farther up her thigh. He stopped at the hem of her nightshirt, then slipped his hand underneath it to continue his journey. When he reached the crisp curls covering her mound, he stopped again. Taking a deep breath, he moved his hand between her legs. The hot, liquid essence of her body covered his fingers. It pleased him to find her so wet.

"Are you dreaming of me, pretty lady?" he whispered.

She shifted on the bed and spread her legs wider, giving him more room to explore her. Pushing his hand farther between the swollen lips, he gathered more of her honey on his fingers, raised them to his mouth, and licked them.

Her taste was every bit as intoxicating as her scent. The sample wasn't enough; he wanted more. He moved between her legs and lay on his stomach. He moaned when his hard cock pressed against the bed. It was making demands for attention, but he had to ignore those demands for now. Her pleasure was more important than his own. Pushing her nightshirt up to her waist, he slipped his hands beneath her buttocks and lifted her to his mouth.

A soft groan escaped her lips. She arched her back and tilted her hips toward him. He stroked the feminine lips with his tongue, licked her clitoris, then darted deep inside her to lap at her cream. "Mmm," she groaned again.

Taking that sexy sound as a sign that she liked what he was doing, he continued the movement of his tongue. She shifted on the bed and spread her legs even wider. He couldn't help moaning at her uninhibited response. Her dreams had given him a glimpse at her passionate nature. Her actions far surpassed the fictional images in her head.

Her juices flowed freely from her vagina, trickling down to her anus. He circled the puckered hole with his forefinger, lubricating her with her own cream, before he pushed that finger inside her.

She gasped. His cock twitched. He rocked his pelvis from side to side, rubbing his cock against the sheet. How he'd love to slide inside that forbidden area! *Soon*, he told himself. *I will do* everything *with her, soon.*

He pushed his finger farther inside her ass while increasing the strokes of his tongue across her clitoris. She began to pump her hips, faster, faster. Another surge of cream gushed from her vagina. He swallowed it greedily as her body shook from her climax.

She wilted on the bed. Breathing heavily, he raised up to his knees and looked at her. Her chest rose and fell rapidly. Her light-colored hair lay spread over her pillow. A thin sheen of sweat coated her skin.

She was the most beautiful thing he'd ever seen.

Able to wait no longer, he gently turned her over. Slipping his arm beneath her waist, he lifted her enough so he could slide the extra pillow underneath her stomach.

"Wha—" she muttered.

He leaned over her body and whispered in her ear. "Shh. Just relax and let me love you, pretty lady."

Gathering her hair in one hand, he dropped a kiss on her nape. The salty flavor of her sweat sent desire coursing through him. His cock grew even harder, and he didn't think that was possible.

He had to have her.

Using his knees, he spread her legs farther apart. With one shift of his hips, he thrust his cock all the way inside her vagina.

"Oh, yesssss…" She opened her legs wider and raised her buttocks. "More, please."

Those raised buttocks, that tight puckered hole, were too much of a temptation. He slipped his thumb completely inside her anus. Holding tightly to her waist with his other hand, he began moving faster, thrusting harder, until his groin slapped against her buttocks. His heart pounded, sweat broke out all over his skin. Still he kept thrusting, wanting—*needing*—to give her pleasure again.

Her body stilled a moment, then she trembled violently. Slamming his cock deep inside her, he followed her into bliss.

* * * * *

Wow, what a dream. Catherine shifted on the bed, and winced when sore areas between her thighs complained. She'd had erotic dreams many times, but none of them had felt so real. If she didn't know better, she would swear her fantasy man had actually been here, in her bed, making love to her…wild, passionate, earth-shattering love.

Too much time staring at that card, Cat.

With a heavy sigh, Catherine rolled to her side toward the window. She liked to look at the early morning sunshine before she rose from the bed. Instead, today she looked into the face of her fantasy man...only he wasn't a fantasy, but very real.

Cat blinked. And blinked again. She must still be dreaming. That had to be the answer. But it didn't seem like she was dreaming. The warmth of the sun touched her face. Her soft feather pillow supported her head. Her silky chemise caressed her skin. Surely all those things wouldn't seem so real if she were dreaming.

Slowly, she reached out and touched his long hair that lay over his shoulder. It was soft, as soft as her own. Her gaze followed her hand as it drifted down his arm. Warm skin overlay firm muscle. A light dusting of hair covered his forearm. That, too, felt real.

Catherine raised her gaze back to his face. His open eyes stared back at her.

"Good morning," he whispered.

The sound of his deep voice spurred her into action. Catherine jumped up from the bed and backed up until she encountered the wall. "Who—who are you?"

He raised up on one elbow. "I am Kane."

"What are you doing in my bed?"

"Did you not wish for me to be here?"

"How could I wish for you to be there? I don't even *know* you!"

"You have been dreaming of me for years. Now I am here."

Through the cobwebs scattered in her head, Catherine recognized the hint of an English accent. She'd always loved hearing an English accent.

Good grief, Cat, there's a naked man *in your bed and you're thinking about his* accent?

At least, she *thought* he was naked.

"Uh, Kane? Are you..." She waved her hand toward his groin. "Are you wearing anything?"

"No."

"Hoo boy." Catherine pushed her hair back from her face with shaky hands. She was losing her mind. That had to be the answer. She'd been designing websites and book covers for erotica authors for the past year. All that exposure to sexy excerpts and handsome hunks had fried her brain.

Kane sat up in bed. "You are not pleased to see me?"

"Well...no. I'm not used to waking up with a naked man in my bed."

His eyes turned smoky. "You did not mind having a naked man in your bed last night...or inside you."

Catherine gulped. It hadn't been a dream. She'd really made love with this man last night...this man she knew nothing about.

All this was too much for Catherine to take before she'd even gone to the bathroom or had a cup of coffee. The exact image of her fantasy man was naked in her bed, giving her looks that said he'd like to devour her. She had so many questions, she didn't know where to start.

"Look, I have to... Uh, I'll be right back, okay?"

"I will be here."

She returned a few moments later to discover Kane still in her bed. She'd hoped he would disappear while she was gone. He lay propped against the pillows, looking as if he would be perfectly content to stay in her bed all day.

That was not an option.

"This has to be someone's idea of a joke. I don't know how you got here, or who's playing this trick on me, but you have to leave."

"I cannot leave. I belong with you. You are my mate."

"Your mate." Great. Not only was a strange man in her bed, but he was as insane as she.

Before she realized what he planned to do, he rose from the bed and walked toward her. Catherine couldn't help it, her gaze involuntarily dropped to his groin. He wasn't standing-up-straight aroused, but close to it. She gulped. She had all *that* inside her last night? No wonder parts of her throbbed this morning.

Kane stopped less than a foot away from her. "I have been waiting for you to find me. We belong together. It is that simple."

His eyes were a glorious dark brown with thick eyelashes. No man had ever looked at her this way...as if she were the most precious and important thing in the world. Catherine swallowed hard, preparing to tell him again that he had to leave, when he touched her. A simple fingertip on her cheek stole whatever she'd been about to say. She stood still, her breathing becoming heavier, as that fingertip glided across her cheek, over her chin, down her neck, and into the neckline of her chemise. It stopped on the curve of her left breast.

"Come back to bed with me and I will show you we belong together."

Chapter 3

The idea was incredibly tempting. If him touching her with that one finger could make her heart pound, she could only imagine how she'd feel if she were fully awake while they made love.

Before she did anything with this man, she had to find out who he was and who sent him here. She pulled his hand away from her. "Kane, we need to talk."

"You would rather talk than make love?"

"For now, yes. I really need coffee. How about if I fix us some breakfast? Are you hungry?"

He nodded. "I am."

"Okay. I'll grab a robe, you put on your clothes, and I'll meet you in the kitchen."

Catherine didn't wait to see if he actually started to put on his clothes before she left the bedroom. She grabbed her robe off the end of the bed as she scurried from the room.

She couldn't imagine who would play this kind of trick on her. Well, actually, she could. Anita loved practical jokes, especially the kind that made her younger sister blush. Sisters shared a lot of private thoughts, and Catherine had told Anita about her fantasy man. But for Anita to be able to find a guy who looked so much like the one in Catherine's head was incredible. Catherine hadn't described him in *that* much detail.

The open card on the table made Catherine stop in her tracks. The saying was still in the bottom corner, but the picture had changed. She now saw only an image of a rumpled sheet.

"Do you believe me now?"

Catherine whirled around at the sound of Kane's voice. He stood close to her, still nude. The sight of all that masculine beauty made her brain stop working for a moment. She'd never be able to concentrate as long as he paraded around in his birthday suit. "You didn't put on your clothes."

"I do not have clothes." He pointed at the card. "I came from there."

"You came from the card."

"Yes. I will try to explain—"

"Wait." Catherine held up one hand to stop him. "Let me start the coffee. I have the feeling I'm going to need caffeine to hear this. And I need to find you something to wear."

Kane frowned. "You do not like me this way?"

"I like you very much this way, but I can't think straight while you're naked."

Kane's frown quickly turned into a devilish smile. Stepping closer, he slipped one arm around her waist. "I like the sound of that."

Catherine moved away from him. "I'll see if I can find something for you to wear. Wait here."

After preparing the coffee to brew, Catherine headed for the laundry room. She searched the cabinets until she discovered a pair of her brother-in-law's sweatpants that he'd left while helping her paint the kitchen. He was not as tall as Kane, but at least Kane would be partially covered.

She found him standing by the counter when she returned to the kitchen. He stared at the coffeepot as if it were an alien being.

"So many things about which I know nothing."

"You've never drunk coffee?"

His brows drew together. "I do not know." He motioned toward the card still lying on the table. "I do know how I came to be there, but my memory of other things is unclear."

Catherine noticed Kane spoke almost formally, as if from a period a long time ago. "Do you remember where you live? Are you from England, or somewhere in the British Isles?"

"I now live here, with you. That is all that matters."

"No, Kane, that *isn't* all that matters." Suddenly realizing she still held the sweatpants, she thrust them at him. "Here, put these on. I'll start breakfast and then we'll talk."

* * * * *

Kane watched her move about the room as she prepared their meal. He couldn't blame her for doubting that he'd come from the card. A sane person wouldn't believe what had happened to him. He'd experienced it, and still had trouble believing it.

He didn't know how to explain it to her.

She set a plate of food in front of him before taking a chair across the table with her own plate. He didn't recognize some of the items, but would be willing to try whatever she prepared for him...as long as she didn't ask him to drink the beverage she called "coffee" again. One sip of the brown liquid had almost choked him, and he'd asked her for water instead.

He was very hungry and ate heartily. She remained silent while she ate. He took his cue from her and ate without speaking. When he finished his meal, he pushed his empty plate aside and sipped his water while waiting for her to finish.

She laid her fork in her empty plate and pushed it aside also. Leaning forward, she rested her forearms on the table.

"Did my sister send you?" she asked.

"I do not know your sister. No one sent me here. You are my mate."

"You don't even know my *name*. How can I be your 'mate'?"

"I do not need to know your name. I know in my heart that we are meant to be together."

"You still want me to believe you came from that card?"

"I am no longer there. What other explanation do you have for that?"

"I don't have any other explanation, but what you're saying is crazy. People don't materialize out of birthday cards!"

"They do if they are under a spell."

"A spell?"

"Yes."

She remained quiet for several moments. "I think you'd better start at the beginning, Kane."

Needing to move after sitting for so long, Kane rose and paced the small area between the table and cabinets. "I told you I do not remember many details from my past. What I do remember is being...involved with someone who cared more for me than I cared for her."

"You were lovers?"

"Yes, for a short while. I told her she was not my true love and I could not marry her. When I tried to end our relationship, she became very angry. She was a sorceress and told me if she could not have me, no one could. She cast a spell that I would remain imprisoned until my true love found me." He stopped by her chair. "You found me and set me free."

"You've been imprisoned in a *greeting card*?"

"I do not know the details of my imprisonment, nor how long I have been captive." Kneeling by her chair, he took her hand in his. "I only know that you found me and set me free. That means you are my one true love."

"Kane—"

He placed one finger over her mouth to stop her words. "My memory may be unclear, but my feelings are not. I knew the moment I saw you how I feel about you. I have waited for you a long time." He cradled her cheek in his hand and rubbed his thumb over her lips. "I know of your dreams of me. I do not know *how* I know, I simply *do*. You would not have dreamed of me for so long if we were not meant to be together." His thumb brushed her lips again. "You are my true love."

* * * * *

Catherine wanted to melt. No man had ever looked at her with so much love in his eyes...not even her ex-husband in the first months of their marriage. A lump formed in her throat, making it burn. She wanted to believe him. She wanted to throw herself in his arms and accept the love he offered her.

But how could she? His story was so incredible.

"Give me the chance to prove how I feel about you, pretty lady."

"Catherine," she said softly, squeezing the words past the tightness still in her throat. "My name is Catherine."

"Catherine," he repeated. "It is a beautiful name."

She held her breath as he moved closer to her. The gentle caress of his lips on hers made her sigh. Her eyes drifted closed when he kissed her again...this time longer. His lips parted slightly and she felt the tip of his tongue touch her lips.

"Mmm..." Catherine murmured.

"Do you like to kiss?" he asked against her mouth.

"Yes, very much."

"As do I."

As if to prove his words, he kissed her again. While his previous kisses had been sweet, this one was passionate and hot. His tongue dove deep inside her mouth to tangle with hers. Advance, withdraw, advance, withdraw, copying the motion of lovemaking. Catherine's mind spun, her blood rushed through her veins, her lungs labored for air. Oh, did this man know how to kiss!

She squealed in surprise when he swept her off her feet and into his arms.

"I want you naked beneath me," he said, his voice husky.

He began walking toward her bedroom. She did nothing to stop him.

Chapter 4

He laid her in the middle of the bed. Catherine watched Kane quickly shed the sweatpants he'd donned mere minutes ago. Once free of the fleece, his cock sprang forward from his body...thick, long, and fully erect.

Kane knelt on the bed and reached for the tie that held her robe together. "I did not see your body last night. I want to see it now."

He helped her sit up and slipped the robe from her shoulders. Catherine stared into his eyes after he drew the chemise over her head. She watched for any sign that he found her slim body lacking. She saw none, and his words confirmed that.

"You're beautiful, Catherine." Cradling both breasts in his hands, he lifted and pushed them together. "These are the perfect size."

"They could be bigger."

"Yes, they could, but I do not want them bigger." He raised his gaze to her face. "Do you?"

Catherine had always wanted D cups like her sister Anita, instead of the B cups she possessed, and Anita's voluptuous body. Right now, with Kane looking at her with so much passion in his eyes, she couldn't imagine why she had. "No."

"Do they taste as wonderful as they look?"

Feeling brave and a bit naughty, Catherine arched her back. "Why don't you find out?"

Kane fastened his mouth over one of her nipples. He scraped the tip of her breast lightly with his teeth, then soothed it with his tongue.

Catherine closed her eyes as he gave the same treatment to her other nipple. So many sensations were zinging through her body. Her breasts felt swollen and tight, her stomach churned, her pussy ached to be filled. She shifted on the bed, opening her legs wider as he moved one knee between them.

"Delicious." He raised his head from her breast and kissed her mouth. "You are delicious everywhere."

His statement brought heat to her face and made her clitoris throb. Catherine had dreamed last night of her fantasy man making love to her with his mouth. Apparently, it hadn't been a dream.

Catherine had had a grand total of three lovers in her life. Telling them what she needed during sex had always been difficult for her. Not now. She felt no shame with Kane, no shyness to tell him what she wanted. She kissed him deeply, then whispered, "Put your mouth between my legs."

Kane smiled. "With pleasure."

Catherine lay back and spread her legs. Kane lifted her knees until her feet were flat on the bed. He ran his hands up and down the outside of her thighs while he looked between her legs. Catherine waited, but he didn't move his hands from her thighs; he just kept staring at her. The tension built inside her body…that burning need for his fingers, his tongue, his cock.

The tension became almost unbearable. Catherine raised her hips and wantonly offered herself to him. "Kane, please."

"I want to look at you." He pushed on her knees to get her legs even farther apart. "A woman is beautiful here, especially when she is aroused. Your lips are dark pink and swollen. I can see how creamy and ready you are for me. I can smell you…that unique scent that comes only from a woman when she wants to make love."

If he so much as breathed on her, Catherine knew she would come right now.

He looked into her eyes. "You said you want my mouth on you. I want to watch you touch yourself first."

Catherine's clitoris throbbed in time with her heartbeat. Pleasuring herself when she was alone was one thing, but she'd never done that with a man watching her…not even her ex-husband.

She was so hot right now, she'd do handsprings if Kane asked her to.

Slowly, she slid her hand over her stomach to between her thighs. She inhaled sharply when she touched the wet, swollen folds.

"Yes, like that," Kane whispered. "Move your fingers over yourself."

She did as he requested, concentrating on her clitoris. Kane wrapped his hand around his cock, slowly pumping it as he looked at her. She'd never seen a man pleasure himself, and it fascinated her. If she didn't want him inside her so badly, she'd ask him to bring himself to an orgasm while she watched.

His pumping increased in time with her fingers. It took only a few strokes before her orgasm rushed through her body.

Kane raised her hand to his mouth and licked her fingers. It was the sexiest thing a man had ever done with her.

Catherine wrapped her hands around his wrists and tugged. "Come here."

He came down on top of her. Catherine reached between their bodies and took his cock in her hand. Lifting her hips, she guided him inside her.

She moaned when they became one. It had been so long since she'd had a man on top of her, inside her...

"You said you wanted my mouth on you," he murmured against her neck.

"I do. Later. Right now, I want this."

"I live to please you, pretty lady."

Kane began to thrust inside her, slowly at first, but quickly picking up speed. Catherine let her hands drift down his back until she reached his buttocks. She squeezed them, enjoying their firmness and fullness. He had very nice buns. Her breath hitched when he drove deeper inside her. He had very nice *everything*.

Kane's skin became damp with sweat. His breathing sounded labored. His heart thudded heavily against hers. His thrusts became harder, faster, pounding into her with a force that shook Catherine's senses. The pressure inside her built and built, until it exploded with a rush of pleasure that rippled through her body.

Catherine dug her short fingernails into Kane's buttocks when she heard the low animal growl in his throat. He thrust once, twice, three times, then lay still on top of her.

She couldn't have moved right then if her house was on fire. Every muscle and bone in her body had dissolved. She wrapped her arms tightly around Kane's waist and closed her eyes.

The touch of his lips on hers made her open her eyes again. "You are incredible," he whispered.

"That goes both ways."

"I pleased you?"

"Very much."

He smiled. "That is all I want." He moved to her side, propped up on one elbow, and draped his arm over her waist. "I would like to bathe."

"Oh, boy, me too."

Lifting his hand, he drew circles around her left nipple with his fingertip. "Is there a place where we can bathe together?"

"I don't think my tub is large enough for two, but we can shower together."

His brows drew together. "Shower? But it is not raining."

Kane had said earlier in the kitchen that there were many things he didn't know about, but Catherine had no idea something as basic as a shower would be foreign to him. "You really don't remember much of your former life, do you?"

"No, I do not, but I am willing to learn. Will you teach me?"

"Yes. And the shower is a good place to start."

* * * * *

"And this is where I work."

Kane stepped into the small room, unsure if he was ready to see more of the things Catherine took for granted but were so strange to him. He'd already seen the rest of Catherine's house and the many things she possessed. The fact that he could relieve himself in the "bathroom", as she called it, amazed him. He liked the shower very much. The warm water flowing over his body had quickly revived him. And the solid wall had been perfect for supporting Catherine as he pounded his cock into her.

The functional kitchen was an ingenious idea with all that space for cooking. He liked the refrigerator, the stove, and the microwave. The coffeemaker, she could keep.

Some things didn't appeal to him. He wasn't sure how the item she called a "telephone" worked, and he couldn't grasp the concept of a "television". Seeing small images of people locked up in a box made him uneasy.

His gaze swept every corner of her work area, noting the shelves full of books, the paintings of scenery on the walls, and the large, U-shaped desk covered with papers and more strange looking equipment.

Stepping closer to the desk, he looked at one of the pieces of equipment. Lights and buttons covered the top, and he saw several sheets of paper in a small tray.

"That's my fax machine."

"Fax machine," he said slowly, hoping he pronounced it correctly. "And what does this fax machine do?"

"It lets me send and receive messages over a telephone wire. They're printed out on that paper."

"Ah, another use for the telephone. Amazing."

"Yes." Catherine sighed. "I'm afraid I'm not a very good teacher, Kane. I don't know how to explain all these things to you. You have to be overwhelmed by all this."

Kane kissed her softly. "You are doing a wonderful job. You have been very patient with me." He glanced around the room again. "Everything is so different, and yes, it is overwhelming. I do not recognize any of these things." His gaze fell on another object sitting on her desk. "What is that?" he asked, pointing to it. "Is it another television?"

Catherine turned and faced her desk. "That's my computer. I use it in my work."

"You make a living with that box?"

She smiled. "I make a nice living with that box. I'm a graphic artist and I design websites and book covers."

"I understand 'artist,' but I do not understand 'graphic'. What is a 'website'?"

"Wow, how do I explain the Internet to you?" Catherine ran one hand through her hair. "I guess the best way is just to show you." She gestured toward the padded chair at her desk. "Sit down. I'll get another chair and be right back."

Kane sat in the chair, but he rolled it back from the desk. He did not want to be near the thing she called a "computer", not if there were small people in it too.

Catherine returned a moment later with her chair. She set it near the desk, then crooked her finger at him. "You need to come closer."

Reluctantly, Kane moved his chair where she indicated. He watched her touch an oval object and move it on the desk. An image of a rose appeared on the computer glass.

Kane backed up his chair a few inches.

Catherine smiled at him. "It won't hurt you, I promise. Here, I want to show you something."

He watched closely as she moved the oval object and pressed a button on it over and over. The image changed several times. Soon, a picture appeared with strange green and blue shapes.

"This is a map of the world." She pointed to a spot on the picture. "We're here, in Texas, in the United States of America. I can't be sure, but I think this is where you came from." She pointed to a different spot on the image with her finger. "This is England. Your accent makes me think this was your home."

England. The word sounded familiar, but Kane wasn't sure. "I do not know."

"No problem. Maybe you'll start to remember things soon." She moved the little oval thing and the image of England became larger. She pointed to another spot. "This is London. One of my clients lives about twenty kilometers outside of town."

"This London, it is far away from here?"

"Yes, it is far away from here." Returning her attention to the computer, she moved the oval thing again. "Let me show you the website I designed for my client."

The image changed while Kane watched. Soon a picture of a man and woman entwined on a bed came into view.

"This is her place on the Internet where people can go to learn about her and the books she writes. I can correspond with people all over the world from right here." He heard a "click" and a white box came up. "This is electronic mail, or e-mail for short. I use this to send messages to my clients and friends."

"You use this to send a message to a woman in England?"

"Yes. I can send a message to anyone in the world if I have their e-mail address."

Kane silently studied the white box for a moment, then looked at Catherine. "If you can sit here in your home and send a message to anyone in the world, you should have no trouble believing I am here because of a spell."

She blinked. Her mouth opened and closed once without her saying anything, then she chuckled. "Well, you have me there, Kane."

He smiled, happy for the first time since she'd begun the tour of her home.

Wanting to understand more about her work and her life, he scooted closer to the desk. "Tell me more about this Internet."

Chapter 5

Catherine saw Anita sitting at a table by the window close to the back of the restaurant. For a moment, she simply stood and watched her sister as Anita wrote in a notebook. Catherine loved her sister fiercely, but she'd always been jealous of her. Anita had it all—the beauty, the voluptuous body, the adoring husband, the three incredible children, the administrative assistant job she loved that netted her a very nice income.

Since Kane had come into her life, Catherine's jealousy had faded dramatically.

He'd become so special to her in such a short period of time. Only six days had passed since she met him...six days filled with easy conversation, quiet times, laughter, and passion. Their lovemaking didn't occur only at night during the cover of darkness. Kane enjoyed looking at her, touching her, and took every opportunity to tell her so...both with words and with his body. He especially liked making love outside in her backyard. Two fenced acres of land covered with large trees gave them all the privacy they needed, making clothes unnecessary.

Catherine had never been happier.

Pushing Kane to the back of her mind for now, she made her way to her sister's table. Anita looked up and smiled as Catherine drew closer.

"Hiya, sis."

"Hi." Catherine set a small gift bag on the table in front of her sister, then gave her a one-armed hug. "Happy birthday."

"Thanks, but you know you didn't have to get me a gift."

"And you know you'd be disappointed if I didn't."

Anita grinned. "True."

Catherine sat in the chair opposite Anita. "Am I late?"

"No, I was early. I took the day off and decided to do some shopping before lunch." She sighed dramatically as she opened the bag and peered inside it. "I had to go *alone* since you said you were too *busy* to go shopping with me."

"Sorry," Catherine said without the slightest bit of remorse. She was used to Anita's dramatics. "I was on a deadline. Take a look at Paulette Owen's site when you get the chance. I uploaded the changes this morning."

"Oh, Cat, I love the votives. Thank..." Anita stopped and looked at her sister, her eyes wide. "Paulette Owen?"

Catherine could almost see Anita's mouth watering at the mention of her favorite erotica author. Her sister hadn't read any type of erotica until six months ago. Now she couldn't get enough of it. Anita leaned forward, her expression eager. "Does she have a new book coming out?"

"Next month. The cover is gorgeous, if I do say so myself."

Smiling wickedly, Anita set the gift bag on the windowsill next to her. "A new book by Paulette Owen makes Jed sooooo happy."

"That's because you turn into a sex maniac."

"True. And the sex just gets better and better. It's hard to believe that, since sex with Jed has been magnificent since the first time with him." Anita sipped her iced tea. "One of these days, sis, you'll find the right guy and turn into a sex maniac, too."

Catherine quickly lowered her head so Anita wouldn't see the huge smile that tried to break free. She'd already found the right guy, and he was at her house right now playing on the computer.

"I see that grin on your face, Cat. What's going on? Have you met someone?"

Catherine concentrated on wiping the smile from her lips before looking at Anita again. "I'm not grinning about a guy, I'm grinning about you. Jed should send me roses once a week for introducing you to erotica."

"He has been a very happy camper the last few months."

"You're lucky, Nita. Jed is a great guy."

"Yes, he is, and I want *you* to find a great guy too."

"I'm fine, I promise. Don't worry about me."

"I'm supposed to worry about you. That's a big sister's job."

"And you take your job seriously, I know that, but I don't want you worrying about me." Catherine reached for the glass of water by her silverware. "Besides, we're here to celebrate your birthday. Let's get the waitress over here and order lunch. I'm hungry."

"I've already ordered chicken salad sandwiches for both of us. I told the waitress to turn in the order and bring you a glass of tea as soon as she saw you."

"Now, how did you know I'd even *want* a chicken salad sandwich?"

"Because you *always* order a chicken salad sandwich when we eat here."

The waitress arrived with Catherine's iced tea. She added a packet of Equal to it and took a sip before speaking again. "Sometimes I think you know me *too* well, Nita. Maybe I need to do something wild and crazy to shake you up."

"Like...what?"

"Like...have an affair with a gorgeous hunk."

"If you do something like that, I'll need complete details."

Catherine made little circles on the table with her iced tea glass while trying to decide how much to tell Anita. She shared everything with her sister, but maybe she shouldn't say anything yet. Maybe she should just show up at Anita's house for supper tomorrow night with Kane on her arm and watch her sister's mouth drop open. *That* would be fun.

Anita glanced past Catherine's shoulder. "While you're deciding about the gorgeous hunk, we can eat. Here comes our food." She returned her attention to Catherine. "You're still coming for supper tomorrow night, right?"

Catherine grinned. "I wouldn't miss it."

$$* \ * \ * \ * \ *$$

Three hours later, Catherine pulled into her driveway. Lunch had been shorter than Anita wanted, but Catherine had some shopping to do before she returned home and got back to work.

She liked shopping for Kane. While she enjoyed watching him walk around naked—which he much preferred over wearing clothes—she couldn't allow the UPS driver to come to her door and see Kane in the buff. He'd been happy with the denim shorts and simple white T-shirts she'd purchased for him, but she wanted to buy him something nicer.

It was while Catherine sorted through racks of dress shirts that she decided she would take Kane with her to Anita's tomorrow evening. Meeting her parents would be too big a step so soon in their blossoming relationship, but she wanted him to meet Anita, Jed, and the kids.

It really would be fun to watch Anita's mouth drop open.

Catherine grinned. She loved surprising her sister. Besides, it was time for Kane to get out of the house. They'd been inseparable for the past six days, but he needed to see other things than her home. She liked having him all to herself, yet she knew that wasn't fair to him. Perhaps driving around, looking at the scenery and buildings, would trigger a memory for him.

The sound of hammering greeted Catherine when she walked in the kitchen door. Kane had found several places on her property that could use some sprucing up and had volunteered to do the repairs. Since Catherine called on Jed to help her only when she had an emergency, she happily agreed to supply Kane with a hammer and nails. He was very good at carpentry, which made her wonder if that's what he had done in his former life.

She found him in her office, putting up a shelf above her computer. Catherine had mentioned to Kane about wanting a shelf there for some of the books she used most often. He hadn't told her he would build one for her, but apparently he had decided to while she was gone.

Leaning against the doorway, she watched him swing the hammer as if he'd done it for years. He wore only a pair of denim shorts. His hair was pulled back in a ponytail. The motion of his arm made the muscles bunch in his shoulder and upper back. Catherine sighed. Simply looking at him made her want him.

She had it bad.

Catherine walked up behind Kane and slipped her arms around his waist. His body jerked. He whipped his head to the side and looked at her over his shoulder.

"Hi," she said with a smile.

"Hello. You startled me."

"I'm sorry." She ran her hands up and down his chest. His skin was covered with a light sheen of perspiration. "I couldn't resist touching you."

Her comment made him smile. He covered one of her hands with his free one. "I will never complain about you touching me."

Catherine stepped closer and pressed her breasts against his back. "Have you been working long?"

"An hour, perhaps a bit longer. I am building the shelf you said you wanted here."

"I see that." She let her hands drift down to his stomach. "That's very nice of you."

Kane sucked in a sharp breath when Catherine's hands reached his crotch. "You are trying to distract me from working."

"Am I succeeding?"

"You are."

"Good." She released the snap, lowered the zipper, and slipped her hand inside his shorts. Finding no underwear didn't surprise her. Feeling him start to harden with just a simple touch didn't surprise her either. He always responded to her quickly.

"That feels good," he said, his voice husky. "I wish to touch you also."

"No. This time *I* get to do whatever I want."

"Have I not pleased you with my touch?"

"You've pleased me very much." She freed his now-hard cock from his shorts. "Now it's my turn."

Chapter 6

Kane faced Catherine and let her push his shorts down his legs. After stepping out of them, he stood still and waited for what she would do next. He desperately wanted to touch her, kiss her, but would respect her desire for him not to.

"Sit down," she whispered.

Pulling out the chair from her desk, Kane sat. He watched Catherine's gaze travel over him from his head to his feet, then up to his groin to linger there. The heat in that look made the blood pound in his cock. He shifted on the chair and thrust his hips forward. He needed to be inside her.

"Catherine, I want you."

"I want you too." She glanced in his eyes a moment before looking back at his groin. "I want to watch you touch yourself."

She had never asked that of him. He couldn't deny her anything she wanted. Wrapping one hand around his cock, he began to pump it slowly. He watched her face as he did. She stared intently at him, her concentration focused on the movement of his hand.

"Does that feel good?" she asked.

"Yes."

"Move your hand faster."

He obeyed her request, adding his second hand to rub over the head while he continued to pump. Release would not be far away at this rate. If she wanted to watch him climax, he would do so for her.

"Would some lotion or oil make it better for you?"

Kane's heavy breathing made it difficult to answer her. "I am fine. Do you wish for me to climax this way?"

"Yes...and no. I want..." Her breasts rose and fell with her sigh. "You are so gorgeous, Kane. I love to look at you." She lightly touched his hand. "Stop, please."

He did, mere seconds before his release would have overtaken him.

Catherine touched his knees and pushed them outward. Kane obeyed her silent demand for him to spread his legs. "I love the way I feel when I'm with you...cherished, loved, beautiful. No man has ever made me feel the way you do."

Kneeling before him, she cupped his cock in her hands. Kane briefly closed his eyes at the intense pleasure, but quickly opened them again so he could watch her. She had cradled him with her hands and her body, but had not yet done so with her mouth. He'd desired it, but hadn't asked that of her in case she found it distasteful.

Her tongue licked the tiny slit on the tip. Kane gripped the armrests so as not to grab her head and drive his cock deep inside her mouth. He was already so close to a climax, but this had to be at her pace...no matter if the waiting drove him insane.

Her lips encircled the head. He could feel her tongue bathing the entire tip, then darting into the slit again. Over and over she repeated the action. Sweat beaded Kane's forehead and he gripped the armrests tighter.

Looking into his eyes, Catherine's tongue slowly made a path down his cock to the base. She licked both balls thoroughly before making the return journey to the tip.

"Do you like this?" she asked.

Kane swallowed thickly. "Yes."

"Do you want more?"

"I want whatever you are willing to do."

She covered the head with her lips again. Kane groaned deep in his throat. Her mouth moved farther down, back up, then down again. With each pass, she took more of him, until at last she had all of his cock in her mouth.

Kane couldn't hold back any longer. Clasping her head, he began gently fucking her mouth. He slowly increased his speed until he developed a rhythm with her. When he was sure he wasn't hurting her, he moved even faster, until he almost left the chair with each thrust.

Catherine's hand slipped between his legs. He felt the pressure of her wet fingertip against his anus. On his next downward motion, her finger slipped inside him.

"Ah, Catherine..."

Pleasure rushed through his body. Kane closed his eyes, lifted his hips, and let the orgasm overtake him.

Long moments passed while Kane waited for his heart to stop pounding. When he finally managed to open his eyes, he saw Catherine still on her knees between his legs. Her tongue kept bathing his softening cock as if she couldn't get enough of his taste. The feeling was incredible, but it was the love shining in her eyes that touched his heart.

He hadn't said the words yet. It was time. Bending forward, Kane took her lips in a passionate kiss.

"I love you, Catherine."

Tears quickly filled her eyes. "I love you, too."

He wiped the tears from her lower lashes. "Why are you crying?"

"Because I'm just...feeling so much right now."

"As am I." He kissed her again, softly this time. "What you did...it was a very personal thing."

"I wanted to taste you. I haven't...done that except with my ex-husband."

"I am pleased you did it for me." He kissed her once more before whispering, "I wish to make love to you with my mouth now."

In response to his request, Catherine pulled her T-shirt over her head and removed her bra. She lay back on the carpet, unfastened her slacks, and pushed them and her panties over her hips. When they reached her thighs, Kane took over. Dropping to his knees, he pulled her clothes over her feet and tossed them behind him.

Kane wasted no time in lowering his face between Catherine's thighs. She was very creamy. It proved that watching him pleasuring himself and having him in her mouth had aroused her greatly. He slid his tongue over her, taking some of her cream into his mouth.

"You are delicious, Catherine. I love the way you taste, the way you smell."

He also loved the way she responded when he flicked her clitoris with his tongue. In the short time they'd been together, he'd learned what she liked and what she didn't like. They'd made love many times already, in many different positions. It got better each time.

The way Catherine moved her hips indicated she was close to her peak. Kane slipped two fingers inside her and increased the flicking of her clitoris, wanting to send her over that peak.

She grabbed his head, raised her hips, and trembled.

Kane rained kisses on her skin as he traveled up her body. He thrust his tongue into her mouth as he thrust his cock into her pussy.

Catherine gasped and arched her back. Kane felt the contractions deep inside her, signaling she'd reached the peak again.

"So soon?" he asked against her lips.

"Yes. God, yes."

"Good. That pleases me."

"It would please me for you to move." She skimmed her hands down his back and clasped his buttocks. "I'm not through."

Obeying her command, Kane began to move again. He didn't rush, but continued to thrust at an unhurried pace while staring into her eyes. He watched the different emotions cross her face...desire, impatience, rapture, completion. When he saw that last emotion, he let his own pleasure engulf him.

Kane moved to his back and drew Catherine to his side. She cuddled up against him, wrapping one arm around his waist and laying one leg over both of his.

"It just keeps getting better, doesn't it?" she asked softly.

Kane chuckled to himself. He'd had that same thought only moments earlier. Tightening his arms around her, he dropped a kiss on the top of her head. "Yes, it does."

"Nita told me sex with Jed keeps getting better the longer they're together."

Sex was a private thing between a man and a woman. The fact that Catherine and her sister talked about it surprised him. "You and your sister discuss something so personal?"

"We talk about everything. We're very close." She tilted her head on his shoulder and gazed at his face. "I want you to meet her."

Kane had been slowly stroking her shoulders and upper back. Her words made him freeze. He couldn't meet Anita. He couldn't meet *anyone*.

Not ready to discuss his situation yet, Kane forced a smile. "I will meet her soon."

"Tomorrow."

"*Tomorrow?*"

"We're going to her and Jed's house for supper."

Kane didn't know what to say. He couldn't go to Anita's house, but didn't want to tell Catherine why. Not yet. Grasping for an excuse, he said the first thing that came into his head. "I have no clothes appropriate to wear."

Catherine laughed. "That old 'I have nothing to wear' excuse belongs to a woman, Kane. Besides, you *do* have clothes to wear. I bought two pairs of jeans and three shirts for you today. Oh, and a pair of running shoes and three pairs of socks. I didn't buy you any more briefs since you don't wear the ones you already have." Her hand drifted down to fondle his flaccid penis. "Not that I'm complaining. I like slipping my hand inside your shorts to touch you."

Unable to lie still any longer, Kane pulled away from Catherine and sat up. He ran one hand over his face while frantically searching his mind for a way out of meeting Anita without making Catherine suspicious.

He didn't want to tell her the truth. If he did, he would lose her.

"Kane?" She sat up beside him. "What's wrong?"

"Nothing is wrong," he said quickly.

"Don't lie to me, Kane, please. Tell me what's bothering you."

Kane reached for his denim shorts. "I will bring you a washcloth."

She grabbed his wrist, keeping him from picking up his shorts. "I don't want a washcloth. I want you to talk to me."

Kane laid his hand over hers. He knew he had to tell her. Despite their glorious lovemaking, she wouldn't want to stay here in her home forever. It was natural that she'd want him to meet her sister, and eventually her friends.

Gathering his courage, Kane looked into her eyes. "I am thirsty. I will prepare us something to drink while you get dressed. Then we will talk."

Chapter 7

Catherine's hands shook as she tugged on a pair of shorts. Whatever Kane wanted to talk about, she had the feeling she wouldn't like it. Kane was always happy, charming, almost carefree, despite knowing so little about this time period. Today was the first time since he'd come into her life that he'd looked uncomfortable.

Maybe he was thinking about leaving her.

No. He *couldn't* be leaving her. They'd just had the most amazing sex, and they'd both said they loved each other. He couldn't *possibly* leave her.

Catherine pulled a clean T-shirt over her head, not bothering with a bra. Kane liked for her to go braless. He liked to come up behind her, slip his hands beneath her shirt, and cup her unbound breasts. He liked to rub his fingertips over her nipples until they became hard, and suck on them until she was begging him to take her.

Kane was the best lover she'd ever had, but it wasn't simply the sex that made her love him. He was considerate, charming, funny, intelligent. He learned quickly, even things like using the computer when he'd had no idea how to turn one on, much less control a mouse.

He found things to occupy himself during the day so she could work, but the evening was their time together. They would sit in the living room after supper, reading, watching television, or simply talking. She loved to hear him speak with that wonderful accent.

She just *loved* him.

Oh God, I can't let him go. Please don't take him away from me.

After running a brush through her hair, Catherine made her way to the kitchen. She found Kane leaning against the counter, drinking iced tea. He lowered his glass when he saw her.

"Your tea is on the table."

Catherine glanced in the direction of the table before looking back at him. "Thank you." She tried to think of what to say, what to ask. She was so afraid he'd discovered from the Internet that there was a huge world out there, and he wanted to see it.

"Please sit down, Catherine."

"All right."

Catherine sat at the table, then picked up her glass of tea and took a healthy sip to wet her suddenly dry throat.

Kane sat down across from her. He laid his hands in the middle of the table, palms up. Catherine took that as a sign that he wanted her touch. Setting down her glass, she grasped his hands tightly.

"I cannot go to your sister's house tomorrow night."

He didn't want to go to Anita's. Catherine didn't understand why he didn't want to go, but perhaps he still felt uncomfortable meeting any of her family so soon. If that was the only thing wrong, she could definitely live with that. The weight on her heart began to lift. "No problem. We can go another time. I'll call her—"

"No, Catherine, you do not understand. It is not that I do not *want* to go, I *cannot* go."

The weight settled back on her heart. "You're right. I don't understand."

Kane looked down at their clasped hands. "You have been busy with your work. I understand that and would never interfere while you are doing something you obviously enjoy." He squeezed her hands before raising his gaze to her face. "I have been taking walks around your property each day while you work. I have not wanted to disturb you, and it is difficult for me to keep my hands off you when I am near you. I only have to look at you to want you."

Catherine smiled slightly, but remained silent. She didn't want to interrupt anything he had to tell her.

"Two days ago, I decided to do some exploring. You had told me that the lane leads to a road and other people's homes. I wanted to see something other than your land." Kane took a deep breath and let it out slowly. "When I reached the edge of your front yard, I could go no farther."

Catherine frowned. "What do you mean, you could go no farther? Why not?"

"Because I was stopped. I tried to take a step off your yard, and it was as if I had come up against an invisible wall. I felt the wall but I could not see it, and I could not get past it." Releasing her hands, Kane leaned back in his chair. "That is when the memories began to come back."

"What did you remember?"

"More about Alexandra's spell. Yes, I remember her name now, although I did not when I first arrived here. She was a beautiful woman, but jealous and possessive. When I turned her away, she placed me under the spell that caused my imprisonment. She said someday I might find my true love, but I would live with her completely alone, cut off from any other people." He leaned forward in his chair again. "No one will be able to see me, Catherine. Your sister could come here, sit at this table with me, and she would not know I exist. I cannot leave your property to meet anyone. I am completely isolated here with you."

The fact of Kane's existence was hard enough to believe; what he said now couldn't possibly be true. How could something that happened years ago — perhaps centuries ago — keep him bound to a house and two acres of land?

"Kane, I'm sorry, but I don't believe this. It's just too incredible."

"I can prove it. Walk with me to the edge of your property."

The doorbell's ring made Catherine jump. She wasn't expecting anyone and couldn't imagine who would be here.

"I'll be right back," she said, rising from her chair.

"I will go with you."

Kane followed her to the front door. He stood right beside her as Catherine opened it to see her regular UPS driver, Scott, with a small package.

"Hi," he said as he held out his clipboard for her to sign. "Looks like you've been shopping on the Internet again."

"Guilty as charged." She signed her name in the space provided, glancing at Kane as she did. He moved so he stood directly in front of the driver, no more than six inches away from him. Scott didn't even blink. Kane waved his hands in front of the driver's face. Still, nothing.

A chill raced down Catherine's spine.

She returned the board to Scott and accepted her package. Closing the front door, she leaned back against it and faced Kane.

Her heart pounded so hard, she could feel it in her temples.

Kane crossed his arms over his chest. "Now do you believe me?"

"I have no other choice." Releasing a heavy sigh, Catherine pushed her hair off her forehead. "So what does this mean? Do you have more to tell me?"

A look of indecision flashed through his eyes. "There is more, but it can wait until later."

"No, I don't think I *want* it to wait. Tell me everything now so I can figure out how to deal with it."

Kane held out his hand to her. "Come sit down with me."

Catherine took his hand and let him lead her to the couch. Instead of sitting beside her, he knelt on the floor before her.

"It is strange that I remember so little of my life, but remember Alexandra so vividly. I have to assume that was part of her spell. If she could not have me, I would not have myself." He took her hands in his. "I will not age, Catherine. How you see me now is how I will remain. I will stay young and strong and…virile for the rest of your life."

It took a moment for Catherine to realize what Kane was actually saying. "The rest of my life? You won't ever change?"

"No."

"I'll get older, but you won't?"

"No, but it will be many years before you will even realize it, Catherine. You're a young and beautiful woman. You will stay beautiful for a long time."

"I suppose."

"We will be together. We will make love as often as you want. Aging will not affect me." He squeezed her hands. "I have read that a woman becomes more amorous as she grows older. I will still be able to satisfy you as often as you want, as I do now."

"There's more to a relationship than sex, Kane. Being with you is wonderful, but I can't share you with anyone. I can't introduce you to my sister, or my parents, or my friends. We can't go anywhere together, not even out to dinner or a movie. I attend two or three conferences a year because of my work. You won't be able to go with me."

"I will be here when you return."

"What kind of life will that be for you?"

"I will have you."

Catherine remained silent several moments. He would wait here for her, no matter how long she had to be gone. Emotion clogged her throat and made her heart feel as if it would swell right out of her chest. How lucky she was to have found him.

Releasing one of his hands, Catherine touched his face. "Well, there's a bright side to all this. When we decide to start a family, you'll be here to take care of the kids until I return."

Kane closed his eyes, tilted his head back, and blew out a quick breath.

His action made Catherine's heart stop.

"Don't you want children, Kane?"

He looked at her again, and she saw pain and unhappiness in his eyes. "Yes, Catherine, I want children. I would like very much to place my hand on your stomach and feel my child moving inside your body. But I cannot. Another effect of the spell is that I cannot father a child."

Catherine's mind spun. All this was happening much too fast. No one would ever know about Kane. She would grow older and everyone would think she was alone since they couldn't see him. He was literally a prisoner and could never leave her property. He would never see the mountains, or the ocean, or the desert, except on television or the Internet.

She would never have the children she wanted.

"We will be together, Catherine. It is enough for me."

It isn't enough for me.

The unbidden thought flashed through Catherine's mind. She quickly pushed it aside. She loved Kane and wanted to be with him. They had problems to work out, but all couples had problems. As long as they loved each other, everything would be fine.

Chapter 8

Catherine stood up and stretched her arms high over her head. Three straight hours on the computer was too much at one time, but she wanted to get her project finished. Her latest client now had a brand new look to her website, one Catherine had worked hard to accomplish. Personally, she would never use orange, green, and blue as the color scheme, but that's what her client had wanted. Making the colors blend into an eye-pleasing scheme had been a challenge.

A challenge always made her blood flow faster.

It also made her hungry. Her stomach growled, reminding her she hadn't eaten anything since a slice of toast hours ago. She headed for the kitchen to prepare something for her and Kane. She stopped along the way to peer into the bedroom, bathroom, and living room in search of him. She didn't find him in any of the rooms.

The house had been silent all morning except for the soft instrumental music she played while she worked. That meant Kane must be outside.

He'd spent a lot of time outside this past week.

Catherine looked through the kitchen window, but she didn't see him. She debated for a moment whether to leave him alone or look for him. The desire to find him won.

He stood on her front yard, his hands in the back pockets of his jeans, staring down the narrow lane that led to the farm-market-road...and points beyond. She watched him for well over a minute, but he never moved; he simply stood still and stared. Tears tightened her throat. No matter how many times he said being with her was enough, he had to be feeling more frustrated every day about being stuck on two acres. He'd already done all the small carpentry projects she had, mowed her lawn, trimmed the hedges, and painted the inside of the garage. Other than adding on a room to her house that she didn't want, she didn't know of any other projects he could do.

She walked up behind him and touched his shoulder. "Hi."

Kane looked at her. The corners of his mouth turned up, but she couldn't call it a smile.

"Are you all right?"

"I am fine."

"What are you doing?"

"Staying out of your way while you work."

"I appreciate that, but I'm taking a break. How about some lunch?"

"I am not very hungry."

That wasn't good. Kane was a hearty eater and never turned down a meal. "Then keep me company while I make a sandwich."

Catherine held out her hand to him. He hesitated a few seconds, then placed his hand in hers.

Halfway to the house, Catherine heard a car coming down her lane. She looked over her shoulder and recognized Anita's car.

Kane released her hand and took a step back. Catherine glanced at him, hurt that he'd pulled away from her. She swung her gaze back to the car when her sister opened the driver's door.

"Hiya, sis," Anita said as she climbed out of her Honda and circled the front to the passenger side.

"Hi. Two Fridays off in a row? Are you special or something?"

"Well, yes, I'm *very* special." She grinned and opened the passenger's door. "I had to take Paige to the doctor."

Anita's five-year-old daughter bounded from the car and ran toward her aunt. Catherine dropped to her knees to accept Paige's hug.

"Hi, Aunt Cat!"

"Hi, sweetie." She looked back at her sister. "Why did she have to go to the doctor?"

"Just a follow-up after she had that nasty virus."

"I'm all better now," Paige said. "The doctor tol' me so."

Catherine smiled. "Well, that's wonderful. I'm glad you're all better." She tickled Paige's tummy, making her niece giggle. "How about a glass of lemonade to celebrate?"

"Yes, please."

Standing, Catherine took Paige's hand and led her toward the house. She looked at Kane to be sure he was following them. He stayed a few steps behind as they made their way to the back door.

* * * * *

Catherine spoke with her sister and shared a glass of lemonade with her niece while Paige sat on her lap, but she kept her gaze trained on Kane whenever possible. He stood next to the sink, ankles and arms crossed. Sometimes he would glance her way, but most of the time he simply stood still and stared at the floor.

Her heart ached for him.

"We need to get going, sis. I just stopped by to get that knitting book."

"It's on my dresser. I'll go get it."

"I can get it, Aunt Cat."

Catherine smiled at her niece and kissed her cheek. "Okay, you can get it."

Paige slipped from Catherine's lap and skipped from the room. Catherine sighed. "She's growing up *way* too fast."

"Don't I know it. My baby isn't a baby anymore." Anita leaned forward in her chair. "If there's another baby in this family, it'll be up to you."

Catherine glanced at Kane. He was staring intently at her. She quickly looked away.

Paige skipped back in the room with the large book. "Here, Mommy."

"Thank you, darling." She took the book from her daughter and stood. "We'd better go. I'll call you tomorrow."

"I'll be here."

Catherine watched Kane finally move away from the sink toward the table. He reached out to touch her niece's head. She gasped as his hand passed through Paige as if she were nothing but air.

Anita frowned. "Cat? What's wrong?"

Catherine swallowed quickly to dislodge the lump in her throat. "Nothing. Just a muscle twinge."

"Hey, *I'm* the one who just had a birthday. You're too young for muscle twinges."

"Tell that to my muscles."

Anita held out her hand to Paige. "Let's go, sweetheart."

"Okay." Paige looked up at Catherine. "Will you come see me soon, Aunt Cat?"

"You bet I will, sweetheart."

Catherine walked them to the door, then turned to face Kane. He sat at the table, twirling her half-empty glass around and around. She sat across from him.

"She's a beautiful little girl," he said softly, not looking at her.

"Yes, she is."

"You two are very close."

"I'm close with all three of Anita's kids. They're all very special."

Kane raised his gaze to her face. "You will be a wonderful mother."

A sharp pain shot through Catherine's heart. She loved her niece and two nephews and longed for children of her own. Falling in love with Kane meant she'd never carry a child, never feel life moving inside her. "You said you can't father a child."

"I cannot, but another man could," he whispered.

"No," Catherine stated firmly. "That isn't even an option."

"Catherine, you deserve to have the chance at motherhood."

"I don't have to physically bear a child to be a mother. We could adopt..."

"There is no 'we' as far as the world is concerned, Catherine. You saw what happened when I tried to touch Paige. I would never be able to hold a child if you adopted one."

"Then I won't."

Kane slammed his palms flat on the table, making Catherine jump. "That is not fair to you. You deserve more than half a life, which is all you'll have as long as you're with me."

"Why are you saying these things, Kane? I thought you wanted to be with me."

"I want that more than anything."

"Then I don't understand why we're having this conversation."

The fire left his eyes, to be replaced with sadness. "I want only your happiness, Catherine."

"I have it." Reaching across the table, she covered his hands with hers. "With you."

* * * * *

Kane lay on the bed, waiting while Catherine finished drying her hair. They'd showered together, as they did every night. He loved soaping her skin, sliding his slick hands over her body, watching the lather disappear as the water cascaded over her. More often than not, they would make love in the small stall, with Catherine's back against the wall and her legs wrapped around his waist while he pounded his cock into her.

Not tonight. Tonight, he'd showered quickly and left her in the bathroom. He needed to be alone to think.

Seeing her with her niece today had made him understand how much she was giving up by loving him. It wasn't only the lack of children, although that was the main thing he considered. She'd said it didn't matter that he could never travel with her, or he'd never grow old, but he couldn't quite believe that. Perhaps it didn't matter to her now, but it would in time. Her family and friends would watch her grow older and believe her to be alone. They would try to set her up with men, even if she told them not to, for they would feel sorry for her.

He could not allow that. He could not allow her to be unhappy because of him.

Kane covered his eyes with one arm. He did not want to leave her, but he knew no other way for her to be happy.

"Kane?"

He moved his arm and saw Catherine standing by the bed. She wore her short, silky robe...the one he enjoyed so much taking off her.

"Are you all right?"

"Yes, I am fine. Perhaps a bit tired."

"You worked hard this afternoon. I didn't know you were building new bookshelves for my office, but I appreciate them."

"I enjoyed making them for you."

She toyed with the belt of her robe. "Are you too tired to make love?"

As Kane watched, she untied the belt and slipped the robe from her shoulders. It fell to the floor, leaving her nude before him. Propping up on his elbow, he reached out, cupped one breast in his hand, and ran his thumb over the nipple. "I am never too tired to make love with you."

She lay beside him and he took her in his arms. For a moment, he simply held her, absorbing her scent, the softness of her skin, the warmth of her breath on his neck. Then he kissed her, softly, so softly. When she responded, he deepened the kiss, using his tongue to part her lips so he could dip inside her mouth. He so loved the way she tasted.

Her response quickly intensified. The frantic way she clutched at him told Kane she was as aroused as he. Rolling to his back, he helped her to straddle his hips. He held his rigid cock while she lowered herself onto it.

Catherine threw back her head and arched her back. "Oh, Kane, you feel so good inside me."

"Move for me, Catherine. Take whatever you need from me."

She did as he suggested, her breasts bouncing as she rode him hard and fast. Kane laid still as long as he could, then he had to move. Clutching her waist, he lifted his hips as she lowered hers, driving his cock as far inside her as possible.

The contractions deep within her, signaling her climax, brought on Kane's own release. He held tightly to Catherine's waist while the pleasure washed over him.

Catherine crumpled on top of him. "Wow."

Kane slid his hands down to her buttocks. "Yeah, wow."

He could feel the rumble of laughter in her chest. "That's the first time I've heard you say 'yeah'."

"I have learned some of your more…relaxed words. What we just did, you call it 'fucking', right?"

This time, Catherine laughed out loud. "Yes, some people call it that."

"You do not?"

"I prefer to call it 'lovemaking'."

"I will call it whatever you wish."

He stroked her back and buttocks, over and over, while their breathing slowed. She felt so good in his arms, so perfect.

The thought of another man holding her like this hurt him more than if someone thrust a knife into his chest.

"You're leaving, aren't you?" Catherine whispered.

Kane's hands stopped. He took a deep breath and let it out slowly. "Yes."

"Why?"

"For you."

Catherine raised her head from his chest and looked at him with tears in her eyes. "Don't say you're doing it for me. I don't want you to leave."

She scrambled from the bed, grabbed her robe from the floor, and hurriedly pulled it over her arms. Kane rose more slowly, until he stood in front of her. His heart ached even more when she swiped tears from her cheeks.

"Catherine—"

She closed her robe with a fast twist of the belt. "I love you! Can't you understand that?"

"Yes, I understand that. And I love you. That is why I must leave."

"If you love me, then leaving me makes no sense! We're so happy together. How can you give that up?"

"Yes, we're happy and you love me now, but that love will not last. You will grow older and watch me stay young. You will be able to come and go as you please while I am here." He spread his arms wide to indicate his "prison". "You will never be able to introduce me to anyone."

"I don't care! No relationship is perfect. Every couple has problems they have to work out."

"But our problems cannot be worked out, Catherine." Kane stepped forward and cradled her face in his hands. "You do not care now, but you will someday. It is better if I leave *now*, while you are still young enough to find someone else to love…someone who can give you the children you want, can live the life with you that you want."

Tears continued to trickle down her cheeks. Kane wiped away each one with his thumbs. "You have to tear up the card."

"I can't, Kane." Her voice sounded thick and husky. "I can't. I don't want to lose you."

Kane released her, walked over to her dresser, and picked up the greeting card. He had looked at it every day for the last week, wondering how he could possibly ask her to tear it and make him disappear. He did not want to leave, but had no other choice. For her happiness later, she had to be unhappy now.

Taking a deep breath for courage, Kane returned to her and held out the card. "Take it. Tear it."

She looked at the card, then back at him. "Wh-what will happen to you?"

"I do not know, exactly. I know I will leave you."

More tears fell from her eyes. "Kane, please, don't do this."

"Catherine, I cannot tear the card myself. I cannot make myself disappear. It has to be up to you. *You* have to be the one to tear it."

"*I can't!*"

"And I cannot watch you grow to resent or perhaps even hate me! I cannot look into your beautiful eyes and watch your love fade!" He grabbed her wrist and slapped the card into her palm. "Tear it!"

With shaking hands, Catherine grasped the card at the fold. She looked into his eyes, and he could see how much this hurt her. Tears filled his throat, making speech difficult. "Please," he whispered.

She tore the card into two pieces.

He felt no pain. That surprised Kane. All he felt was peace and serenity. He gazed at Catherine. A halo of light surrounded her. He caught a glimpse of her future...marriage, two children, a larger home, a successful career.

And a man who loved her deeply.

"I love you, Catherine. I always will."

Catherine stood still, unable to move, while she watched Kane slowly fade from her sight. She opened her hands and the card pieces fell to her feet.

What have I done?

"Kane? Kane!"

She reached out a hand to where he had been standing. Nothing. There was no warmth, no scent, no sound...nothing to indicate Kane had been here.

"*Kane!*"

Catherine fell to her knees and frantically grabbed the card pieces. She clutched them to her chest, over her heart.

"Kane, I'm sorry! Come back to me. Please come back!"

All that greeted her wish was silence.

Chapter 9
Six Months Later

"Take care of your plants," Anita said, ticking off the details on her fingers. "Bring in the mail and stack it on your desk. Download your e-mail into the 'pending' folder you made. Check the answering machine for messages." She wiggled four fingers. "That's it, right?"

"That's it. I've already stopped the newspaper, so you don't have to worry about that."

"Great. Okay, then I guess you're ready to go as soon as you finish your packing." Anita picked up a sweater from the bed and started folding it. "I'll help you."

Catherine took the sweater from her sister's hands and laid it in the large suitcase. "I can do this, Nita," she said softly.

"Right. Of course you can." She folded her arms beneath her breasts. "Are you sure there isn't *something* I can do to help?"

"You're doing it, just by being here."

Pushing the pile of clothes to the side, Anita sat on the bed and watched Catherine place more items in the suitcase. "Going away will be good for you. You've been working too hard lately and spending too much time in this house. The fresh air will be good for you."

Catherine chuckled. Anita was beginning to repeat herself, a sure sign that she wasn't saying what she actually wanted to say. She straightened and looked at her sister. "What do you want to ask me that you aren't asking me?"

Anita clasped her hands together in her lap. "Are you ever going to tell me why you've been so unhappy the last six months?"

Catherine looked away from Anita's inquiring gaze. She hadn't confided in her sister, mainly because her story was so unbelievable. She had no proof that Kane had even been here, except for the carpentry work he'd done and the few items of clothing that she kept on the top shelf of her closet.

And she still hurt too much to talk about him.

Six months should've been enough time to heal, or at least to start the healing process. After all, she'd only known Kane for two weeks. But six months wasn't nearly enough time to forget him. Catherine's heart felt as heavy now as it had when she tore up the greeting card.

She missed him so much.

"I've just been...frustrated and tired, Nita. I took on too many new clients because it's hard for me to say no and I got overwhelmed. I really need this vacation."

"But Thanksgiving is next week. What did you tell Mom about not coming to the big family shindig?"

"I told her the truth. She said as long as I'm back by Christmas, all will be forgiven."

Anita grinned. "Sounds like Mom." Her grin quickly faded. "You don't know anyone in Colorado."

"That's the whole point. I'm not even taking my laptop. I have twenty books downloaded on my eBookMan and I'm taking a few paperbacks too. I just want to read, relax, and recharge."

"Can I go with you?"

Catherine laughed. "Not this time." Taking Anita's hand, she pulled her up from the bed. "Now get out of here so I can finish packing. My plane leaves in four hours."

"Okay, okay." Anita hugged her fiercely. "Are you sure you don't want me to drive you to the airport?"

"I'm sure. I've already told you I'm riding with Mrs. McPherson. Her son is flying in for a visit just about the time my flight leaves."

"Well, okay then. I guess...there's nothing else for me to do but say goodbye."

Anita's last words faded off and tears flooded her eyes. Seeing her sister crying made Catherine's eyes fill also. She hugged Anita again. "I'll be back, I promise. Don't worry about me."

"I *have* to worry. I'm the big sister."

"So you keep telling me." She hooked one arm through Anita's and led her toward the back door. "I'll call you when I get to the lodge."

"You'd better."

After one more hug, Catherine ushered her sister out the back door and closed it behind her. Peace, finally. Anita had been here all morning, hovering like a mother hen over her chick. Catherine loved her sister dearly, but she was glad to see her go so she could be alone.

Alone with her memories of Kane.

Stop it, Catherine. He's been gone six months. You have to get on with your life.

This vacation had been a spur-of-the-moment decision, but a decision Catherine was glad she'd made. Getting away from this house would be good for her. She hadn't been lying to Anita when she said she'd been working long hours. Working helped keep her mind off Kane.

After preparing herself a cup of hot chocolate, Catherine returned to the bedroom to finish her packing. She planned to get over Kane once and for all...starting today.

* * * * *

Catherine knew better than to go into any of those stores at the airport. Despite her eBookMan holding twenty books and the three paperbacks in her suitcase, she hadn't been able to resist buying more books and some souvenirs for Anita's kids. With her carry-on slung over her shoulder, her shopping bag in one hand, and the large suitcase on wheels behind her, Catherine made her way down the hall. She looked at each door number, certain her room had to be close.

She rounded the corner—and ended up on her butt when someone knocked her off her feet.

"I'm so sorry!" a deep, masculine voice said. "Are you all right? Please, let me help you up."

Goose bumps erupted all over her skin. She knew that voice. She'd listened to it whisper words of love to her every night for two weeks.

Catherine looked at the hand stretched out to her. It was sturdy and strong, with calluses on the palm and fingertips. This was a hand that did a lot of manual labor. She let her gaze travel up his sweater-clad arm to a broad shoulder, dark brown hair that brushed that shoulder, then to his face.

Catherine gasped.

"You really are hurt, aren't you?" he asked, concern evident in his voice. "Do I need to call a doctor?"

His mentioning a doctor snapped Catherine out of her shock. "No, no, of course not. I'm fine, really." She hesitated another moment before placing her hand in his.

Catherine almost jerked it back when she felt that same electric sensation she'd experienced the first time she'd touched Kane's greeting card. He tugged gently until she stood on shaky legs.

She gazed up into Kane's face.

He still looked worried. "Are you sure? There's a doctor on staff here in the lodge..."

"No, that isn't necessary. My pride is more bruised than my bottom."

She attempted to smile. It wasn't easy when her heart pounded so hard and her lungs fought for oxygen. Her attempt must have looked real, for he smiled back.

"That'll teach me to watch where I'm going instead of daydreaming about hitting the slopes." He squatted and began to pick up the items that had spilled from her shopping bag. "The least I can do is help you carry this stuff to your room."

Catherine started to tell him he didn't have to help, but stopped before speaking. If he wanted to be a gentleman and carry her luggage, she would gratefully accept.

And she wanted more time with him.

"Thank you. I appreciate your help."

"No problem." He rose with her shopping bag in one hand, and took her wheeled luggage in his other. "Can you grab your carry-on?"

"Sure."

"Which one's your room?"

"Number fourteen."

He smiled. "How about that? Mine's fifteen. I'm right across the hall from you. Here, I'll show you."

Catherine followed him around the corner and down the hall. She tried not to stare at his bottom in those tight ski pants, but it wasn't easy. She'd always loved looking at Kane's buttocks, especially when he hadn't been wearing anything.

"Right there," he said, nodding toward the door to room fourteen.

"Thank you." Catherine unlocked the door with her card key, which wasn't easy when her hands were shaking. She pushed it open and stood to the side. He entered the room and set her bag on the dresser and her suitcase on the floor. Every movement, every gesture he made, looked exactly like Kane's.

Her heart constricted in her chest.

"There you go," he said with another smile. "And you're okay, right?"

"I'm fine, thanks."

He stood still, his hands at his sides. Catherine felt as if he wanted to say something else and waited for him to speak.

"Since I practically ran over you, I guess I should introduce myself. I'm Keene."

Keene. Oh, God, even his *name* was similar! Catherine ignored the tightening in her throat. "I'm Catherine."

"It's nice to meet you, Catherine."

"You too."

After several moments of him staring at her, he gestured at the door. "I'd better go so you can unpack. I'll, uh, see you on the slopes."

That possibility wasn't likely since she'd be on the beginner's slope and he was probably an expert, but Catherine returned his smile and said, "See you."

Keene headed for the door. Before he stepped out of her room, he turned back to face her. "I know this is going to sound like a pick-up line, but I would swear I know you. Is it possible we've met?"

Catherine let her gaze wander over him. She looked at his thick brown hair, shorter than Kane's but still brushing his shoulders. She looked at his dark brown eyes, the hint of a five-o'clock shadow. Broad shoulders and chest, trim waist, sturdy legs, and the large bulge that ski pants couldn't hide, all received her perusal. He could pass for Kane's twin brother, yet he was also different. His voice was a bit deeper, his body not as husky, and a thick moustache covered his upper lip.

Alike, yet different.

The heaviness in her heart disappeared, leaving Catherine feeling lighter and more carefree than she had in six months. She *knew*. She didn't know how, but she knew Keene and Kane were one and the same. Their love was strong enough that he'd found a way to come back to her.

Catherine smiled. "Yes, I believe it's *very* possible."

ONE THING TO GIVE

Chapter 1

Samuel McKeifer dropped a slice of lime in the gin and tonic he'd prepared before glancing up again. She still sat at table six. She'd been sitting there, alone, for over an hour, nursing a plain Coke.

She hadn't been alone earlier this evening. He'd seen her with three other women in the restaurant when he'd arrived at 7:00, sitting at a table close to the bar. Having to go right to work meant he couldn't pay as much attention to her as he'd liked, but he'd taken every opportunity he had to look at her.

She'd left with the other women shortly before 8:00. At 9:00, he'd looked up to see her at the table twelve feet away from him.

His heart had skipped at least three beats.

With his employee Monte Gaines now helping mix drinks, Sam had more chances to admire her. Dark brown, wavy hair fell well past her shoulders. Her high cheekbones, straight nose, large eyes, and generous lips combined to create a stunning face. The long-sleeved dark red T-shirt she wore showed off her full breasts. He couldn't see below her waist because of the table, but what he *could* see stirred his interest.

It'd been a long time since a woman stirred his interest.

Monte reached past Sam to pick up a towel from the bar. "Where did all these people come from? It's almost eleven and the restaurant is still packed. Is it a full moon or what?"

"Actually, there *is* a full moon tonight."

"Shit. I should've stayed home. All the crazies come out when the moon is full."

"Those crazies give good tips."

"Yeah, I guess." He wiped up the few drops of scotch he'd dribbled on the bar. "Did you see the gal at table six? Man, those tits are big enough for their own ZIP code!"

A flash of irritation made Sam frown. He and Monte had been friends for a long time. They often told lewd jokes and made comments about the people in the restaurant and bar, but Monte's disrespectful remark about her made him angry.

He didn't understand why.

"Look at all that long hair," Monte continued. "I'll bet she's got a bush—"

"Watch it," Sam said softly.

Monte's eyebrows drew together. "What's wrong?"

Not wanting to tell Monte the truth and appear foolish when he didn't even know that woman, Sam nodded toward the couple standing a few feet away. "Customers."

"Oops. Sorry." He grinned. "You gotta admit, she's hot. And alone. I wonder what she's doing when I get off?"

Sam wondered the same thing, only for himself. He'd never been a fan of one-night stands; he'd rather be involved with one woman. Lately, the relationships he'd become involved in had turned sour quickly. It'd been several months since he'd been with a woman. After his last relationship ended, he'd sworn off them…at least for awhile.

Looking at her sitting there alone made him think it might be time to reconsider his beliefs on one-night stands. If one night was all he could have with her, he'd take it.

Cheryl Heppler, his weekend waitress, set her tray on the end of the bar. "Hey, Sam, I need two bourbons and seven, a Manhattan, a scotch on the rocks, two gin and tonics, a Sex On The Beach, an Agent Orange, a Diamond Fizz, two Cayman Sunsets, and a Bailey's."

Sam reached for a glass to begin preparing the Manhattan. "And you remembered all that without writing it down?"

Cheryl grinned. "That's why I'm worth every cent you pay me. Oh, and a plain Coke too."

The mention of a plain Coke had Sam glancing at table six to see if she was still there.

"Is the Coke for table six?"

Cheryl glanced over her shoulder at the table Sam mentioned. "No, she said she was fine." Returning her attention to Sam, she began loading her tray as he completed each drink. "She's been nursing that Coke for a long time. It should be pretty flat by now."

"Maybe I should take her a fresh one, just to be nice," Monte said.

"Maybe you should finish Cheryl's order and *I'll* take her a drink."

Monte frowned. "Why should *you* go?"

"Because I sign your paychecks."

"Good reason. Why don't I finish Cheryl's order and you take her a drink?"

* * * * *

Lindsay Cunningham couldn't resist looking at the handsome bartender again. She'd sat here for over an hour, sipping a watered-down Coke, just because her heart fluttered every time she glanced his way.

How silly for a thirty-year-old woman to be obsessed with good looks. She knew better than to let a set of bedroom eyes or kissable lips make her melt. Her experiences with good-looking men had only led to heartache.

But then, she hadn't seen a man so absolutely edible in a long time.

He had dark brown hair that covered his ears, swept across his forehead, and touched his collar in back. There was a hint of wave in it, enough to wrap around a woman's fingers as she ran her hands through it. That same brown hair was repeated in his thick mustache. He wore a medium blue, button-down shirt with the long sleeves rolled up to his elbows. The top two buttons were loose, letting her catch a glimpse of dark chest hair when the lights above the bar hit him just right. Broad shoulders filled out that shirt to perfection. A wide, strong chest tapered down to a trim waist and flat stomach.

She wondered if he was as gorgeous from the waist down.

Lindsay propped her elbow on the table and leaned her head on her fist. She swished her straw within the small slivers of ice while she released a heavy sigh. It didn't make any difference what he looked like anyway, since she'd never see him again. She didn't frequent bars on a regular basis, even if that bar was connected to her favorite restaurant.

Her three best friends had brought her here to the Sweetwater Saloon for dinner to celebrate her thirtieth birthday. Located on the West Side close to Capital Mall, it had opened two years ago and had quickly become the most popular eating establishment in Olympia. A raised floor under the bar separated it from the restaurant. The overhead lights were a bit dimmer here, and every table held a pillar candle inside a hurricane glass. The service was fast and friendly, the food scrumptious. The décor was eclectic — incredible scenery paintings hung next to cartoon characters of the Old West, shelves held silk flower arrangements sitting next to antique coffeepots and scrub boards, photographs of animals and people lay on the tables beneath clear plastic. Lindsay liked coming here simply to sit and look at the decorations, for they changed often.

She did *not* like coming here to celebrate another birthday.

Despite growing up with her parents constantly sniping at each other, an older sister and brother who were both divorced, and most of her friends either divorced or separated, Lindsay had hoped she could be different...that she could find that special someone to fill the loneliness in her heart. She'd tried. She'd dated, she'd had lovers, even fallen in love twice. Every relationship she'd ever been involved in ended in heartache.

Hitting the Big Three-Oh with no one to celebrate it except girlfriends had finally made Lindsay realize that's the way it was meant to be for her. Some people got the short end of the stick when it came to happily ever after. She just happened to be one of those people.

So here she sat, alone in a bar, feeling sorry for herself.

Well, no more. She didn't need a man in her life; she didn't *want* a man in her life. She had a job she loved, a small house that would be hers in seventeen years, and wonderful friends. Other than for sex, what good was a man anyway? He left the seat up, his dirty clothes on the floor, and a mess in the kitchen. Lindsay had better ways to spend her time than picking up after a slob.

But there were times, like now, that she craved a man's touch.

A masculine hand holding a glass of Coke came into her view. He set the glass on the table next to her almost-empty one.

"I thought you might like a fresh drink."

Lindsay looked up into the face of the bartender. She couldn't help but let her gaze travel down his body to his crotch. He wore black pants that were tight enough to show the impressive bulge of his penis. Yep, just as nice from the waist down.

"Thank you." She reached for her small purse lying on the table. His gentle touch on her shoulder stopped her.

"It's on the house."

That voice was absolutely mesmerizing. Rich and deep, it flowed over her like heavy syrup. She'd be happy to sit and listen to him talk for the rest of the night.

Well, maybe talking wouldn't be the *only* thing she'd be happy to do with him…

"Thank you again."

"My pleasure."

She watched his gaze drop to her breasts and linger there for a moment before he looked at her face again. Lindsay was used to men ogling her large breasts. Normally, she ignored their rude stares. The way *he* looked at her didn't feel rude. It felt sensuous and hot and made her long for his hands on her.

"Hey, Sam."

He turned his head toward the other man behind the bar. "Yeah?"

"Can you grab a bottle of Johnny Walker Black out of the storeroom?"

"Sure." He looked at Lindsay again. "Duty calls."

"I understand."

Lindsay watched him walk toward a door halfway between the restrooms and the bar. The view of his back and buttocks was every bit as nice as the view of his front. And she'd always loved the name "Sam".

He took a key ring from his pocket, unlocked the door, and went into what she assumed was the storeroom. *I wonder what he'd do if I went in there with him, closed the door, and attacked him?*

Chuckling, Lindsay took a sip of her fresh Coke. As if she'd ever do anything like that. She couldn't possibly consider sex with a man when their entire conversation had consisted of less than ten sentences.

But then, why not?

Lindsay had never been shy, but she was conservative. She'd never had sex with a man on the first date. She'd never asked a man out, believing he should be the one to take the first step. Her girlfriends all said she was too old-fashioned, that she should move into the twenty-first century.

Maybe she should. Maybe it was time for her to do something she'd never done, something totally out of her character.

Lindsay unzipped her purse and peeked inside at the three condoms her girlfriend Rita Moore had pushed across the table at dinner. The four women had been talking about sex—one of Rita's favorite topics—and she had calmly laid the condoms on the table with instructions for Lindsay to "use them."

Her other friends had giggled while Lindsay quickly scooped them up and stuck them in her purse. Part of her was mortified that Rita would do that in a public place. Another part of her was intrigued by the thought of picking up a man she'd just met and having wild, uninhibited sex.

Glancing toward the bar, she saw that Sam had returned to work. She felt a strong attraction to him, there was no doubt of that. And the way he'd looked at her when he brought her the Coke made her believe he felt an attraction, too.

So, what's stopping you, Lindsay?

Sam no longer being in the storeroom, for one thing. She couldn't very well start tearing off his clothes with customers watching their every move.

Lindsay looked at her watch. Eleven-twenty. There were still a few people in the bar, but the restaurant had finally emptied except for two couples. The Saloon closed at midnight. She had forty more minutes left of her birthday. She wanted it to end with a special present.

She wanted it to end with Sam coming inside her.

Chapter 2

Five more minutes. Just five more minutes and Sam could lock the doors. The restaurant was empty and there were only three people left in the bar. Closing on time wouldn't be a problem, despite it being Friday.

"Last call for drinks, folks," Sam said.

The couple at table four stood and reached for their jackets draped over the back of their chairs. Sam looked over at table six. She was staring into her half-empty glass, a slight frown turning down her lips. He had to start closing up, but he didn't want to ask her to leave.

Cheryl walked up next to him and leaned back against the bar. "Do you want me to tell her we're closing?" she asked softly.

"No, let her finish her drink. Why don't you get out of here?"

"Don't you want me to help you restock?"

"Monte can help me." He smiled and tweaked the end of her nose. "Close the curtains for me, then go home and put your feet up."

"Amen to that. Thanks, Sam."

He watched Cheryl head to the restaurant and begin closing the curtains, then shifted his attention back to table six. His gaze met hers and held for several moments before he cleared his throat.

"Would you like your Coke freshened?"

"No, thank you." She swished her straw around the glass. "You're closing, aren't you?"

"Yes, but I won't run you off. I have to clean up and restock before I leave."

She sat up straighter in her chair. "Restock?"

Sam nodded. "It won't take us long. Go ahead and finish your drink."

She drew her bottom lip between her teeth. Sam almost groaned. The action made him think of other ways she could use her lips and teeth...

Sam turned and faced the back wall to start taking a mental inventory. It had been a typical busy Friday evening, so it would take him awhile to bring the stock back up to what he'd need for Saturday night.

Reaching into his pocket for his key ring, Sam headed for the storeroom.

* * * * *

Lindsay drew her bottom lip farther between her teeth when she saw Sam unlock the door to the storeroom. She glanced around the bar, searching for the other bartender. She didn't see him, but she could hear what sounded like dishes being shifted and stacked from the kitchen.

She had no idea how long Sam would be in that storeroom. If she was going to do something, she had to do it now.

Don't be a wimp, Lindsay. Go for it.

Lindsay sipped her Coke and took a deep breath. Grabbing her purse, she rose and strode to the storeroom.

It was a large room, larger than she'd expected. Long and wide, there were shelves along all the walls and down the middle, all holding boxes of liquor and glassware. She saw a door straight ahead of her that she assumed led to the kitchen, or perhaps was used for deliveries. She couldn't see Sam, but she could hear bottles rattling.

Laying her purse on top of a case of bourbon, she pushed the door shut and flipped the deadbolt.

The rattling stopped. "Monte?" Sam called out.

Lindsay leaned back against the door, her hands behind her for support. "No, it isn't Monte."

Several seconds passed before he appeared at the end of the middle shelves.

Lindsay said nothing and neither did he. She watched his gaze slowly move over her from head to feet and back again. Her heart pounded as if she'd just done an hour of hard exercise. Sweat formed on her palms while her mouth became dry. She waited for him to move closer, but he remained still.

The first move had to be hers.

She took a step toward him and stopped. One step was all she could manage on shaky legs. She wished she could think of something witty to say, something that would make him melt at her feet, but her brain seemed to have deserted her.

His gaze focused on her face, he walked closer, stopping an arm's length away from her. At five-seven, Lindsay didn't consider herself short, but he stood five or six inches taller. She looked up into eyes the color of a stormy sea.

Sam touched her chin with a fingertip. Lindsay held her breath as he slowly drew that fingertip down her neck and chest. His movement stilled at the neckline of her shirt.

"Why are you here?" he asked.

Lindsay swallowed. "You know why I'm here. Do I have to say it?"

"I think you'd better."

Needing to touch him, she reached up and ran one hand through his hair. It was as soft and thick as she'd expected.

"Today is my birthday. I came here earlier and had dinner with some friends. After I went home, I decided to come back by myself because I..." She stopped, not wanting to admit her disgusting self-pity. "I took one look at you and wanted you. That doesn't happen to me. I sat at that table and sipped on a Coke I didn't even want just so I could look at you." Taking a chance that he felt the same as she, she laid her palms on his chest. "I still want you."

Since she'd already taken more chances tonight than usual for her, Lindsay took another one. Rising up on her toes, she kissed him gently.

He didn't respond at first. She was about to pull away from him when he cradled her face in his hands and returned her kiss. While her kiss had been soft, a polite introduction, his kiss held no softness; it held fire and passion, and made her toes curl.

When his tongue slipped between her lips, Lindsay moaned. The sound must have done something to Sam for his arms encircled her tightly. Tilting his head, he deepened the kiss, using his lips and tongue in an erotic dance that stole her breath and made moisture gather between her thighs.

He stepped even closer to her, pushing Lindsay against the door again. The move made her gasp. Her gasp turned into another moan when Sam's tongue touched hers. She slid her hands up over his shoulders and into that glorious mane of hair, wanting to get as close to him as possible.

Lindsay wasn't a stranger to physical love. She'd kissed many males since her first game of Spin the Bottle at age twelve. She'd never kissed a man who made her feel so hot so quickly. Desire rose inside her faster than a river during a heavy rain.

Sam broke off the kiss and rested his forehead against hers. "Wow. You're quite a kisser, lady."

"I could say the same thing about you."

He raised his head and smiled. "I'm Sam."

"Hi, Sam. I'm Lindsay."

"Spread your legs for me, Lindsay."

She didn't hesitate to obey him. Letting the door support her, she spread her legs until her feet were almost a yard apart. Sam stepped between them and pushed his hips into hers. The feel of his thick, hard cock made her shudder. He shifted forward, driving his cock farther between her thighs. It grazed against her clit. Lindsay drew in a sharp breath at the electrifying sensation.

"Are you all right?" he whispered against her ear.

"Yes. Oh, yes." He moved his hips from left to right and back again. Each pass brushed her clit. "That feels so good."

"It would feel even better without clothes."

Lindsay drew back so she could look at his face. "So why are you still wearing any?"

*   *   *   *   *

Sam swallowed hard. She was even more sensual, more sexy, than he'd thought when he first saw her. He'd seen the desire in her eyes when he approached her, yet he'd also seen wariness and hesitation. He had the feeling she wasn't in the habit of picking up strange men.

That knowledge made him desire her even more.

Wanting more of that luscious mouth, he kissed her again. Each time his tongue touched hers, shafts of fire flew straight to his cock.

Sam let his hands slowly glide down her back to her buttocks. Full, round, firm, they filled his hands perfectly. Squeezing her ass, he lifted and pulled her even more tightly against his pelvis. He began to rock his hips slowly, imitating the act of lovemaking. Each time he pressed against her, he heard her breath catch.

If she was this hot while still wearing clothes, he couldn't wait any longer to be inside her.

A loud pounding on the door made Lindsay gasp and Sam jump.

"Hey, Sam, are you gonna restock, or are you gonna play footsie with the customer?"

Sam watched a deep blush creep into Lindsay's cheeks. "Damn that Monte," he muttered.

"Sam!"

"Go home, Monte," he said loudly enough to penetrate through the door.

"Don't you want me to help you in there? Two guys can get things done faster, you know."

The laughter in Monte's voice made Sam want to punch him. "We're doing just fine, Monte. Go home. And lock the door on your way out."

"Will do, boss. Have fun."

Sam tried to look into Lindsay's eyes, but she kept her head lowered. Monte knowing they were together in the storeroom had obviously embarrassed her.

Sam sighed to himself. Maybe that was for the best. It wasn't like him to become carried away so quickly with a woman, and he never had sex without using a condom. Simple common sense demanded it.

Damn it.

"Lindsay."

She raised her head.

"I don't have a condom," he said softly.

"I do," she whispered.

That surprised him. He'd been so sure she wasn't the type of woman who picked up men in bars.

"My girlfriend gave them to me."

"*Them?*"

Her cheeks turned even redder. "As a joke. My girlfriend gave me three tonight at dinner with instructions to…use them."

He understood how a friend would do that as a joke, especially on someone's birthday. "So you decided to use them with me?"

117

"No! I mean, yes, I did." She released a heavy breath. "I didn't *purposely* decide to use them with you. They're in my purse."

Sam glanced to his left and saw her purse lying on top of a case of bourbon.

"I'm sorry," Lindsay whispered, closing her eyes. "I shouldn't be here. This isn't me at all. Please let me go."

Her voice sounded thick, as if she were about to cry. Sam's heart melted. He'd been right all along; Lindsay didn't normally pick up men in bars. That had to mean she felt as strong an attraction for him as he did for her.

He squeezed her buttocks. "I don't want to let you go."

"Sam, I'm not..." She looked at him. A hint of tears shone in her dark brown eyes. "I'm not like this. I don't pick up men, I don't try to seduce them. I was just feeling..."

When she didn't continue, he prompted, "Feeling what?"

"Sorry for myself. I turned thirty and wanted to do something I've never done." She ran her hands over his shoulders and upper arms. "You're a very handsome man. I can't help being attracted to you."

"Then I don't understand why you asked me to let you go." Sam slid his hands over her hips and up to her waist. His action caused her shirt hem to lift, exposing the button and zipper of her slacks. Gazing into her eyes, he released the button and began to lower the tab. "I think we should pick up where we left off, don't you?"

Chapter 3

Lindsay's breath hitched when Sam's fingers brushed her abdomen. He never looked away from her eyes as he unfastened her slacks and slid his hand inside the opening. He laid his palm against her tummy, slowly rotating it in a small circle.

"Your skin is soft." His index finger slipped inside the waistband of her bikini panties. It dipped even lower, until she could feel it ruffling her pubic hair. "Mmm, nice."

Lindsay swallowed. Just that simple graze with a single fingertip raised her blood pressure several points He didn't seem to be in any hurry to touch her more intimately. He merely...explored.

Sam kissed her neck while his other hand skimmed inside her panties and cupped her buttock. "What do you want me to do?"

Lindsay tilted her head to give him easier access to her neck. "You're doing great right now."

She could feel his chuckle against her breasts. "You said something earlier about me wearing too many clothes."

That's true. She'd said that during one of her "brave" moments as a daring woman. That woman had disappeared when Monte pounded on the door.

Lindsay knew no reason why that daring woman couldn't come back.

She wanted Sam and he wanted her. She longed to let go and be totally free with him, do some of the things she'd always dreamed of doing with a lover but never had.

After all, she wouldn't see him again after tonight.

"Yes, I believe I did." Lindsay reached for the top button on his shirt. Sam's hands stilled for a moment, then began their slow coasting over her buttocks and hips as she reached for the second button. Each button released let her see a bit more of his chest, and the dark hair that covered it.

Lindsay released the last button and pulled the tails from his pants. Pushing his shirt open, she moved her hands over his chest and stomach. Smooth, hair-dusted skin stretched over firm muscle. She'd dated men who had the lean body of a runner, but she preferred a man's body to be more husky.

Like Sam's.

She unfastened the snap on his pants. When she reached for the zipper, her hand brushed against his fabric-covered cock. Abandoning the zipper, she switched her attention to that fascinating hardness. She cupped it in her palm and squeezed lightly. Hearing Sam's sharp intake of breath encouraged her to continue. She ran her hand up and down his cock, over and over. Even through his pants, the length and breadth of him made her mouth water.

Sam laid his hand over hers, stilling it. "If you keep doing that, I'm not promising how long I can last before I have to be inside you."

"I *want* you inside me."

Her statement must have been all Sam needed. He kissed her again, greedily, while sliding his hands inside her slacks and panties. One tug and they fell past her hips. Another tug let them pool at her feet.

Lindsay used Sam's shoulders for support as he removed her boots and socks along with her clothes. Slowly, his gaze traveled up her legs to between her thighs. Her breath caught when he leaned forward and kissed the nest of curls.

"You smell good," he whispered.

"Sam, please," she croaked.

"Please what?"

His warm breath caressed her skin. She opened her mouth to say she needed him inside her. Her plea turned to a moan as his tongue touched her intimately.

Closing her eyes, Lindsay leaned her head back against the door. Sam touched her again with his tongue, licking her clit before delving deeper.

Lindsay whimpered in need and spread her legs wider.

"You taste even better than you smell." Sam parted her feminine lips with his thumbs and licked her again, slow and easy. Lindsay tilted her hips forward, silently asking him for more. He gave it, spearing his tongue between her lips. That nimble tongue caressed her clit, then dipped inside her before returning to her clit. Again and again he repeated that action, until Lindsay was panting and her legs grew weak.

Her climax was *there*, hovering on the brink of breaking. Just when Lindsay didn't think she could possibly take any more without screaming, Sam suckled her clit. Stars exploded behind her eyes. Waves of pleasure washed over her, making her tremble.

Lindsay struggled to open her eyes. She'd barely had time to float back to earth before Sam stood and kissed her deeply. She could taste herself on his lips. Lindsay drew his tongue into her mouth, sucking it the way she longed to suck the hard cock pressed against her stomach.

Sam broke off the kiss and moved his mouth to her neck. "Condom."

"Purse."

He fumbled for her purse on top of the case of bourbon. Lindsay took it from him and unzipped it. Sam grabbed one of the foil packages and quickly tore it open.

Lindsay watched, engrossed, while Sam unzipped his pants, pushed down the front of his shorts, and sheathed himself. She had but a moment to admire his masculine beauty before he bent his knees and thrust deep inside her.

It had been much too long since she'd experienced that feeling of fullness. She clenched her internal muscles, trying to pull him to the mouth of her womb.

"Wrap your arms around my neck," he whispered.

Lindsay did as he said. Sam cupped his hands behind her thighs and lifted her. The new position opened her legs wider and let him drive even deeper. His thrusts were easy at first, but quickly gained speed. Lindsay tightened her arms around his neck, holding him as close as possible while he pounded his cock into her.

Having an orgasm didn't always happen when she had sex. The fact that she'd had one was wonderful. A second one building inside her was a pleasant surprise. Lindsay bit her lip to keep from groaning aloud as the pleasure rushed through her.

Sam pressed his pelvis into hers and moaned from his own release.

Moments passed, moments when Lindsay attempted to catch her breath while analyzing what she'd done. She'd had mind-blowing sex with a man she'd never seen until a few short hours ago. She knew nothing about him, not even his last name.

She had absolutely no regrets.

Sam lifted his head from her neck. "Wow."

"I'll second that."

"If that was an appetizer, I don't think I could survive a full meal."

Lindsay chuckled. She liked his sense of humor. "Maybe that *was* the full meal."

"A full meal isn't complete without dessert." Slowly, he withdrew from her and let her feet touch the floor. "Are you game for dessert?"

"I'm game for anything."

Sam smiled, then kissed her softly. "I'll get rid of this condom and be right back. Okay?"

"Okay."

She moved away from the door so he could open it. Sam tipped up her chin and kissed her again, then left the room.

Once he was gone, Lindsay closed her eyes and took a deep breath. She couldn't remember a time when sex had been so...staggering. Perhaps it was the spontaneity, the situation, or the fact that Sam kissed so yummy. Whatever the reason, Lindsay couldn't imagine how "dessert" could be any better.

Goose bumps pebbled her flesh, a reminder that she was naked from the waist down. She didn't know whether to stay in here or go out in the bar. If she left the safety of this room, she certainly couldn't do it like this.

Untangling her panties from her slacks, Lindsay drew them on and smoothed down her T-shirt. She couldn't help wondering why Sam hadn't even touched her breasts. Maybe he wasn't a breast man, or maybe he didn't like large ones. That hadn't been a problem for her in the past; men couldn't wait to get their hands on her breasts. She remembered one date even making the comment that he had to check if they were real.

He'd ended up in the emergency room with a broken finger.

Lindsay stepped out of the storeroom, turning off the light behind her. She blinked to adjust her eyes to the dimmer lights in the bar. Once they had adapted, she looked around for Sam, but didn't see him anywhere.

A sound to her left made her turn. Sam came out of the men's room...totally naked.

Chapter 4

Sam spotted her as soon as he stepped from the men's room. Lindsay stood in the doorway to the storeroom, leaning against the frame with her hands behind her back. The position made those luscious breasts jut forward, as if begging for his touch.

He'd neglected them earlier. He planned to correct that mistake very soon.

Slowly, Sam walked toward her. He watched Lindsay's gaze travel over his body. Even in the dim light, he could see the desire in her eyes, as if she'd like to lick every inch of him.

He had no objection about that.

He stopped before her, cradled her face in his hands, and kissed her deeply. His cock stirred at the taste of her, anticipating when it could have "dessert." Sam silently told his hormones to behave. There were things he wanted to do to her, with her, first.

She clutched at his back a moment, then he felt her hands slide downward. They coasted over his lower back, his buttocks, his hips, his outer thighs. Each caress with her soft hands made him long for more of them.

"I like touching you," she whispered against his neck.

"I like touching you too." Sam cupped her breasts and squeezed gently. Lindsay hitched in her breath. He took that as a sign of acquiescence and squeezed them a bit firmer. "Like that?"

"Yes."

Sam ran his hands under her shirt and unhooked her bra. Now he could touch her without any hindrance. Her breasts were full and round, the skin silky smooth, her nipples hard little points in his palms. "These feel incredible."

"You didn't..." She made a strangled sound deep in her throat when his thumbs brushed her nipples. "You didn't touch them earlier. I didn't think you liked large breasts."

"I made an unforgivable mistake, ignoring these. I'll be more than happy to try and make it up to you."

"How do you plan to do that?"

"I'm sure I can think of a few ways that will please both of us."

Lindsay arched her back, which thrust her breasts more fully into his hands. "Go for it."

Sam grinned to himself. He liked her passion, and he liked her spunk. This was a woman who could make him laugh while driving him crazy with desire.

She was exactly the type of woman he'd been looking for all his life.

"Let's start by getting rid of these clothes." He drew her T-shirt over her head. "Why are you wearing your panties?"

"I didn't know if anyone else was still here."

"It's just you and me." Sam tossed her T-shirt on a bar stool and reached for her bra straps. "We can do whatever we want." Her bra joined the shirt, then her panties. Taking a step back, Sam simply looked at her. She was exquisite.

His cock rose to full attention.

"You're beautiful, Lindsay."

She pushed her hair behind her ears and lowered her eyes, as if his compliment embarrassed her. Passionate, funny, and a touch of shyness too.

It wouldn't take much more for Sam to lose his heart.

"I'm ready for my dessert," he said.

Lindsay's gaze shot up to his.

"Come here."

She closed the short distance between them. Sam scooped her up in his arms, turned, and laid her on top of the bar.

"It's cold!" Lindsay shrieked.

Sam didn't give her the chance to say anything else before kissing her again. It took no more than a second for her to relax and respond to him. She tunneled her fingers into his hair and made love to his mouth with her lips and tongue.

This woman certainly knew how to kiss.

Sam kissed his way down her neck and chest until he fastened his lips over Lindsay's right nipple. He heard her groan of pleasure as she arched her back again. Oh, yes, he had definitely made a mistake ignoring these beautiful breasts. Lindsay's passionate response proved that.

Her nipple grew harder and longer in his mouth. Sam circled it with his tongue, suckled it, then circled it again. He covered her left breast with his hand and could feel her heart pounding.

She was obviously turned on, but he wanted her even higher.

Sam raised his head. "Are you still game for anything?"

She nodded.

"What's your favorite liqueur?"

"I'm...not much of a drinker."

"Then I'll pick one for you, okay?"

She nodded again. Sam took a bottle of amaretto and a shot glass off the shelf. "Do you like almonds?"

"Yes."

"Good. So do I." Tipping up the bottle, Sam filled the shot glass with the amber liquid. He set down the bottle, then dipped his finger into the glass. Looking into her eyes, he spread the liqueur over her lips. Lindsay parted them, letting his finger slip inside her mouth. He left it there but a moment before gathering more amaretto on his finger and returning it to her mouth. This time she closed her teeth, gently trapping his finger between them.

He watched her eyes drift closed while she sucked on it. Her tongue curled around his finger, as if she were trying to lick off every bit of the amaretto.

Heat flared in his cock.

Lindsay opened her eyes and released his finger. "It's good."

"You've never tasted amaretto?"

"Not by itself."

"It's good mixed with Bailey's over ice. I serve that drink to a lot of women." Dipping his finger in the shot glass again, Sam spread more liqueur over her lips. He dipped once more and drew his finger down her chin. Again and again, he gathered more amaretto on his finger and painted her with it—down her chest, around each nipple, zigzagging across her stomach, venturing into her navel.

Reaching the top of her pubic hair, he set down the shot glass and made the return journey up her body with his tongue.

Sam fastened his mouth over her right nipple again. He sucked firmly, and was rewarded by Lindsay's whispered, "Yesssss." She cupped her breast in her hand and offered it to him. Sam accepted her gift, licking and suckling her nipple even harder. He listened to her breathing, her moans, and noted the shifting of her body.

She was almost ready to come.

When he suspected the time was right, he pulled on her nipple as he quickly pushed two fingers inside her pussy. He pressed upward into her G-spot, and she shattered.

Sam watched Lindsay's face as the orgasm took over her body. He loved giving a woman pleasure, and especially loved watching the different emotions cross her face when she experienced those few moments of intense sensation.

Although he enjoyed her orgasm, his cock was making demands for its *own* pleasure.

Leaving Lindsay to recuperate, Sam went back in the storeroom. He located the other two condoms in her purse and returned to the bar.

He saw Lindsay's gaze drop to his pelvis as he walked toward her. "Like what you see?" he asked.

"Very much. You're gorgeous, Sam."

"Do you want me inside you again?"

"Very much."

"Any way I want?"

Her throat worked as she swallowed. "Any way you want."

Sam lifted her from the bar and set her on her feet. She wobbled, and he quickly grabbed her arms to steady her.

"Are you all right?"

"My legs are weak."

Sam grinned. "Ah, words a man's ego loves to hear."

Lindsay wrapped her arms around his neck. "Here are some more words for your ego. That was incredible." She tugged on his neck until he lowered his head. Her lips met his in a voracious kiss.

The few moments away from her while he went in the storeroom had allowed Sam's ardor to cool a bit. Lindsay's kiss brought it back in seconds. He had to get inside her.

Still kissing her, Sam walked her backward until she bumped against the end bar stool. The sudden stop made Lindsay jerk.

"What—"

He ended whatever she was going to say with a hard, fast kiss. "Turn around and bend over."

She asked no questions, but did as he said. Lindsay rested her elbows on the stool, arched her back, and spread her legs.

Her pussy was rosy, swollen, and wet with her cream. The animalistic urge to mate reared up within him. Picking up one of the condom packages he'd dropped on the bar, he quickly tore it open and prepared himself. Holding her hips, he buried his cock deep inside her with one thrust.

Her walls milked him as he pushed forward, withdrew, and pushed forward again. The rational part of Sam's brain told him to slow down so Lindsay could come once more. The animal part dictated him to move faster toward his own orgasm.

The animal won.

Sam increased the speed of his thrusts, until his hips were slapping against her bottom. Sweat formed on his face, chest, and arms as he pounded into her. Lindsay took everything he gave her without a whimper of protest.

The orgasm traveled down his spine, through his balls, and into his cock. Sam groaned loudly, pulled her hips hard against him, and let the pleasure engulf him.

Moments passed while Sam tried to catch his breath. Knowing Lindsay was probably uncomfortable, he attempted to move back so he could let her stand. His shaky limbs refused to cooperate.

"Now *my* legs are weak," he said with a chuckle.

Lindsay looked at him over her shoulder. "Serves you right for being so rough."

Her words made his blood run cold. He'd hurt her, something he'd never intended to do. His shaky legs forgotten, Sam pulled out of her, slipped his arms around her waist, and helped her stand.

"God, Lindsay, I'm sorry. I didn't mean to hurt you."

She wrapped one arm around his neck. "You didn't hurt me, Sam. Not at all."

Sam's released his breath in a long *whoosh*. He tightened his arms around her and dropped a kiss on her nape. "Good. I wouldn't do that for anything."

He held her then, enjoying the feel of her back and buttocks against him. Slowly, he caressed her breasts, her stomach, her hips...not in a sexual way, but simply to touch her silky skin.

He wanted to touch her for the rest of the night.

The urge surprised him. He hadn't invited a woman to his home in over six months. He wanted Lindsay there, in his arms, in his bed.

Sam kissed her nape again. "Come home with me."

Lindsay turned and faced him. Her gaze traveled over his face as if she were trying to memorize every feature. Sam felt a pang deep in his gut. She was going to refuse him.

Cradling his cheeks in her hands, Lindsay kissed him tenderly. "Yes, I'll go home with you," she whispered.

Sam smiled. "Let's get dressed and get out of here."

"Don't you have to restock?"

"I'll come in early tomorrow." He touched her waist, letting his hands glide up and down her sides. "I don't want to waste any more time here. I just want to be with you."

Chapter 5

Lindsay pulled out of The Saloon's parking lot and followed Sam's SUV. He'd told her he lived close, and had made the offer for her to ride with him. She'd politely refused. She had to have her car with her in case she needed to make a fast getaway.

She'd almost said no when Sam asked her to go home with him. Being with him at the bar was supposed to be all that happened between them. She'd wanted a special ending to her birthday, and Sam had definitely given it to her. But looking at that handsome face, staring into those blue-gray eyes, had made it impossible to say no. She wanted this whole night with Sam, for she knew there could be no others.

Coward! a tiny voice in her head shouted.

You're damn right I'm a coward. I've had my heart broken too many times. More than one night with Sam isn't even a remote possibility.

Oh, but how she'd like it to be!

There was something about him...something that called to her. She didn't understand it, and couldn't possibly explain it to anyone if they asked her to describe how she felt. It wasn't simply mind-boggling sex, but something deep inside her, a place no man had ever touched. She'd been in love twice, so knew how that felt.

Or at least she *thought* she knew how love felt.

You're getting way ahead of yourself, Lindsay. You aren't in love with Sam. You don't even know him, so you can't possibly love him. You're just on hormone overdrive.

Lindsay shivered. Yes, she was definitely on hormone overdrive. Sam's lovemaking was the most intense she'd ever experienced. What he'd done with the amaretto was the best "dessert" she'd ever had. He made her feel sexy and free to do whatever she desired, however she desired it.

She wanted to keep those feelings as long as possible.

Sam led her up Cooper Point Road. He pulled down a graveled drive overgrown with fir trees. His headlights bounced off a large, split-level house with cedar siding. Security lights came on as he parked in front of a three-car garage. Lindsay stopped her car next to his SUV and shut off the motor.

He met her as she opened her door and held out his hand to help her from the car. The security lights allowed her to see the house and a small portion of the surrounding area. Although minutes from the Westside, Sam's home sat in the middle of huge trees in complete privacy.

"It's lovely, Sam."

He smiled. "Thanks. I consider it my little piece of heaven." He squeezed her hand. "It's getting cold. Let's go inside."

Sam led her through a heavy door next to the garage and flipped up a light switch. Lindsay saw a large den complete with overstuffed couches and chairs, a rock fireplace, and a big-screen television. The room practically oozed testosterone.

"Very nice," Lindsay said. She gestured toward the TV. "I'll bet the Seahawks look great on that."

"I don't get the chance to watch them here very often since I'm usually at The Saloon when they play." He grinned. "But I do watch the Super Bowl every year. Since I make up the schedule, I always give myself that day off."

Lindsay returned his grin, then wandered around the room. She stopped at the dark brown recliner and ran her hand over the headrest. The butter-soft leather invited a person to curl up in front of a roaring fire with an afghan, a cup of hot cocoa, and a good book.

"I don't spend much time down here." Sam walked up to Lindsay and she turned to face him. "There's a small kitchen over there," he said with a nod of his head, "and a bedroom and bathroom down the hall. The main living area is upstairs. Would you like the tour?"

Lindsay assumed the "main living area" included his bedroom. "I think the upstairs tour will be enough for now."

Sam took her hand again and led her to the circular staircase next to the fireplace. Lindsay followed him up the stairs to the spacious kitchen. She had only a moment to admire the stainless steel appliances and country blue color scheme before he led her out of the kitchen and into the living room. Her boot heels sank into the thick gray carpeting. While the leather furniture in the den was dark brown, this furniture was natural in color. A rock fireplace, identical to the one downstairs, filled one wall. Floor-to-ceiling bookcases flanked a large picture window. Lindsay wasn't sure of the directions, but she thought the window faced east. If that were the case, Sam had a magnificent view of Mount Rainier.

"Can you see the mountain?"

Sam nodded. "And Budd Inlet."

"I'm insanely jealous. The sunrise on a clear day must be unbelievable."

"It is, but I don't get to see many of them. I usually go to bed after two, so I sleep through the sunrises." He brushed her cheek with one fingertip. "Would you like a glass of wine?"

His caress alone was enough to make her head spin; she didn't need anything alcoholic to add to it. "I'd be happy with some water."

"One glass of cold water coming up. Sit down and make yourself comfortable."

Lindsay watched Sam leave the room, then turned her attention back to the décor. A large seascape — similar to the ones at The Saloon — hung over the fireplace. It was the only thing in the room that she would call an adornment. Whoever decorated Sam's house neglected to add any feminine touches. Maybe he didn't *want* any feminine touches. After all, he was a single man. But Lindsay thought this beautiful room would be so much more inviting and comfortable with some silk flower arrangements, candle holders with tapers and large pillars, fluffy throw pillows on the couch and chairs...

Lindsay chuckled to herself as she sat on the couch. She was mentally refurbishing Sam's house and she'd never see it again.

"Here you go."

Lindsay accepted the glass of water from Sam as he sat beside her. "Thank you." She took a healthy drink, not realizing the extent of her thirst until she'd taken her first sip.

When she lowered the glass, Sam took it from her, turned it, and placed his mouth where hers had been. He watched her over the rim of the glass while he drank.

She'd never met a man who exuded sex appeal as much as Sam.

He set the glass on the coffee table and wrapped his arm around her shoulders. "Are you ready for the rest of the tour?"

Lindsay touched his lips. They were cool from the water. "Right now, I'm ready to kiss you."

Sam smiled. "I like the way you think."

Cradling her cheek in his hand, Sam kissed her. Lindsay sighed and relaxed back against his arm. She loved the feel of his mouth on hers, the way his tongue peeked out to play over her lips and with her tongue. His mustache brushed her upper lip, his breath caressed her cheek. His kisses made everything within her go all soft and liquid.

Desire flared up inside her as hot as what she'd experienced at the bar.

Sam ended their kiss with one last nip of her lower lip. "Now are you ready for the rest of the tour?"

"What tour?" Lindsay asked, struggling to open her eyes. His kiss had scrambled her brain.

A crooked grin tipped up one corner of Sam's mouth. "The tour of my house."

"Oh, yeah. *That* tour."

Sam stood and helped her to her feet. "I'll warn you ahead of time that you won't see much. I bought this house six months ago. My schedule at The Saloon is crazy, so I haven't had time to do any decorating. And frankly, I'm not sure what to do. I had help with the restaurant, and I enjoy doing the paintings, but other than that I — "

"Wait a minute." It took Lindsay a moment to realize what he'd said. "You're an artist? You did all those wonderful paintings at The Saloon?"

"I did the paintings, but I don't call myself an artist."

"Why not? Sam, you're immensely talented. I *love* your work."

He lowered his eyes, then looked back at her again and smiled. "Thanks. It's nice to have a fan."

Lindsay had come here for heart-pounding sex. She hadn't expected to feel any tenderness toward Sam, or want to know more about him. His complete lack of conceit about his incredible talent drew her closer to him, made her want to know more about him.

"Do you have a studio?"

Sam chuckled. "Not exactly. I turned the extra bedroom on this floor into an office where I paint, work on the computer, stuff like that."

"May I see it?"

"Sure, if you want to."

Stepping closer to Sam, Lindsay dropped a soft kiss on his lips. "I want to very much."

Chapter 6

No one but very close friends and his parents had seen where he worked. Sam enjoyed painting, but didn't share that fact with many people. His art was private, something he did to relieve the stress of sixty-hour work weeks.

He wanted to show his art to Lindsay.

Sam walked across the hall to the bedroom he'd turned into a studio/office. Flipping the light switch, he stood to the side so Lindsay could enter the room. It didn't take her long to locate the easel. He had set it up at an angle to catch the natural light from the window. Lindsay walked around it and gazed at the canvas sitting on it. Her lips parted and she laid one hand on her chest.

Sweat broke out on his forehead as he waited for her to comment.

"Sam, it's gorgeous," she whispered. She looked at him over the top of the canvas. "Is this the view you have?"

"Yeah."

"The mountain and the water and the clouds... It's incredible." She glanced past him into the living room. "You can see it from here?"

He nodded. "It was one of the features that sold me on the house. I can see the mountain from every room on this floor."

"Now I'm even *more* jealous." Lindsay peered more closely at the painting. "It looks wet."

"I finished it this afternoon."

"Darn. I can't steal it if it's still wet."

Sam walked over to stand beside her. "Sorry, I can't let you steal this one. It goes in my dad's office by special request."

"You could do another one for your dad."

He liked this game. The way Lindsay's eyes sparkled with laughter showed Sam she liked it too. He encircled her waist with one arm and tugged her a step closer to him. "And what do I get in return for making my dad wait?"

"My eternal gratitude?"

Trying not to grin, Sam shook his head. "You'll have to do better than that."

Lindsay slid her hands up his chest to his shoulders. "How about a kiss?"

"That'll do for a start."

Sam tightened his arm around Lindsay's waist when her lips touched his. Each time she kissed him was better than the last. Wrapping his other arm around her, he let his hand glide down to cup one round buttock and pull her between his spread legs. Those luscious breasts pressed against his chest.

She fit perfectly in his arms.

Lindsay kissed his chin, his cheek, his jaw. "How was that?" she whispered in his ear.

"Not bad. You're definitely getting warmer."

"Well," she said as her hands drifted toward his groin, "maybe I can do something to turn up the heat."

He inhaled sharply when her fingers moved between his legs and squeezed his balls. "I'd say that definitely turns up the heat."

"Am I hot yet?"

"I think you're on your way to scorching."

Lindsay unbuckled his belt. "Any ideas on how I could put out the fire?"

"I don't want you to put out the fire." He lifted her in his arms. "I want us both to burn up."

＊ ＊ ＊ ＊ ＊

A squeak of surprise passed Lindsay's lips when Sam lifted her. With her voluptuous body and above-average height, there were few men who would even consider lifting her, much less actually *do* it. Sam carried her as if she were petite and slender.

He walked down the hall and into a dark room she assumed was his bedroom. He confirmed that assumption when he lowered her to a king-sized bed. The thick down comforter surrounded her, releasing Sam's scent.

Soft light filled their corner of the room when Sam turned on the bedside lamp. Lindsay lay still and watched him unbutton his shirt. It fell to the floor, followed by his belt. Propping up on one elbow, Lindsay prepared herself to enjoy the strip show.

"Having fun? Sam asked as he unfastened his slacks.

Lindsay grinned. "Immensely."

"Do you expect me to take off everything while you lie there and watch?"

"Absolutely."

"Well, if that's what the lady wants…"

The rest of his clothes quickly vanished, leaving him standing before her nude and fully aroused. Lindsay rose to her knees and scooted across the bed to him. First she simply looked. Forget the scenery paintings; a painting of *him* should be hanging where every woman could admire it. The broad shoulders, hair-dusted chest, flat stomach, strong thighs, and thick cock all combined into one mouth-watering, knee-weakening man.

A few moments of looking was all Lindsay could manage before she had to touch.

His chest beckoned. Lindsay laid her hands on him, letting her fingertips trace the well-defined pectoral muscles. She watched the movement of her hands as his shoulders and upper arms received her attention next, then his stomach. She bypassed his cock and caressed his thighs and hips instead.

"Lindsay," Sam said, his voice sounding strangled.

She looked into his eyes. "What?"

"Touch me."

"I *am* touching you."

"You know what I mean." Taking one of her hands, he wrapped it around his straining cock. "*Touch* me."

Lindsay tightened her hand around him. "Like that?"

"A little harder. Move your hand more… Yeah, like that." Closing his eyes, Sam tilted his head back. "Yeah, just like that."

The bliss on Sam's face made Lindsay want to please him even more. She added her other hand, fondling his cock and balls with both hands as her gaze moved from his face to his groin and back again.

"God, babe," Sam groaned.

Hearing the endearment made a delicious thrill skate up her spine. Lindsay increased the movement of her hands, sliding them up and down the hard shaft and over the velvety head while Sam pumped his hips back and forth. Sweat beaded his skin. His breathing became heavier. Lindsay had never brought a man to a climax with only her hands, but she would now if that's what Sam wanted.

Sam suddenly grabbed her hands and jerked them away from him. "Stop!"

"Why?"

"Because I was about to come."

"I want you to."

He shook his head. "Not without you." Leaning forward, he kissed her once, twice. "I want you with me when I come." He reached for the hem of her shirt. "I need you naked."

Her shirt and bra joined the pile of Sam's clothes on the floor. He gently pushed on her shoulders. Lindsay lay back on the bed and let Sam finish taking off her clothes. When she was nude, he nudged her knees apart and lay on top of her. His erection felt hot and hard against her stomach.

"I like having you in my bed."

"I like being here."

Sam plowed his fingers into her hair and held her head while he kissed her hungrily. Lindsay had never been with a man who kissed as much as Sam.

She loved it.

He kissed his way to her breasts. He lavished each one with his tongue and teeth...licking, nipping and sucking until Lindsay writhed on the bed.

Sam pulled one nipple hard between his lips, then soothed it with his tongue. "Can you come from having your nipples sucked?"

The few men she'd been with had never taken the time for her to find out. "I...don't know."

He licked her nipple again, and Lindsay inhaled sharply. "Do you want to try?"

She wanted to try everything with him. "Yes."

"Put your arms over your head."

Lindsay stretched her arms over her head and arched her back. Sam stared at her breasts for several moments, his breathing heavy and deep, before rising to his knees between her legs. Looking into her eyes, he cradled her breasts in his hands and began a soft kneading motion.

Lindsay tried to lie still, but the sensation of Sam's hands on her was too strong. She arched her back, needing more. Sam must have understood her silent request. His kneading became firmer as he lowered his head and swiped his tongue across one nipple, then the other.

"These are so beautiful," he whispered. "Firm, full, big. Your nipples... God, I love your nipples." His warm breath flowed over her skin. He took one hard peak in his mouth, sucking firmly while coating it with his tongue. Switching to the other peak, he gave it the same generous treatment as the first. Back and forth, back and forth, kneading her breasts the entire time his mouth loved her nipples.

Lindsay jerked when the pulse pounded between her thighs. She released a long moan as the orgasm enveloped her body.

When she managed to find the strength to open her eyes, she looked directly into Sam's lust-filled ones.

"That was... Wow. I don't have any words."

"You don't need any words." Sam kissed her deeply, then moved away from her and opened a drawer in the nightstand. Lindsay watched him tear open a condom package and prepare himself. He stretched out on top of her, slid his hands beneath her buttocks, and entered her.

Lindsay wrapped her arms around his neck, her legs around his waist, and held him as his thrusts quickly increased in speed.

"You feel so good. You're so hot, so wet. I can't get deep enough."

Unwrapping her legs, Lindsay set her feet flat on the bed and pumped her hips to meet his thrusts.

"Yeah, like that." Sam bit her earlobe. "Harder. Push up harder. *Harder. Shit!*"

He shuddered and groaned loudly. Smaller tremors shook his body for several moments before he finally lay still.

Chapter 7

Sam couldn't move, and he wasn't sure if he'd ever be able to move again. His heart pounded so hard, he could feel it in his temples. His lungs burned from breathing so fiercely. An orgasm left him weak, but he'd never had one completely shatter him.

He wondered how long it'd take him to recover so he could do it again.

Slowly, Sam withdrew from Lindsay's arms and her body. He fell to his back beside her and threw one arm over his eyes. In his estimation, his heartbeat should return to normal by Tuesday.

The gentle touch of Lindsay's hand on his chest made Sam move his arm so he could look at her. She lay on her side, a satisfied smile touching her lips. "Hi," she said softly.

"Hi."

"Are you okay?"

"I figure I will be by Tuesday."

Lindsay chuckled. "I'm sorry, but you kept saying 'harder.'"

"I did, and you did everything *exactly* like I wanted."

She slid her hand over his chest and stomach. "Thank you."

Sam smiled. "My pleasure." He lifted his arm over her head. "C'mere."

She moved next to his side. Sam drew her even closer and wrapped his arms around her. He felt...content.

His contentment vanished when she tried to pull away from him. "Where are you going?"

"To get that glass of water. I worked up a thirst."

"Me too. You stay here, I'll get the water. I need to get rid of the condom anyway."

Sam made a detour into the bathroom before heading for the living room. He had to use the wall for support since his legs were still weak. While he doubted he'd been with as many women as his friend Monte,

Sam hadn't lacked for sex ever since he'd discovered at sixteen how good it felt.

He'd never experienced the intense feelings he'd experienced with Lindsay.

Sam picked up the glass in the living room, drained it, then took it to the kitchen to refill it. Sex with Lindsay was incredible, but incredible sex wasn't the only thing that drew him to her. In the few hours they'd been together, he'd learned she had a great sense of humor, a touch of shyness, and a love of some of the things he loved. While he didn't believe a man and woman had to like all the same things, he did believe they should have some things in common for a relationship to work.

Sam stumbled at that thought. The word "relationship" was too strong to use so soon.

Then again, why not?

Sam started down the hall. This little bit of time with her wasn't enough. He wanted more. He wanted to learn her favorite foods, favorite color, favorite season…all the things two people learned about each other while falling in love.

Seeing Lindsay lying on his bed, all that glorious hair spread out around her head, her voluptuous body nude and shiny from perspiration, made his heart jump up in his throat.

He suspected he was already well on his way to falling in love with her.

She sat up as he approached the bed. Sam handed her the glass, then sat beside her while she drank.

"Oh, thank you," Lindsay said after lowering the glass from her mouth. "I needed that."

"Are you hungry? I could whip us up an omelet or something."

"I'm fine." She touched his cheek, her thumb lightly caressing his chin. "I'd better go."

Sam frowned. "Why?"

"It's after three o'clock."

"Do you have to work tomorrow? I mean, today?"

Lindsay shook her head.

"Then stay with me." He took the glass from her and set it on the nightstand. "I want to hold you until we wake up, then I'll fix us a huge brunch. I make a mean ham and cheese omelet, if I do say so myself."

"With hash browns?"

"You bet."

She smiled. "You're trying to tempt me."

"Then let me tempt you some more." He cupped her breasts in his hands while kissing her neck. "We'll make love when we wake up. Then after brunch, we'll make love again. I have a hot tub downstairs."

"Mmm." She tilted her head, and Sam kissed his way up to her ear. "I've never made love in a hot tub."

"You'll love it. The warm water, the jets, the bubbles...they all feel *so* good."

He kissed her, trying to tempt her even further. When she relaxed and returned his kiss, he knew he'd convinced her.

"So, do we have a deal?"

"That ham and cheese omelet with hash browns does sound awfully good."

"Hey!"

Lindsay laughed, and Sam joined her. He liked her quick wit. It was one more thing to add to the growing list of things he liked about her.

Her laughter died and she shivered. Sam frowned. "Are you all right?"

"Just a little cold, now that I'm not...occupied."

Sam squeezed her breasts. "Wanna be 'occupied' again?"

One eyebrow arched as she glanced at his flaccid penis. "Now?"

"I'm good, but I'm not Superman." Sam rose from the bed. "I'll go turn off the lights and lock up while you get in bed."

He returned to the bedroom a few minutes later to find Lindsay beneath the covers. After turning off the lamp, he slipped into bed beside her and drew her into his arms. She cuddled up next to him and wrapped one arm around his waist.

"Thank you," Lindsay whispered. "You made my birthday very special. Or I guess I should say you made the day *after* my birthday very special."

Sam caressed her shoulder and upper arm. "You're welcome," he said softly. "I enjoyed it too, and it isn't even close to my birthday."

She kissed his chest. "That thing with the amaretto... Do you do that often?"

"I've never done it."

"Why not?"

"Well, for one thing, I've never had a naked woman on top of my bar."

"You've never had sex with a woman in your bar." Sam could hear the disbelief in her voice.

"I didn't say that. "

"So you admit you've had sex with a woman there?"

"All new businesses must be initiated. Just like a house. When you move into a new house, you're supposed to have sex in every room. It's a law."

She released an unladylike snort of laughter. Sam thought it was cute. "Oh, really. So that means you've had sex in every room of this house?"

"No."

"Why not?"

"I haven't been involved with anyone important enough to me for that to happen." He kissed the top of her head. "I was involved with someone when I opened the restaurant, so yeah, we had sex in the office. But I didn't have this house then, and I haven't been seriously involved with anyone since I bought it. So I guess you could say my house is still a virgin."

"Your bedroom is no longer a virgin."

"That's true."

Lindsay slowly caressed his chest and stomach as they talked. Sam loved the feel of her hand touching him. It wasn't sexual, but comforting.

"You said when *you* opened the restaurant. Is The Saloon yours?"

"Only about twenty percent. The bank owns the rest of it."

"It's a wonderful place."

"Thanks. I'm proud of it. It's been more successful than I ever imagined it could be."

"Good food and good service will do that."

"I insist on both."

Her hand dipped lower on his body. Sam closed his eyes briefly when she caressed his cock. If she kept doing that, it wouldn't take him long to recover...

"You mentioned your dad earlier, but not your mother. Are they divorced?"

Her question snapped his attention away from his cock and back to her. "Still very happily married after thirty-five years."

"That's amazing."

"*They're* amazing." He touched her hair, letting the silky strands flow through his fingers. "I had a twin brother, Lindsay. He was killed in a car accident shortly after our twenty-first birthday." He heard her gasp softly. Not wanting to hear the inevitable "I'm sorry," he continued before she could speak. "The grief was... I can't even describe how much I hurt. To say my parents were devastated is a vast understatement. Something like that has torn a lot of couples apart. They leaned more on each other, and it made their relationship even stronger." He kissed the top of her head. "They have the kind of relationship I want with the woman I marry."

"That kind of relationship is rare."

"True, but not impossible if a couple is willing to work at making their marriage a success. I won't have any other kind."

"You expect a lot from a woman."

"I only expect her to give me one thing, and that's her heart. If she does that, anything is possible."

"It sounds nice, Sam," she whispered.

"It can be, if we're willing to try."

"*We?*"

"Yeah, *we*. I want a lot more of you, Lindsay. I want you physically, but that isn't all. I want to spend time with you, get to know you better. You made quite an impression on me, lady. And that was before we made love."

"You're rushing things, Sam."

"Maybe, but I'm being honest. I don't consider this a one-night stand."

"It's morning. This can't be a one-*night* stand."

"Smartass."

She giggled, then rubbed her hand over his chest. "This discussion is much too serious to have when I'm so sleepy."

"Okay. Discussion on hold until later. Let's get some sleep."

Lindsay turned her back to him. Sam curled up behind her and draped his arm over her waist. Content once again, he closed his eyes.

* * * * *

Lindsay lay as still as possible, watching the minutes tick off on Sam's digital clock. She could hear Sam's steady breathing. He must be asleep, but she had to be sure.

His idea of making love in the hot tub and having brunch was a wonderful one. Lindsay had agreed to stay without thinking of the consequences. She couldn't stay here until Sam awoke. Spending more time with him would just make it more difficult to leave him.

Lindsay waited a full twenty minutes before she gently lifted his arm from her waist and slid from the bed.

Gathering up her clothes, she crept from the bedroom. A nightlight in the hall gave her enough illumination to make her way to the kitchen. She dressed quickly and descended the staircase. Luckily, Sam had a nightlight in the den too, so she had no trouble finding the back door. He hadn't mentioned setting an alarm. Praying she wouldn't hear bells or sirens, Lindsay flipped the dead bolt and opened the door.

Silence.

Lindsay released her breath as she headed for her car. She slid beneath the wheel and opened her purse for her keys.

The tears didn't start until she backed out of Sam's driveway. They flowed down her cheeks as fast as she could wipe them away. She didn't understand why she was crying. Finding a man to love her forever wouldn't happen. She'd gone home with Sam knowing there could be nothing for them beyond this one night.

Sam's version of marriage was beautiful but unrealistic. Lindsay refused to be a divorce statistic like the rest of her family and friends. Trying to build something with Sam would only end in heartache, just like all her other relationships. Remaining single, and alone, was the only way to keep her heart in one piece.

Chapter 8

Consciousness slowly seeped into Sam's brain. He fought it, wanting sleep to overcome him again. But he knew once he'd awakened, there was no going back to sleep. He never set an alarm since his internal clock knew exactly how much sleep he needed.

He wished that internal clock had an "off" button.

Sam rolled to his back and realized two things at once – he had a full bladder and a raging hard-on. He figured he could manage the full bladder for a few minutes longer, enough to take care of the hard-on. Grinning, he opened his eyes and reached for Lindsay.

She wasn't there.

His grin faded as he sat up and looked around the bedroom. "Lindsay?" A glance at the floor showed him her clothes were gone. "Lindsay," he said louder.

Nothing.

Throwing back the covers, Sam bounded from the bed and hurried out of the bedroom. He didn't find Lindsay in any of the rooms upstairs. A search of the downstairs produced the same result. He opened the back door and looked in the driveway. Her car wasn't there.

His heart started pounding from fear. Lindsay couldn't be gone. After what they'd experienced together, she wouldn't have left him without saying something to him.

The feel of the cool breeze on his skin made Sam realize he stood nude in the doorway. Slowly, he closed the door and leaned his back against it. *How could she have left me?*

As soon as that thought entered his mind, Sam disregarded it. She probably went out for donuts or lattes. She'd be back at any minute, demanding to know why he didn't have her brunch ready.

Get your ass in gear, McKeifer.

Sam hurried back upstairs. Deciding to take a fast shower, he headed for his bathroom. Ten minutes later, wearing a pair of gray sweats and thick socks, he returned to the kitchen to start brunch.

Coffee came first, then he took potatoes and onions out of the pantry for the hash browns.

By the time he had the vegetables peeled, sliced and diced, he'd finally accepted that Lindsay wasn't coming back.

Anger surged up inside him. Wadding up the dish towel he'd been using to wipe his hands, he hurled it toward the dining room. It landed silently on the floor. How dare she leave without saving a word? What they'd shared wasn't a cheap, fast fuck. He truly wanted more time with her, a chance to find out if she could be "the one."

She'd stolen that from him by sneaking off like a thief.

Leaving the potatoes and onions on the cutting board, Sam wandered into the living room and flopped down in his favorite chair. Leaning his head back, he closed his eyes while remembering everything that had passed between the two of them. He'd meant it when he told her last night wasn't simply a one-night stand for him. He had no doubt that his feelings for Lindsay were different than any he'd ever felt for a woman. While he wasn't sure if he could call it love yet, it was definitely strong.

"*Damn* it, Lindsay, why did you leave?"

He'd find her. He'd find her and they'd talk, share more of their feelings, make love again...

And how do you plan to find her when you don't even know Lindsay's last name?

Sam snapped his fingers. A credit card receipt. She said she'd had dinner there last night. Maybe he'd find a credit card receipt with her last name. Once he knew that, finding her would be easy. After all, his father could find *anyone*.

Thinking of Lindsay having dinner at The Saloon made him remember what happened between them *after* dinner. He'd wanted Lindsay in his bed so badly, he hadn't restocked or cleaned up afterwards...

"*Shit!*"

Sam jumped up from the chair and jogged down the hall to his bedroom. He didn't think he'd poured any amaretto on the bar when he'd painted Lindsay's body with it, but he couldn't take that chance. He had to get to The Saloon and clean up the evidence of his and Lindsay's lovemaking before anyone else saw it.

* * * * *

Sam arrived at The Saloon shortly before 11:30. Customers already sat at several tables in the restaurant. Luckily for him, few customers sat at the tables in the bar before happy hour. He'd have time to clean and stock before anyone patronized the bar.

Nodding to the customers as he passed them, Sam made his way through the restaurant. Out of habit, he automatically looked at the glass shelves behind the counter to check the stock. The bottles were restocked, the glasses clean and stacked or hanging in racks. A glance at the countertops showed Sam they were also clean and shiny.

Puzzled, Sam looked back into the restaurant. Michelle and Dianne, two of his best waitresses, were working. Michelle was his lunchtime manager. Perhaps she had cleaned up his mess.

He hoped not. He didn't want his employees knowing what he'd done here last night.

Unable to solve the mystery now, Sam grabbed a cup of coffee from the wait staff's station before continuing on to his office. A large envelope lay on his desk, proof that Michelle had already gathered up the receipts from yesterday for him. He sat at his desk and booted up his computer, then removed the contents from the envelope. He sorted through the paperwork until he found the paper-clipped credit card receipts.

Searching for the name "Lindsay," Sam carefully examined every receipt. When his search didn't produce what he wanted, he started over again. His second search still didn't produce a receipt with Lindsay's name.

"*Damn* it!" Sam ran both hands through his hair. Dropping his head forward, he hooked his hands behind his neck and exhaled loudly. What now?

"Trouble, boss?"

The sound of Monte's voice made Sam raise his head. Since Monte always worked the late shift, seeing him here well before five p.m. surprised Sam. "What are you doing here?"

"I came by earlier to check out the bar. I suspected you might've been too...busy last night to restock and clean up." Monte took something out of his pocket and tossed it on Sam's desk. Sam looked down at Lindsay's third condom.

"I found that next to an open bottle of amaretto." Grinning wickedly, Monte slouched in the chair before Sam's desk. "She must've been one hot piece for you to leave empty shelves. I need details."

"You aren't getting any details, Monte."

"Oh, come on, let me have some fun. I didn't get laid last night, so at least let me enjoy what happened to you."

"I said no."

Monte's eyes narrowed slightly. Sam recognized that expression on his friend's face — it said he wasn't buying whatever Sam was saying. While Sam didn't believe in being disrespectful toward women or sharing personal information, as best friends he and Monte did joke about and share sexual experiences in general. Sam refusing to do so had to make Monte suspicious.

Monte gestured toward the disorderly pile of paperwork on Sam's desk. "Yesterday's receipts?"

"Yeah."

"Something special about them? You aren't usually that messy with your stuff."

"I was looking for something."

When he didn't continue, Monte prompted, "Like?"

Sam frowned. "You're being awfully nosy today."

"That's because you aren't being yourself." Monte's voice softened. "What's going on, man?"

Sam leaned back in his chair, trying to decide whether or not to confide in his friend. Maybe he should. Maybe Monte would have an idea on how to find Lindsay.

"I was looking for a credit card receipt from Lindsay."

"Who's Lindsay?"

"The woman I was with last night."

"The woman with the need-their-own-ZIP-code tits?"

"Jesus, Monte. Try not to be a jerk just once, okay?"

Monte held up his hands, palms forward. "Sorry." Propping one ankle on the opposite knee, Monte lowered his hands and laced his fingers over his stomach. "So, why were you looking for a receipt from Lindsay?"

"I thought it might help me find her, but there's no receipt with the name Lindsay on it. She said she came here with her girlfriends, so one of them must've bought her dinner."

"Okay, you've lost me again. What do you mean, it might help you find her?"

Needing to move, Sam stood and walked over to his window. He drew back the curtains and looked out at the passing traffic on Cooper Point Road. "She was gone when I woke up this morning. We didn't exchange last names, so I don't know how to find her."

"Why do you want to find her? Was her pussy that tight?"

Fists clenched, Sam whirled around to face his friend. "Goddamn it, Monte, knock it off. I've had enough of your filthy mouth."

Monte remained silent for several seconds. "I didn't know I was stepping on sacred ground, Sam. You've never been this touchy about a woman. You're acting like you're in love or something." His eyes widened. "My God, is that it? Are you in love with her?"

"I just *met* her, Monte. I can't be in love with her."

"That's bullshit. Love can slap a man in the face when he least expects it. That's when he starts thinking about marriage and kids and station wagons." Monte shuddered. "No thanks."

Sam couldn't help chuckling at his friend's obvious distaste of matrimony. "I think it's minivans now instead of station wagons."

"Whatever. I want nothing to do with it. I plan to stay happily single."

"Sounds lonely."

"I'm alone only when I want to be."

"There's a difference between alone and lonely, Monte."

"Not in my book." Monte lowered his foot to the floor and leaned forward. "Enough about me. Let's figure out how to find this gal."

"I don't think it's possible. All I know about her is her first name. She drove a silver car, but I can't tell you the make or model." Sam returned to his chair. "I thought if I could find out her last name from a credit card receipt, my dad could find her."

Monte scratched his chin. "What about an Internet search?"

"With what? I don't even know if she lives in Olympia. Maybe she lives in Chehalis, or Tacoma, or even Seattle. Maybe Lindsay isn't her first name, maybe it's her *middle* name."

"So let's concentrate on the little bit you *do* know. You said she came here with girlfriends. That's plural." He nodded toward the stack of credit card receipts. "Go through the receipts and take out the ones that are signed by a man, or have only two dinners charged."

Willing to try anything, Sam divided the stack of receipts and handed half of them to Monte. He worked silently with his friend, taking out the receipts that were obviously not from Lindsay's dinner and making a separate stack of them. When they were through, Sam still held almost fifty receipts.

"You had a good Friday night," Monte said.

"Great for my bank balance, lousy for my love life." Sam thumbed through the receipts. "Lorna Aish, Celia Greenland, Twila Hollier, Rita Moore, Emma McGuire, Bev Thornton. Any of these women could be Lindsay's friend, or it might not be *any* of them. Maybe they paid cash instead of using a credit card." Frustrated at his inability to do anything, Sam tossed the receipts back on his desk. They skittered across the shiny surface, some of them falling at Monte's feet.

"I wish I could be more help, man," Monte said as he gathered up the receipts from the floor and replaced them on Sam's desk.

"Me too." Sam released a heavy sigh. "You probably think I'm crazy to be so obsessed over finding Lindsay."

"No, I don't think you're crazy. I think you're in love. And don't tell me it's too early. You've never acted like this about a woman."

"No, I haven't." He fanned the receipts, hoping the answer to finding Lindsay would jump out at him. "I'm not like you, Monte. I *want* the marriage and the kids and the minivan."

"Yeah, I know." Monte stood. "Give me a call if there's anything I can do."

Once his friend left, Sam again leaned back in his chair. Quitting wasn't in his vocabulary. His father had taught him to never give up on his goals, no matter how hard they might be to obtain.

Perhaps Lindsay wouldn't turn out to be the woman of his dreams, but he wanted the chance to find out.

I'll find you, Lindsay. Somehow, I'll find you.

Chapter 9

Lindsay added a final burst of hairspray to Mrs. Bain's white hair. She was Lindsay's favorite customer, and Lindsay truly enjoyed Mrs. Bain's weekly appointment.

Lindsay held up the large hand mirror so Mrs. Bain could see the back of her head. "How's that?"

"Perfect. You always do a good job."

"It's easy to do a good job on such beautiful hair." Lindsay laid down the mirror and removed the cape from her customer. "Same time next week?"

"I'll be here."

"I'll tell Sharon to put you down in the appointment book."

"Thank you, dear." Mrs. Bain opened her purse, took out a twenty-dollar bill, and handed it to Lindsay. "Goodbye."

"Goodbye."

Smiling, Lindsay watched Mrs. Bain toddle out to the reception area. Her son stood and offered his arm as she reached him. Every Tuesday at 10:30, Mrs. Bain's son brought her here so she could have her hair washed and styled. He waited until she was through, then he took her to lunch.

If he wasn't sixty-one years old and married, Lindsay would snap him up in a second. Any man who did so much for his mother had to have a good heart.

No, that wasn't true. She wouldn't snap him up in a second. She wouldn't snap up *any* man. Despite the popular cliché, she didn't believe the third time was the charm.

With a sigh, Lindsay turned back to her cubicle to prepare it for her next customer. Gathering up Mrs. Bain's cape and towels, she dropped them in the laundry hamper. She closed the lid as her friend and co-worker Rita swept through the cubicle's saloon doors.

"I checked the appointment book and we're both free until twelve-thirty. Let's take an early lunch. I'm *starving*."

Lindsay chuckled. "You're *always* starving. I don't know how you stay so slim when you eat enough for three people."

"Good genes," Rita said with a grin. "So, what'd ya say? Let's go to The Saloon and get one of their—"

"No Saloon," Lindsay said quickly. "How about Chinese? We haven't—"

"What do you mean, no Saloon? It's your favorite restaurant. It's *my* favorite restaurant."

"I want to do something different." Lindsay took her broom from the corner and began to sweep, even though Mrs. Bain hadn't received a trim today and there was no hair on the floor. It gave her the excuse to avoid Rita's penetrating eyes.

"Chinese isn't different."

"It is if we try that new smorgy in Lacey."

"Fine. I won't argue with you when my tummy is making noise. My car or yours?"

*   *   *   *   *

Lindsay shook her head when she saw the stack of food on Rita's plate. "You keep eating like that, your good genes are going to desert you."

"Oh, pish tosh, as my grandmother says. Don't spoil my good mood." Rita picked up an egg roll and took a healthy bite. "Mmm, nummy. You had a good idea." She finished her egg roll and washed it down with hot tea. "We haven't chatted since your birthday. Did you use the rubbers?"

Lindsay almost choked on her tea. "Rita!"

"I want to know."

"It's none of your business."

"Aha!" Rita pointed her fork at Lindsay. "That means you *did* use them."

Hoping to get her friend's mind off her love life, Lindsay lifted the teapot. "More tea?"

"Don't try to change the subject. You've been alone for too long. I know you got burned once—"

"Twice."

"Okay, twice, but that isn't any reason to spend your life alone."

"I don't need a man in my life. I'm perfectly happy with my own company."

"Yeah, well, your fingers or a plastic dildo are no substitute for warm lips and a hard cock."

Heat flooded Lindsay's face...not at Rita's words, but at the images they brought to her mind. The memory of Sam's hard cock inside her made desire rush through her body. She remembered how he thrust so deeply, licked her clit, sucked her nipples...

"That red face isn't from drinking hot tea, Lindsay. Who was he?"

Lindsay scooped up some chicken chow mein on her fork. "No one you know."

"Someone special?"

Lindsay paused while swallowing. Yes, Sam was special. That didn't mean he wouldn't break her heart. "No, no one special."

"Do you still believe that ridiculous notion that you aren't meant to be happy?"

"It isn't a ridiculous notion. Everyone in my family is divorced. So are my friends, including you."

"That's because I married a jerk."

"You didn't think he was a jerk when you married him or you never would've married him."

Rita dug back into her lunch without comment, which proved to Lindsay that she was right.

"Something happens when two people get married, Rita. All the love, the passion, the longing to be together, disappears. Once they sign that marriage contract, they start to change."

"Yes, people change, Lindsay. They grow, they get older. That happens to *everyone*. It doesn't mean every marriage is doomed for failure. My folks were happy until my dad died, and my mom's been happy since she remarried. Don't you know *anyone* who has a happy marriage?"

She thought of what Sam had said about his parents. They'd been happily married for thirty-five years, despite losing a child.

"My marriage failed because I was so young when I got married," Rita said. "I started to grow up, become more independent, and Brady couldn't handle it. He wanted to keep the sweet, naïve eighteen-year-old he married. When she disappeared, he started staying out late and drinking heavily. I refused to be married to a drunk, he refused to stop drinking. So we divorced. There was no other option for us."

"So why haven't you remarried? You've been divorced for five or six years."

"I haven't fallen in love again. I haven't met the man who makes my heart pound with just a look. It's that simple."

Lindsay had met that man. One look from Sam's stormy eyes had made her heart pound, her nipples tighten, and moisture dampen her panties. Despite being in love twice, she'd never felt such a strong attraction to a man.

But it went beyond physical attraction. She had actually fantasized about a wedding, a honeymoon, decorating Sam's house, the birth of a child…

Lindsay sighed silently. None of those fantasies would come true. She wasn't willing to take the chance.

* * * * *

"I can't believe I let you talk me into this," Sam grumbled as he held open the door for Cheryl.

"Don't be such a grouch. You know you love Chinese."

"Yeah, I do, but I have a ton of paperwork to finish. Am I at my desk taking care of it? No. Instead of working on the Westside, I'm at a Chinese smorgasbord in Lacey."

"Ya gotta eat."

"I own a *restaurant*."

"Which is closed today."

"You are the only woman, besides my mom, who can twist me around your little finger."

Cheryl smiled. "I know. That's why we're such good friends."

"The place is packed."

"So we'll wait a few minutes. Besides, you needed some time away from The Saloon to get your mind off Lindsay."

Hearing Cheryl say Lindsay's name surprised Sam. "How do you know about Lindsay?"

"Monte told me."

"What?"

"It was obvious you were down last night at the bar. You didn't even pay any attention to the game on TV. So I asked Monte if he knew what was bothering you. I'm sorry, Sam," she said softly. "Is there anything I can do to help?"

"Not unless you can find her."

"I would if I could. You're a nicer guy to work for when you're happy."

"Gee, thanks," Sam said dryly.

Cheryl grinned, then wandered over to the counter and picked up a to-go menu. "Nice selection. I've heard the food is great." She replaced the menu before tapping one fingernail against a large brandy snifter next to the register. "Hey, Sam, do you have a business card with you?"

"Yeah, why?"

"They have a drawing once a month for a free dinner for two." She held out her hand. "Give me one of your cards."

Sam reached in his shirt pocket. "You'll never win. There must be a hundred cards in there."

"It's worth a shot." She dropped Sam's card in the snifter, then removed another one. "Hmm, The Hair Salon. I've been looking for a new hairstylist. I wonder if Rita Moore is any good?"

Sam frowned slightly. "Rita Moore? That name is familiar." He watched Cheryl slip the card into her purse. "You can't take that card."

"I just did. I'll copy down the info and drop the card back in the snifter when we go." She grabbed Sam's arm and tugged him toward the dining room. "A couple is leaving. C'mon, let's eat."

Chapter 10

Rita whipped the cape off of Lindsay. "Voila! Ze hair is beeootiful again."

Lindsay decided it was the worst French accent she'd ever heard. But she had to admit Rita was a wonderful stylist. She shook her head. Her hair fell perfectly over her shoulders. "Thanks for the trim."

"Anytime. I'll expect you to return the favor when I need a trim."

"Deal." Lindsay stood and straightened the crease of her slacks. "Can you go shopping with me?"

"I have a new customer due at any minute. Give me a rain check?"

"Sure. See you later."

Lindsay left Rita's cubicle, stopping at the receptionist's desk to double-check her schedule. Friday and Saturday were booked solid from nine o'clock on, but her first customer didn't come in until ten-thirty tomorrow and the rest of the day was light. Good. Maybe she'd be able to get some extra sleep.

She certainly hadn't been able to sleep at night.

It was hard for her to believe it had been less than a week since she'd been in Sam's arms. Not an hour passed that she didn't think of him and long to be with him again. She often thought she should go see him and apologize for leaving the way she had. The idea no more than formed before she disregarded it. If she went to see him, she wouldn't ever want to leave.

The tinkling bell over the front door signaled someone entering the shop. Lindsay glanced in that direction and saw an attractive thirtyish woman with beautiful auburn hair. She looked in Lindsay's direction with a smile, but that smile quickly faded. She stopped in her tracks and her eyes widened.

Lindsay didn't have the chance to try and figure out the woman's strange reaction before Rita appeared and introduced herself. Lindsay watched as Rita showed the young woman to her cubicle. Before she disappeared through the saloon doors, the woman looked back at Lindsay again.

Goose bumps erupted on Lindsay's skin. She had the feeling she knew that woman, or the woman knew her. But she couldn't remember ever meeting her. Surely she'd remember a woman with that glorious auburn hair. In her profession, a person's hair was the first thing Lindsay noticed.

It was probably a case of mistaken identity. Mentally shaking her head, Lindsay decided not to worry about it. She had shopping to do.

* * * * *

Sam examined the inventory list again. "Do you think I should buy extra bourbon?" he asked Monte. "Halloween is on a Friday this year."

"If Halloween is on a Friday, I think you should buy extra *everything*."

"Good point. How are the—"

Sam stopped when the door to his office flew open. If there hadn't been a doorstop attached to the baseboard, the doorknob would've punctured a giant hole in the wall.

"Cheryl, what the hell—"

"Remember that card I took out of the snifter at the Chinese place, the one with Rita Moore's name on it? I made an appointment with her to have my hair done." She fluffed her auburn curls. "Nice, huh?"

Sam glanced at Monte. His friend gave him a look that said, 'Yeah, she's nuts, but we put up with her anyway.' "It's lovely, but what—"

"Thanks. Anyway, when I walked in the door, imagine my shock when I saw Lindsay."

Sam stared at her, his mouth open. "What?" he managed to push past his heart that had wedged in his throat.

"Isn't that incredible? So while Rita was working on my hair, I pumped her for information. Subtly, of course."

"Of course."

She took a piece of paper from her jeans pocket and slapped it on top of Sam's desk. "Lindsay Cunningham, age thirty, drives a silver Nissan Sentra, works as a hairstylist at The Hair Salon on 4th Avenue, lives in a small house close to St. Peter's."

Sam's gaze traveled from Cheryl to the piece of paper and back again. Cheryl was grinning as if she'd just won the lottery.

"Rita Moore was one of the names on the credit card receipts, Sam," Monte reminded him.

That's why that name had seemed familiar when Cheryl read it off the business card. He'd been closer to finding Lindsay than he'd known.

"So, is that info worth a nice Christmas bonus, boss?" Cheryl asked, still grinning.

"Is it ever!" Sam rounded his desk and lifted Cheryl off the floor in a bear hug. When he set her back on her feet, he cupped her face in his hands and gave her a smacking kiss. "I gotta go to that salon. What's the address?"

"She isn't there right now. But I did see her schedule in the appointment book and her first customer is at ten-thirty tomorrow morning. Rita said Lindsay usually gets there about half an hour before her first customer."

"I can't wait until tomorrow. I have to see her tonight. You said she lives near St. Peter's."

"Yeah, but I don't have her address. I couldn't get *that* much information."

"Maybe she's in the phone book."

Cheryl scrunched up her nose. "She's a single woman, so might have an unlisted number."

"Not a problem," Monte said. "I happen to have friends in the right places. I'll have it for you in five minutes."

Monte picked up the telephone receiver. Cheryl hit Sam lightly on his arm. "Isn't it great to have crooks working for you, boss?"

Hanging up the phone after his short conversation, Monte handed Sam another piece of paper. "Here you go."

"I'm not even going to ask how you did that." Sam studied the pieces of paper in his hand. He was only minutes away from finding Lindsay. Raising his head, he looked at Monte again. "I might be late tomorrow —"

"I'll cover you. Go find your woman."

* * * * *

158

Sam sat in his SUV three doors down from Lindsay's house. The dregs from his large coffee had grown cold long ago. He thought about leaving long enough to go get another cup, yet didn't want to miss Lindsay in case she came home while he was gone.

He'd been here for almost two hours. The amount of time didn't matter. He'd sit here for two *days* if he had to in order to speak to Lindsay.

As long as a policeman didn't come by and arrest him for stalking Lindsay, he'd be fine.

A silver car rounded the corner. Sam sat up straighter in the seat. The garage door to Lindsay's house rose as the car drew closer. She pulled her car into the driveway across the street, then backed into her garage.

Hoping she wouldn't close the door before he could get in the garage, Sam left his vehicle and jogged through the light mist to Lindsay's house. He peeked inside the garage. The trunk to Lindsay's car was open, and also a door into her house. Sam walked up to the back of her car. He saw three large sacks with a Target logo. Picking up the sacks, Sam quietly shut the trunk, stepped inside her house, and pushed the door closed with his foot.

He found himself in her laundry room. His gaze swept over the cabinets, the matching washer and dryer, the basket full of towels on the floor, before he continued through the door into the breakfast nook. Lindsay knelt in front of the refrigerator, placing a head of lettuce in the crisper.

His heart swelled at the sight of her, but so did his anger. She had left him without a word, and she owed him one doozy of an explanation.

Sam set the sacks on the counter that separated the breakfast nook from the kitchen. Lindsay jerked to her feet and turned toward him, her eyes wide.

"I thought you needed some help with your bags."

"Sam! You scared me." He saw her throat work as she swallowed. "How-how did you find me?"

"With help from some very good friends." He rounded the counter and moved closer to her. "We have a lot to talk about, Lindsay." Reaching past her, he pushed shut the refrigerator door. "Don't you agree?"

Chapter 11

Lindsay's legs grew weak and sweat beaded her palms. She never expected to see Sam again, and especially not in her house. She took a step back while frantically trying to think of what to do.

Sam took off his leather jacket and tossed it on the counter next to the sacks he'd brought in. "No comment, Lindsay? No explanation why you left me without a word?"

Lindsay could feel anger radiating from him. The anger didn't make him any less attractive. He stood straight, his legs slightly apart, his arms crossed over his chest. The black sweater and jeans he wore fit his body perfectly. He looked incredible, but she remembered how incredible he looked without any clothes at all.

Right now, she'd love to feel his arms around her, his hands on her skin, his lips on hers. She couldn't allow that to happen. She didn't want to hurt Sam, but she had to protect her heart. Lifting her chin, she countered his anger with her own. "I don't owe you any explanations. We both enjoyed the sex."

"It was more than just sex to me and you know it. I told you I wanted more time with you."

"Did you ever think that maybe *I* didn't want more time with *you*? It was a one-night stand, Sam."

"No, it wasn't. Your response was too strong for only a one-night stand."

That was true. Lindsay had never responded so strongly to a man, which was precisely why she ran. Falling in love with Sam wouldn't have been difficult at all.

"You've never had amazing sex with another woman?"

"Yeah, I've had amazing sex with other women. What you don't seem to hear me say, or don't *want* to hear me say, is that it was more than sex to me." He uncrossed his arms and let them hang at his sides. The new position made him seem less angry, and more vulnerable. "I felt a connection with you, Lindsay, a connection I've been looking for with a woman for a long time. I don't know if it's love yet, but I want the chance to find out if it could be." He stepped closer and ran his thumb over her cheek. "We're good together, Lindsay," he said softly, "*really* good. Why do you want to throw that away before we see where it can go?"

His touch made her close her eyes in pleasure. She stopped herself short of moaning. "I can't, Sam," she whispered.

He remained silent for several moments. When he spoke, the tone of his voice sounded flat, no longer gentle and caring. "So it was nothing but sex to you, a one-night stand."

The loss of his touch made her look at him again. She gazed into eyes blazing with anger.

"Since the sex was so 'amazing', there's no reason why we can't have it again."

"What?" Lindsay squeaked.

She didn't get the chance to say anything else before Sam pushed her back against the refrigerator and kissed her roughly, his tongue diving past her lips. Shocked at his manhandling, Lindsay laid her hands on his chest to push him away. He grabbed her wrists and lifted them over her head.

A sliver of fear skated down her spine. It soon disappeared. This was *Sam* kissing her. He would never hurt her, nor force her to do anything she didn't want to do.

He transferred both her wrists to one hand and cradled her breast in his free hand. His thumb slid over her nipple, sending shards of pleasure between her thighs. He seemed to know instinctively how to touch her, and when, to make her want him desperately. He began massaging her breast, and Lindsay couldn't stop the sound of pleasure from escaping this time.

"I love to hear you moan," he whispered against her lips.

His massaging became firmer as he kissed her again. He pressed his hand against her, lifting her breast as he thumbed her nipple. Lindsay struggled to free her wrists, wanting desperately to touch him also. His hold was too firm. His mouth covered hers so she couldn't talk, his body held her against the refrigerator so she couldn't move. She was completely at his mercy for anything he wanted to do.

She'd never felt so helpless...or so aroused.

Sam broke off the kiss and released her wrists at the same time. The lack of support made Lindsay sag against him. He quickly wrapped his arms around her waist and pulled her to him. His erection pressed into her belly.

"I've got to get inside you." He bit the side of her neck, and Lindsay moaned again.

In the next instant, she yelped when Sam dipped, placed his shoulder in her stomach, and lifted her over his shoulder. She hung upside down, staring at his butt, as he walked. "What are you doing?" she managed to choke.

"Taking you to bed."

She couldn't say anything else since all the air had been squeezed out of her lungs. She watched the carpet as Sam walked through the living room. He paused outside her office, then continued down the hall to her bedroom. Her head had begun to spin from her position when Sam dropped her on the bed.

Pushing her legs apart with his knees, Sam stretched out on top of her. Lindsay barely had time to gulp in some oxygen before he kissed her again. He held her head in his hands and devoured her mouth.

Lindsay couldn't breathe, and it had nothing to do with the way Sam had carried her. His kisses, his caresses, made her heart pound and her stomach churn. Heat traveled through her body and pooled between her thighs. A pulse throbbed in her clit. She felt...surrounded by Sam. He not only filled her arms, but also her mind, her soul.

Her heart.

Sitting back on his heels, Sam pulled off his sweater and tossed it to the floor. Lindsay ran her hands over that glorious hair-dusted chest. She didn't get nearly enough time touching him before he took her hands and tugged her to a sitting position. He pulled off her sweater, then unhooked and removed her bra. Both garments joined his sweater on the floor. Sam caressed her breasts while kissing her again. He rolled her nipples between his thumbs and forefingers, making the heat in her body intensify.

Sam pushed her back down on the bed and unfastened her slacks. "God, I want to fuck you."

Lindsay had never heard Sam use that kind of language. It excited her even more. She lifted her hips to make it easier for him to take off the rest of her clothes. Slacks, panties, socks, and shoes soon fell to the floor.

Propping up on one elbow, Lindsay watched Sam shed his clothing. As soon as he was nude, he joined her on the bed again. She didn't even have the chance to inhale before he entered her.

Sam slipped his arms underneath her knees and bent her legs toward her chest. Lindsay gripped his shoulders while he drove his cock into her. She couldn't call this lovemaking. This was too raw, too animalistic, to be called making love. The sound of flesh slapping against flesh filled the room. Sweat formed on his body. His breathing became more labored. His heart pounded against her breast. Lindsay wrapped her arms tightly around his neck and hung on as the pleasure built inside her. Closer, closer...

Sam released a long groan and shuddered. Disappointment pierced her that he had climaxed so soon, and frustration made tears blur her vision. She blinked quickly to stop them from falling.

Raising his head, Sam stared into her eyes. He kissed one eyelid, then the other. "Don't be upset. I'm nowhere near through with you."

✽ ✽ ✽ ✽ ✽

Sam rained kisses on her chin, her neck, her collarbone, continuing down her body until he closed his mouth over one nipple. He suckled hard, wanting Lindsay as hot as he could make her. He'd been selfish rushing toward a climax, but having Lindsay in his arms again had made him lose control. Now he wanted to do everything possible to give her pleasure...while he ravished her.

He lavished attention on her other nipple before moving lower. Her musky scent reached him first. Parting the feminine lips with his fingers, he inhaled deeply. Nothing smelled so good as an aroused woman. He inhaled again, then swiped her slit with his tongue.

Lindsay gasped and lifted her hips. She obviously wanted more from him. He was only too happy to give it to her.

Sam thrust his tongue inside her pussy. She was wet, her cream thick and plentiful from her own body and from his cum. *Delicious*, he thought. He licked her from clit to anus and back again. Each time his tongue swiped her clit, Lindsay raised her hips and he heard that sexy moaning sound she made.

He loved that sound.

Tasting Lindsay soon rekindled his desire to a frantic level. Sam moved his tongue wherever he could reach. He suckled her clit, pushed his tongue into her ass, darted inside her pussy, then returned to her clit. Lindsay's moans became louder, her movements more frenzied. Holding her hips still, he pulled her clit between his lips and worked it with his tongue.

She emitted a strangled sound and grabbed his head. Tremors wracked her body for several moments before she lay still.

Sam didn't give Lindsay a chance to recuperate. Flipping her over to her stomach, he jerked her up to her knees and lunged inside her.

"Oh, God, Sam!"

"Take it, Lindsay." He held her hips, keeping her buttocks tight against his groin. "Take every inch of me."

Lindsay looked at him over her shoulder, her eyes narrowed and sultry. "I can take anything you give me."

Sam smiled. He liked that saucy, sexy attitude. Beginning with slow, long strokes, he pumped his cock into her creamy pussy. When she reached back and grabbed his hip, he increased the speed of his thrusts.

"More, Sam. Harder, please."

"Whatever you want. Spread your legs wider."

Sam moved even faster, until he was hammering his cock into her as hard as he could. Sweat poured off him. Still he kept pumping, determined to bring her to another climax.

He licked his thumb, then pushed it inside her ass. Lindsay arched her back and tossed her head. "*Yesss!*"

The contractions inside her milked him. With a final lunge, Sam followed her into paradise.

Chapter 12

Lindsay awoke to the smell of ham and onions. She rolled to her back and managed to open her eyes after three tries. A glance at her digital clock showed her it was almost eight-thirty. She blinked and looked at it again. Eight-thirty? It was dark in the room; it couldn't possibly be eight-thirty.

Struggling to a sitting position, she pushed her hair out of her face. An ache between her thighs made the memories come flooding back. It was eight-thirty at night and she had fallen asleep after incredible sex with Sam.

Or she'd passed out.

"Wow." Lindsay fell back on the bed, threw one arm over her eyes, and released a deep breath. "Incredible" didn't begin to describe what she'd experienced a short time ago. The sex had been bone-melting hot. Other lovers had brought her to a climax. None of those orgasms had dissolved her limbs until she could barely move.

A sound like a drawer closing in the kitchen made Lindsay uncover her eyes. She sniffed the air, and again detected the aroma of ham and onions. Sam was cooking. Her stomach rumbled. She was ravenous after what they'd shared, but didn't know if she could face him. She'd run away from him without a word, then spread her legs the first time he tapped her shoulder.

The need for a bathroom finally forced her to rise. She used the facility, ran a brush through her hair, and rinsed her mouth. After pulling on her thick terry cloth robe and slippers, she padded out of the bedroom.

She found Sam standing before the stove. He was barefoot, wearing his black jeans that he'd zipped but left unsnapped. He looked so sexy…and perfectly at home in her kitchen.

He must have sensed her presence for he turned his head toward her. A slow, sexy smile formed on his lips.

"Hi, sleepyhead."

"Hi."

"Are you hungry? I was starving, so did some snooping. Luckily, you'd bought a canned ham and I found a block of cheddar in the frig." Scooping up a large omelet from the skillet, he placed it on a plate next to a huge pile of hash browns. "I told you I make a mean ham and cheese omelet. Grab some forks, okay?"

Lindsay watched him carry the plate to the breakfast nook. She noticed he'd already set the table with napkins and glasses of orange juice. He set the plate on the table before facing her. Realizing he was waiting for her before he sat down, Lindsay gathered up the forks and joined him at the table.

She sat in the chair on Sam's left. After handing him one of the forks, she took a bite of omelet. The flavors of egg, ham, and cheese exploded on her tongue. He hadn't lied when he said he made a mean omelet. "It's wonderful, Sam."

Lindsay took one more bite, laid down her fork, and burst into tears.

✳ ✳ ✳ ✳ ✳

Seeing a woman cry always turned Sam to mush, especially when the woman was someone important to him. He dropped his fork and cradled Lindsay's cheek in his hand, gently wiping away the tears as they streamed from her eyes.

"Baby, what's wrong?"

She didn't speak. Sam continued to wipe away her tears while waiting for her to tell him why she was crying.

"I'm so ash-ashamed, S-Sam."

"Why?"

"I left you af-after you'd been so wonderful t-to me." She raised her gaze to his. "I'm s-sorry."

The soft lighting in the room made the tears in her eyes shine like diamonds. Her pain touched him, making him hurt for her.

If he hadn't already suspected he loved her, he knew it for sure now.

Sam sat back in his chair to give her some space. "Why did you leave me?"

Lindsay's chest rose and fell with her deep breath. She wiped the last evidence of tears from her face. "I was scared."

"Of what?"

166

"Of you."

Sam frowned. "Of me? Why?"

"Because of the way you made me feel." She sniffed loudly. "I need a tissue."

Sam went back in the kitchen, returned with a paper towel, and handed it to Lindsay. She blew her nose and stuffed the soiled towel in the pocket of her robe. "Thank you."

"Drink some of your juice," he said softly.

Her hand shook slightly as she raised the glass to her lips and sipped the juice. Afraid she might drop it, Sam took the glass from her and returned it to the table. "Okay, you've blown your nose and drunk your juice. Now talk to me."

Lindsay pulled the lapels of her robe closer together. "My parents are divorced, and so is my brother. My sister has been divorced twice. All my close friends are divorced or separated. It's all I've ever known, Sam. People get married and their relationships fizzle."

"That isn't true. I told you about my parents, how happy they've been despite losing a son. Just because your family and friends have had bad relationships doesn't mean you're destined to do the same."

"I know that in here." She touched her temple. "In here..." She touched her chest, over her heart. "...I know how much it hurts when the relationship ends. I've had my heart broken twice, Sam. I can't put it together a third time."

Lindsay crossed her arms over her stomach. "You were so kind and funny and sexy. The way you kissed me and loved me... No one else has ever made me feel the way you did. I couldn't take the chance of falling for you."

"Not even after I told you how I felt, that I wanted more time to get to know you better?"

"Not even then."

Sam ran one hand through his hair in frustration. "I don't know what to say, Lindsay. I won't make promises I can't keep."

"You can't promise me you won't break my heart?"

The pain in her voice caused a lump to form in his throat. Leaning forward, he pulled her arms away from her stomach and took both her hands in his. "Lindsay, I can't guarantee the sun will rise tomorrow, but I have faith it will. You have to have faith, too, that my love will only grow stronger as time passes."

Her gaze traveled over his face. "Your love?"

"Yeah, my love. I love you, Lindsay." He kissed her softly. "That I *can* guarantee you."

She withdrew one hand from his and touched his lips. He kissed her fingertips. "You really love me?"

"I do. And before you say something about me not knowing you long enough to be sure it's love, don't even bother. I fell in love with you the second I saw you. I know how I feel."

"Oh, Sam." Tears filled her eyes again. "I love you too."

"How could you help it? I'm a studmuffin."

Lindsay laughed, which was exactly what Sam wanted her to do. Standing, he pulled her to her feet and into his arms. She clung to him as if she'd never let him go.

He didn't mind that at all.

"Speaking of you being a studmuffin..." she whispered in his ear.

Her warm breath made goose bumps rise on his skin. "Yeah?"

She pulled back enough to look at his face. "That was pretty wild earlier."

"Yeah, I know." He blew out a breath. "I was angry at you. I never should've touched you before we talked. If I hurt you — "

She laid her fingertips over his lips. "You didn't hurt me. It was hot and intense and incredible. In fact..." She glided her hands over his shoulders and chest. "...I was wondering if I could get a repeat performance."

She stepped back and unbelted her robe. Slowly, she slid the robe off her shoulders and let it fall to the floor.

Sam's cock quickly tightened in anticipation of being inside her again. He would gladly give her as many repeat performances as she wanted.

Scooping her up in his arms, Sam walked toward the bedroom. "That, my beautiful lady, won't be a problem at all."

The End

UNEXPECTED

Chapter 1

Linc Carter propped Nyle up against the doorframe. Placing one hand on his friend's chest to hold him in place, he fumbled in Nyle's jacket pocket for the key to the back door.

It would've been easier to go through the front door instead of practically carrying Nyle to the back door, but his bedroom was closer to the rear of his condo. Going around the condo instead of through it meant Linc could avoid all obstacles, like walls and furniture. All he wanted to do was put Nyle to bed before he passed out.

Linc pushed open the door and reached inside to flip up the light switch. Nyle's knees buckled. Quickly grabbing his friend, Linc pulled Nyle's arm over his shoulder to stop him from sliding any farther.

"Hold on, buddy. I've almost got you there."

Nyle opened one bloodshot eye. "Linc?"

"Yeah."

"Where're we?"

"We're at your condo." Linc dragged Nyle inside the door and pushed it shut behind them.

"I don' wanna be home. I wanna party."

"You've partied enough for one night."

"But it's my birfday. I should get t' party on my birfday."

Linc turned his head, trying to get away from the fumes coming out of Nyle's mouth. All Linc had to do was add a match and that breath could be used as a blow torch. "Your birthday was over two hours ago."

"Oh. Okay. Then I guess I can go home."

Linc managed to get Nyle to the bedroom and lower him to the bed without running him into any walls or furniture. He turned on the bedside lamp. Nyle blinked at the sudden light. "Linc?"

"Yeah."

"How-how come you don' party wif me on my birfday? The other guys party wif me."

"Because I'm the designated driver."

"Thaz no fun." He grinned drunkenly. "I like having fun."

That's an understatement. "Get some sleep, man."

"See you tomorrow?"

"Nope. I'm going up to my cabin."

"Oh, yeah." Nyle closed his eyes. "I don' know why you go up there all by you'self."

Linc wasn't about to try to explain the reason, not with Nyle ready to pass out at any moment. Instead, he pulled up the quilt from the end of the bed and covered his friend. By the time he switched off the lamp, Nyle was already snoring softly.

Linc shut the back door behind him, jiggling the doorknob to be sure it was locked. It had been the same for four years. He and three friends took Nyle out to celebrate his birthday. Every year, Linc made sure his friend got home safely. Nyle didn't usually drink so heavily, but he did like to get smashed on his birthday.

Nyle paid for it with a hell of a hangover, but he certainly had a good time while it was happening.

Everyone gave so much attention to Nyle's birthday that they completely missed Linc's birthday one day later. He didn't mind. With his crazy work schedule and so little time he could call his own, he was happy to spend his birthdays alone in his cabin.

A cold mist had begun to fall while he was inside the condo. An unseasonable cold front had dropped down from Canada two days ago, lowering the normal temperature in Northern California twenty degrees. Combine that with moisture pouring in from the Pacific, and the rain would probably be snow by the time he got to his cabin north of Pollock Pines. He hoped so. Getting snowed in was his idea of paradise.

Stuffing his hands in the pockets of his denim jacket, Linc jogged to his Silverado. Although it was after two a.m., he wasn't the least bit tired. Instead of going home, he decided to take off now for his cabin. All he had to do was pick up a few supplies and he could be on his way.

* * * * *

The mist turned to tiny flakes east of Camino. Linc beat a rhythm on the steering wheel while he sang along with The Four Seasons on the radio. The flakes grew bigger as he climbed in elevation. If it kept coming down like this, there would be several inches on the ground in the morning.

Linc grinned. He had his notebook and plenty of groceries. He had the next eight days to be alone and work on his book. The possibility of getting snowed in didn't bother him at all.

Turning off Highway 50, Linc began the ascent into the foothills. The road narrowed and all evidence of civilization disappeared. The only light Linc could see came from his headlights. They reflected off the falling snow, making the flakes look iridescent.

Linc loved winter. Even though it wouldn't officially be winter for another month, the feel of it definitely filled the air. The below-average temperatures, the snow, the—

A light to his right made Linc glance in that direction. The sky was cloudy and there were no houses or streetlights on this road, so he shouldn't see any kind of light. It became brighter and larger, as if it were getting closer. Stepping on the brakes, Linc leaned forward to get a better look outside the windshield.

The light seemed to be moving incredibly fast. Linc's eyes widened and he swallowed hard. What the hell...

It zipped in front of his vehicle and into the trees to his left.

"Holy shit!"

The shock of what he'd seen froze Linc for a moment. Shaking his head to bring his thoughts back into focus, he pulled over to the side of the road and shut off the motor. Grabbing his flashlight from the glove compartment, he jumped out of the pickup.

Linc stood still a moment, listening for any sounds. Nothing. Whatever had flashed by his truck had either kept going, or had crashed in the trees.

Turning on the high-powered flashlight, Linc crossed the road and trudged into the tall, snow-dusted grass. He had a general idea of where the light had disappeared. That general idea covered several square yards, perhaps even acres, of thick trees and underbrush. His chances of finding the...whatever, were slim.

Slim chances always made him work harder.

Linc shone the flashlight in a wide arc as he walked. The light dusting of snow on the ground hadn't been disturbed. Making his way into the thicker pine trees, he raised the light and shone it above his head. Still no sign that anything had come through here.

I didn't imagine it. I saw something.

Turning around, Linc looked toward his truck. He estimated he'd walked at least seventy-five yards. The "thing" couldn't have traveled much farther, not the way it was falling.

It *had* to be close.

Maybe he'd miscalculated and had gone too far to his left. Linc retraced his steps halfway to his truck, then started again at a thirty-degree angle to his right.

He'd gone no more than twenty yards when he saw it at the base of a large pine tree.

A pale purple light glowed from a crumpled box the size of a bedroom nightstand. He couldn't tell the color of the box, but it looked metallic in his flashlight's beam. No sound came from it, just the faint purple glow.

Linc's heart began to pound.

He didn't know what to do with it. He didn't know what it was, where it came from, or if he should even touch it. That glow might be radioactive.

Okay, Linc, you've seen way too many sci-fi flicks.

On the chance that something living might be inside it, he couldn't just leave it here. Debating with himself for a moment, he decided he had to take it with him. It was too dark out here to tell anything, and he'd feel more comfortable examining it inside his cabin.

Linc crouched next to the box. Sticking his flashlight under his arm, he wiped his palms on his jeans and slipped his hands underneath the box. The purple glow intensified. Swallowing the lump in his throat, Linc ignored the glow and lifted the box as he stood. He staggered with the weight of it.

Whoa! Geez, what is this thing?

Unable to answer that question yet, Linc shifted the box in his arms for a better hold. By the time he made it to his pickup, sweat covered his body, despite the cold temperature and falling snow. He set the box on the ground so he could open the tailgate. He had to shake his arms to start up the circulation again before lifting the object into the bed of his truck and shutting the tailgate. Jogging to the driver's side, he climbed into the cab and started the motor.

Linc glanced frequently at the object as he made his way farther up the hill. He kept trying to figure out what it could be. Perhaps it was some kind of weather tracker. Or maybe a remote-control toy that escaped from a kid.

Or it could be something not of this world.

Oh, yeah, I've definitely seen too many sci-fi movies.

Forty minutes later, he pulled up in front of his cabin. The snow fell heavily and the temperature had been steadily dropping. Linc knew his first priority had to be building a fire in the fireplace. Figuring the groceries would be fine outside in the cold, he brought in the box and set it on the kitchen table.

Linc draped his jacket over the back of a chair and took care of the fire first. Then, opening a drawer in the kitchen cabinets, he removed several tools and laid them on the table. Screwdriver in hand, he studied the box for the best way to open it. He examined it from every angle, but saw no screws or nails. Deciding he'd have to pry it open, he laid down the screwdriver and picked up a hammer and chisel. He located a place that looked like a seam in the metal. Placing the chisel in the seam, he tapped it with the hammer.

A loud hum came from the box. The glow returned, even brighter than in the woods. Linc had to squint his eyes to keep looking at it. The hum intensified, and the box started to vibrate. Linc dropped his tools. They fell to the table with a loud clatter. He stepped back, unsure if he should stay in the cabin or run like hell.

As quickly as it had started, the hum and glow stopped. Linc waited for several moments, but nothing happened. He took a step toward the table.

The top of the box slowly opened like a clamshell.

Swallowing hard, Linc moved even closer and peered inside the box. His mouth dropped open.

"Holy shit."

Chapter 2

Linc took another step forward so he could see her better. At least, he thought it was a "her". The being inside the box was nude. She had pale purple skin, an oval, feminine face, dipped-in waist, and a small-boned frame. She had no hair anywhere on her body, nor any breasts, but Linc still suspected she was female.

She couldn't be more than fifteen inches tall.

Needing to sit before his legs gave out, Linc flopped down in a chair. He had no idea what to do now. Owning a fast-growing, successful computer and software company didn't prepare him for anything like this.

Linc had a basic knowledge of first aid, but that didn't include any medical help for an alien.

Alien. The term made him shiver.

Linc leaned forward and placed his forefinger against her neck. He could feel a faint pulse. Taking that as a good sign, he looked at her chest and detected the slight rise and fall as she breathed. Another good sign that she lived.

Now what?

The fire hadn't completely warmed the cabin yet and her skin felt chilled. He had no idea if her body temperature should be cooler. An episode of *The Munsters* flashed through his mind, where Marilyn had been ill. Her temperature had been 98.6 and Lily considered that a fever.

Linc couldn't help chuckling. His last visit to his brother's place in Portland had included watching a *Munsters* marathon with his six-year-old twin nieces.

Wondering what to do next made Linc's laughter quickly fade. Maybe her body temperature was naturally cooler, but instinct told him he should keep her warm.

Gently, he lifted her from the box and cradled her in the crook of his arm. He felt as if he were holding a Barbie doll. He carried her to the bedroom and placed her on one side of the queen bed. After covering her, he stood and looked down at her face.

What do I do with you? Do I tell someone? If I do tell someone, who should I tell? And what do I do with that...spaceship?

All the questions made his mind spin. Fatigue hit him like a brick. The sun would be rising soon and he hadn't slept in almost twenty-four hours. Clear thinking right now was impossible.

Maybe it would be easier to make decisions after some sleep. Linc didn't feel right staying in here with her, despite the bed that would easily hold both of them, so he returned to the living room. He added another log to the fireplace, slipped off his boots, and stretched out on the couch. All the muscles in his body sighed from relief.

Linc pulled the afghan from the back of the couch over his chest and closed his eyes.

* * * * *

The signal had completely disappeared. He punched several keys on his notebook, but couldn't get any sign of its location.

"Goddamn it," he muttered.

Dwight and Garry stopped talking and faced him. "Did you say something, Cap?" Dwight asked.

"I've lost the signal."

Garry frowned. "That's not possible."

"Come see for yourself."

The two men approached Cap's desk and peered at his computer screen. "What happened?" Garry asked.

"I don't know. One second the signal was sharp and easy to see, the next second it was gone."

Grinning, Dwight nudged Garry in the ribs. "Maybe it turned and landed at Roswell."

Cap glared at him. "Wipe that smirk off your face. I don't find that comment the least bit amusing."

Dwight's grin quickly faded. "Sorry, Cap." He cleared his throat. "What do you want us to do?"

"What do you *think* I want you to do? *Find* it!"

* * * * *

Linc groaned as he sat up on the couch. The short piece of furniture certainly wasn't meant to hold his six-foot frame, at least not in a reclining position. He couldn't have gotten more than three hours of sleep.

A glance at his watch showed him it was almost noon. He hadn't opened any of the curtains last night, so the cabin remained dusky. Linc stood and stretched his arms over his head, trying to work some of the kinks out of his body. Coffee. He desperately needed coffee. His stomach rumbled. Food would also be a good idea.

Thinking of coffee and food made him remember he'd never brought in his groceries. Linc stuffed his feet into his boots and stumbled to the front door. He opened the door, and blinked at the sight of a foot of snow on the ground. The sky looked like one solid gray cloud, a good indication that more snow could fall later.

"Cool," Linc said with a grin.

Since he hadn't bothered to put on a coat, Linc quickly gathered up his sacks of groceries and hurried back into the cabin. He set them on the floor inside the door long enough to throw another log on the fire, then continued on to the kitchen. The sight of the box on the table stopped him in his tracks. He needed to check on her before he did anything else.

Linc took the time to make a detour to the bathroom before he peered through the bedroom door at her. She remained in the same position he'd left her. He moved to the bed and touched her neck. He could still feel a pulse, and it seemed to be stronger than last night. That had to be good.

Releasing a heavy breath, Linc ran both hands through his hair. He needed help. Finding an alien in a spaceship was news, big time news, but he didn't want to report it to anyone in the media. He could imagine what kind of circus something like this could create.

He didn't want anyone to hurt her.

Nyle had dozens of connections. He worked as a sports columnist for *The Sacramento Bee*, but Linc didn't consider him to be part of the media. Writing about the latest 49ers' trade didn't seem like "news" to Linc.

His stomach rumbled again. Linc wanted to shower and shave, knowing he'd be able to think better if he were clean, but his stomach demanded attention first.

Linc started coffee, put away his groceries, and started scrambling eggs before he dialed Nyle's number. Five rings later, he heard his friend's slurred voice.

"'Lo?"

Linc chuckled. Apparently, Nyle hadn't quite slept off his birthday bash. "Good afternoon."

"Aw, hell, Linc, can't you let a guy die in peace?"

"You aren't dying, my friend."

"Couldn't prove it by me."

Linc spooned his eggs onto a plate and dropped two slices of bread into the toaster. "Listen, I need your help."

"You can't expect anything from me until I've had a pot of coffee."

"I'm serious, Nyle. I really need your help."

Linc could hear the covers rustling as his friend moved on the bed. "Okay, I'm sitting up. That's the best I can do right now. What's going on?"

"I need you to come up to my cabin."

"Your *cabin*? *Now*?"

"Yeah, now. Something…unexpected happened to me, Nyle."

"Are you all right?"

"Yeah, I'm fine. I just… I need someone to talk to about this."

"Okay, sure, I'll drive up there. Let me grab a quick shower and I'll be on my way. Do you need me to bring anything?"

"No, I have everything I need," Linc said, taking his toast from the toaster. "Just bring yourself."

"Will do. See you in a couple of hours."

Linc hung up the phone and picked up his plate of food. Sitting down at the table, he dug into his breakfast while peering into the box. It looked like something out of *Star Trek* after a Klingon attack, only in a much smaller version. Although crumpled from the crash, he could make out a control panel with more buttons and levers than a jet plane. It held only one reclining chair where she had been sitting. Wherever she had come from, she'd come alone.

Linc placed his plate in the sink and refilled his coffee mug. He wandered toward the bedroom as he sipped and ended up next to the bed. Her head was turned toward him on the pillow. His heart sped up when he realized she had moved. That must mean she had improved.

Other worlds, other life forms, must be out there. Linc had often wondered what might be outside their solar system. To think Earth had the only living beings in the entire vast universe seemed unrealistic to him.

Perhaps Nyle wouldn't have any better answers to this problem than he did, but Linc had to share this with someone else. If his brother Abe were closer, Linc would call him. Since Abe lived six hundred miles away, Linc saw no reason to confide in his brother when Abe couldn't possibly do anything.

Nyle would be here in a couple of hours. Until then, Linc could do nothing but watch her and wait.

Chapter 3

A silent scream formed on Chandra's lips, one she couldn't utter for fear of being discovered. She knew the change would come, as it always did, and it would be painful. She hadn't expected it to be so excruciating.

Hot. Her skin was so hot. She could feel her bones stretching, getting longer and wider. Digging her fingers into the bed, she arched her back and bit her bottom lip to keep from crying out. An unfamiliar wetness formed in her eyes, blurring her vision and rolling down her temples. Another strange type of moisture covered her entire body. The pain rolled over her in waves.

Stop! Oh, please stop! I can't take any more!

A burning sensation filled her head, then…nothing.

* * * * *

"Come in," Linc called out when he heard the sharp rap on the front door.

Nyle pushed open the door. Frowning, he stomped his boots on the porch before stepping inside. "Thanks for telling me about the snow, Carter."

"What's the problem? Your SUV has four-wheel drive."

"That's beside the point. I *hate* driving in snow."

"And this from a man who loves to ski."

"Skiing is different than driving. The roads are *clear* on the way to the slopes." Nyle closed the door and crossed the floor to where Linc stood in the kitchen. "I'm here. What do you need?"

"I need you to help me decide what to do about that." He pointed to the box on the table.

The confused look on Nyle's face didn't surprise Linc. "What is it?"

"You'd better sit down before I tell you. Want some coffee?"

"Yeah." Nyle sat at the table and peered inside the box. "Is this some kid's toy you're using as a model for a new software game? The inside looks like a spaceship."

"Funny you should say spaceship." Linc placed a mug of coffee on the table in front of Nyle, then sat in the chair to his friend's left. "That's exactly what it is."

"A toy?"

"No, a spaceship."

Nyle's eyebrows shot up. "A spaceship?"

Linc nodded.

"As in from outer space? I still have a hangover, so I might not be hearing things right."

"Your hearing is fine."

Nyle leaned toward Linc and looked in his coffee mug. "How much whiskey did you add to your coffee?"

"I am stone-cold sober."

Snorting with laughter, Nyle leaned back in his chair. "You want me to believe that thing came from space?"

"It flew right in front of my truck about thirty miles from here and crashed in the trees. There's an alien in my bedroom to prove it."

"An alien." Nyle's tone of voice said he clearly didn't believe a word Linc said. "You have an alien in your bedroom."

"She's purple and about fifteen inches tall." Linc set his mug on the table. "Don't you think I *know* how crazy this sounds? But before you call the guys in the white coats with the padded wagon, come with me."

Linc led the way to the bedroom. He stood still and watched his friend stop in his tracks, then creep toward the bed. With each step, his eyes widened more.

"Holy shit," Nyle whispered.

"My exact words when I saw the spaceship."

Nyle picked up a corner of the covers as if to lift them. Linc hurried forward and pulled his hand away. "Hey, man, don't."

"You can't show me something like this and not expect me to want to *see* it."

"Yeah, I know, but she deserves some privacy."

Nyle looked back at the alien. "How do you know this is a she?"

"She doesn't have a cock. She doesn't have breasts or any body hair either, but I just *feel* that she's female."

Nyle scratched his chin. "I expect to hear *The Twilight Zone* theme any second." Bending closer to the bed, he openly studied the lump under the covers. "You said she's about fifteen inches tall. She looks bigger than that to me, more like a couple of feet tall."

At Nyle's comment, Linc looked at her again. She did appear to be bigger. Maybe he had simply misjudged her height last night.

"Shouldn't we be afraid of this, Linc? I mean, we're looking at an *alien* who came here on a *spaceship*. We should be scared out of our gourds."

"I think shock is greater than fear right now."

"I guess." Nyle ran a hand over his face. "You got some whiskey to go in that coffee?"

"I thought you have a hangover."

"I do, but this is more than I can handle without some help."

Linc chuckled. "Yeah, I have a bottle of Jim Beam. Adding some to my coffee sounds like a good idea."

$$* \quad * \quad * \quad * \quad *$$

"I think I found it, Cap."

Cap stepped up behind Garry and gazed at the computer screen. "Where?"

"I reconfigured some of the data, picking up the stats from—"

"I don't need to know how to build the goddamn clock, Fisher, just give me the time."

Pissing off Cap was the last thing Garry wanted to do. He glanced at the forty-five automatic on Cap's hip and swallowed hard. "Northern California."

"*Where* in Northern California?"

"I'm still working on that."

Cap placed his hand on the butt of his pistol. "Then I suggest you keep working."

Chapter 4

Chandra opened her eyes and looked around the unfamiliar room. The excruciating pain had finally faded to a dull ache. She shifted on the bed, and groaned when everything in her body protested the movement. This transformation had been more difficult than usual.

Where was she?

She frowned as she tried to figure out her location. She'd left the Fourth Quadrant three tentons ago, heading for To'Ar to rendezvous with the other Travelers from her planet. They were to complete their reports, turn them over to the Commander, then prepare for their next journey.

Something had gone terribly wrong.

Suddenly warm, Chandra pushed the covers off and slowly sat up. Her head spun. She remained still, her chin almost touching her chest, while things came back into focus. The first thing she noticed was her skin. She lifted her hands, turning them palms up, then backs up, as she studied the color...or lack of color. No longer a deep lavender, her skin was now pale ivory.

Chandra tried to stand so she could examine her body further. Her first attempt ended with her back on her bed. A wooden object sat on the floor next to the bed. Using it for leverage, she pushed herself to her feet.

She saw a strange being across the room.

Chandra gasped silently. She immediately dropped into a fighting stance, and noticed the being made the same movement. Chandra straightened, and the being did too.

It was her own reflection in a mirror.

Moving closer, Chandra studied her new form. A cap of auburn covered her head. That same color was duplicated in a triangle between her thighs, and a slash above each eye. Large, round bumps sat on her chest. A ring of pink in the center of each large bump held smaller nubs. Chandra touched one, and gasped again when a pleasurable sensation shot down her body to between her thighs. She touched both nubs, plucking at them with her thumbs and forefingers to make the sensation return. It grew, intensified, until she fought to draw her next breath.

She'd never felt anything like it.

A strange throbbing at the apex of her thighs made her press her legs tightly together. When that didn't cease the throbbing, she slid one hand between her legs to try and stop it. A creamy wetness covered her fingers. She brushed against a small, hard protrusion. Touching it gave her a greater thrill than tweaking the nubs on her chest. She spread the cream over it, again and again, pressing it a bit harder with each pass of her fingers.

Chandra threw back her head and moaned when the breath-stealing pleasure rushed through her body.

*   *   *   *   *

"You have to hide it," Nyle said, motioning toward the spaceship still on the table. "Bury it in the backyard."

"I don't want to bury it, Nyle. What if she needs it?"

"For what? It's a wreck. There's no way she can fly it again."

"There might be…stuff in it she needs."

"Okay, don't bury it, but you have to hide it. You don't know who may be looking for it."

"You mean, like NASA?"

"NASA, FBI, CIA, Homeland Security, *somebody*. It must have shown up on some government agency's radar."

Linc rose to get the coffeepot. "Sounds like I'm not the only one who's been watching too many sci-fi movies. I doubt if the FBI runs out to check every little bleep on radar."

Nyle raised his mug so Linc could fill it. "Okay, maybe I'm overreacting, but maybe I'm not. You're out here in the boonies. Anybody could show up, knock you out – or worse – and steal the ship and her."

The thought of someone hurting her brought forth all his protective instincts. He would *not* let anyone near her.

"Maybe some of the computer nerds you have working for you could fix it."

Linc shook his head. "I don't want to tell anyone else about this. Then there *would* be people trying to get to her." He replaced the coffeepot on the burner and returned to his chair. "She'd be poked and prodded, maybe even killed. I can't let that happen."

"You can't hide her here forever, Linc."

"Yeah, I know." Blowing out a heavy breath, he looked inside the ship. "I gave myself a week's vacation. Maybe I can fix it. I'm the biggest computer nerd I know, and I'm a pretty good mechanic."

"What can I do to help?"

"I'll need some tools. I have my notebook here, but I'd like to have my PC from the office."

"Make a list of what you need and I'll go get it."

"It'll take you hours to go to Sacramento and back here."

"Make a list. I want to help too."

"I'll give you some money for gas—"

"And I'll give you a black eye if you reach for your wallet. Go make your list."

"How about if I cook you a T-bone when you get back?"

"Deal."

* * * * *

Chandra's breath finally evened out and her heart stopped pounding. She didn't know what planet she'd landed on, but the inhabitants here had some wonderful inventions.

As she became less aware of her body and more aware of her surroundings, she could hear strange sounds coming from the next room. She couldn't understand it, but recognized the tone. Two beings from this planet were communicating with each other.

The ability to transform into someone who blended in with the other beings on the planet was crucial to To'Ar's mission. Learning to communicate in their language took much longer. Chandra rarely had time to learn the planet's language before she had to leave for her next mission.

Speaking with these inhabitants, making them understand her, wouldn't be easy.

She heard a sound like a door closing. Perhaps they had left. Now would be a good time to explore.

Chandra stepped through the doorway and stopped. A being knelt before a large rock framework that held fire. He stood and turned toward her.

"Whoa!"

Chandra frowned, unable to understand what the being said. Her frown deepened when she realized she'd thought of this being as "he." She had no way to know if he actually was male, but instinctively knew it.

She watched his gaze travel over her body. His body was covered while hers was not. Travelers had never worn covering. They would transform once they reached their destination and then the covering might not fit or be inappropriate for that planet. As time passed, more and more of To'Ar's inhabitants had picked up the Travelers' way, until few of them bothered with any type of covering. The year-round mild climate of To'Ar made it unnecessary.

The being moved toward her. The closer he got, the more aware she became of her body. The nubs on her chest hardened. The protrusion between her legs began to throb. The creamy wetness formed inside her and trickled out to dampen her thighs. She didn't understand what was happening to her, but somehow knew this male could help her end the raging torment in her body.

Instinct guided her. When he was close enough to touch, she laid her hands on his chest. The soft covering pleased her, as did the faded blue and gray colors. The warmth underneath the covering pleased her also. She ran her hands over his chest and shoulders, down his arms, and back again to his chest.

The throbbing between her thighs grew stronger.

"Who are you? Can you tell me your name?"

Chandra shook her head, trying to tell him without words that she couldn't understand him. Speaking would be useless for he wouldn't be able to understand her either. She didn't want to talk anyway; she wanted to continue touching him.

She wanted him to touch her.

She let her hands drift farther down his body. A bulge between his legs drew her attention. She laid one hand over it. Bliss engulfed her in a rush.

He took her wrist and pulled her hand away from him. "Hold it, lady. Let's not get carried away here."

Everything he said sounded like gibberish to her. Frustrated, Chandra jerked her wrist away from him. Slipping her arms around his neck, she pulled down his head and covered his lips with hers.

Chandra had never touched a male's lips with her own. She had no idea why she felt such a strong urge to do so, nor why it gave her so much pleasure.

She loved it, but she needed more.

* * * * *

Her kiss shocked him. Linc froze, unsure what to do. Despite his surprise, his body responded. Blood rushed to his cock, making it hard in seconds.

While her kiss aroused him, it wasn't the most skillful one he'd ever received. A bit off-center, the kiss was hesitant and uncertain. It almost seemed as if it were the first time she'd kissed a man. He gripped her elbows, determined to pull her away from him.

The brush of her tongue stopped him.

Her kiss no longer felt untutored. Linc hesitated a moment before desire took over. Wrapping his arms around her, he returned the ravenous kiss. His tongue slipped between her lips to duel with hers. A soft moan came from her throat. The sound fueled his lust, raising it to a pitch he'd never reached.

Her skin was so soft, softer than velvet. Linc's hands wandered over her back, her sides, her buttocks. The firm mounds drew his attention again. *Perfect*, he thought. He massaged her ass, then dipped his fingers between the cleft.

She broke off the kiss and threw her head back. Linc took advantage of her position to kiss her neck, her shoulder, her collarbone. She clutched his hair with both hands and pulled his head lower. Obeying her silent request, he covered one nipple with his mouth and suckled.

He'd had his share of lovers, but never one so hot. She rubbed her mound against his cock while he continued to love her luscious breasts. Full, round, big nipples...beautiful.

He wanted her flat on her back so he could devour them.

She dragged one of his hands between her legs. Linc swallowed hard when he felt the wet, swollen folds. He pushed a finger inside her, then two. She pumped her hips, drawing his fingers farther inside her.

"My God, you're hot."

Her pussy milked his fingers when she came. He watched the rapture cross her face as she continued to pump against his hand. Her hips slowed, then stopped. She opened her eyes and looked at him.

Green. Her eyes were a pure emerald green, surrounded by long, thick, auburn lashes. Linc gazed at her creamy complexion, straight nose, full rosy lips, short auburn hair.

She was absolutely stunning.

Lifting her lips, she kissed him again. Desire quickly flared higher.

Apparently, it struck her too. She grabbed the lapels of his flannel shirt and jerked the snaps open. She attacked the button and zipper on his jeans next. Linc barely had the chance to catch his breath before she pulled down his jeans and shorts enough to free his cock. Her soft hands wrapped around it, surrounding it in warmth.

Linc sucked in a hard breath between his teeth. Her hands certainly didn't feel unskilled. She stroked, caressed, fondled his cock with those wonderful slim fingers. He could easily stand here and let her bring him to orgasm.

Simply having a climax wouldn't be enough. He had to get inside her.

Pulling her hands away from him, Linc held them while he walked backward to the couch. She followed him down, straddling his legs when he sat. Holding his cock straight up, he watched her impale herself.

She gasped. He groaned. Linc cupped her breasts in his hands, kneading them while she rode him. Her movements were slow and awkward at first. They quickly gained speed. In moments, the only sounds he heard were her moans and her flesh smacking against his.

Leaning forward, she pressed her breasts against his chest and emitted a sharp, keening sound. The contractions deep inside her squeezed his cock. Holding tightly to her ass, Linc thrust upward and followed her over the edge.

Chapter 5

Cap paced back and forth while Garry fiddled with the computer. This waiting had to stop. He had to do *something* to find that spaceship.

"Haven't you found anything yet?"

"I'm trying, Cap. The signal is so weak, I can't pinpoint the exact location."

Cap stopped by Garry's chair. "So you could find it if we were closer?"

"I…think so."

"Just *thinking so* doesn't cut it, Fisher. Could you find it if we were in California?"

"Yes, Cap, I could."

"Then you and Dwight start packing up your equipment. We leave at dawn."

* * * * *

Chandra slowly raised her head from his shoulder. Her chest hurt from breathing so hard. Her legs were cramped from the unfamiliar position. She had no idea what had made her do the things she'd done. This male had his…something inside her. She could feel it, although not as easily as a few moments ago.

She didn't know it was possible to have *anything* inside her.

His head lay back on the couch, his eyes closed. It gave her the chance to study him. His looks pleased her. Whereas she had a short auburn cap on her head, his was blond and longer, almost touching his shoulders. His chest had a scattering of the same substance, only in a darker shade. The small nubs she possessed were even smaller on his chest, and brown. She touched them with her fingertips. They hardened like hers.

She returned her gaze to his face. His eyes were now open. As blue as To'Ar's three moons, they studied her face as she studied his.

"What did you do to me?" he said softly.

Frustration made her bite her bottom lip. She still couldn't understand him. The Commander had told her she would be able to communicate with the beings on other worlds if she spent enough time with them. She had no idea how much time she needed.

He placed his hands beneath her arms and lifted. Chandra straightened her legs and stood. He stood next to her. She watched him place the thing that had been inside her back in his covering. It looked different than when she'd touched it, when she'd lowered herself over it. Now smaller and softer, she could hold it in one hand. She didn't understand the change.

There were so many things she didn't understand.

He wiggled one forefinger, then started toward the room where she'd slept. Halfway there, he stopped, looked at her over his shoulder, and wiggled that finger again. Chandra assumed that meant he wanted her to follow him.

She stepped inside the doorway and watched him open drawers in a tall wooden object. He removed what looked like some of his covering. He tossed the items on the bed, then walked over and stood in front of her. His gaze passed over her face before he left the room, pulling the door shut behind him.

It appeared the inhabitants of this planet wore covering as a rule. She'd have to get used to that for as long as she remained here.

Chandra sat on the bed and moved the covering to her lap. A lump formed in her throat. Moisture formed in her eyes. She didn't know where she was, or what had happened to her ship. She didn't know how to communicate with the male. She didn't know why her chest felt so heavy.

All she knew is that she hurt deep inside, and she wanted to go home.

* * * * *

Linc eyed the bottle of Jim Beam on the counter. It was tempting to drain the rest of it now, and without diluting it with coffee. Knowing he couldn't do that when he needed a clear head, he recapped the bottle and stuck it in the cabinet.

His mind spun enough without adding any alcohol.

He couldn't believe he'd had sex with her, and unprotected sex at that. But when he's first seen her, desire had hit him with the force of an earthquake. She'd gone from a little purple alien to a full-grown, gorgeous woman in a matter of hours...a woman who called out to everything male inside him. Touching her, kissing her, fucking her, had been the only things on his mind.

Linc loved sex. He loved a woman's body...the curves, the softness, the scent, the way it fit next to him. He'd never made it a habit to sleep around indiscriminately, yet hadn't lacked for lovers. He was always careful. The fact that wearing a condom with her hadn't even entered his mind confused him. She was from *another world*. He knew absolutely nothing about her, other than she fascinated him and he hadn't been able to keep his hands off her.

Maybe she'd cast a spell on him. Maybe she had some kind of supernatural powers that made men fall at her feet and obey her every command.

Linc ran a hand through his hair and chuckled at the ridiculous thought. *This has to be a dream. Something this crazy can't possibly be real.*

Being inside her had felt real...and perfect, as if she were made especially for him.

She walked into the kitchen. Even wearing a set of his green sweats and gray socks, she was beautiful.

"I wish you could understand me. Can you at least tell me your name?"

Her puzzled look made him sigh. Linc pointed to his chest. "Linc. My name is Linc." He pointed to her chest. "Who are you?"

She shook her head. "Uguop forry nom."

"Oookay, I understand you about like you understand me. We have a problem, don't we? I don't know anyone who can translate alien."

She chafed her arms. He'd given her his heaviest sweats, but maybe they weren't enough.

"Are you cold?" He stepped closer and rubbed her arms from shoulder to elbow and back. "I like it cooler than a lot of people do, but I can add more wood to the fire if you're cold."

Her eyes widened, then narrowed and turned sultry. She laid her hands on his chest and licked her lips.

Desire punched him in the gut again. "Yeah, we communicated just fine a short time ago, didn't we?" Ignoring the tightening in his groin,

Linc released her arms and stepped back. "Unfortunately, having sex won't help us figure out a way to help you."

She bit her bottom lip. He understood her frustration for he was experiencing the same thing. He'd love to sit her on top of the cabinet and slide his cock inside that sweet, wet pussy.

She stuck out her tongue and pointed inside her mouth.

"Are you thirsty? Here." Grateful for something to do to get his mind off sex, Linc drew her a glass of water and handed it to her. She drank half the glass in one gulp. She lowered it and gazed around the room, stopping at her ship. Her eyebrows drew together. Setting her glass on the cabinet, she moved closer to the table. Slowly, she sank into a chair.

Linc could practically feel her frustration at this huge setback. She couldn't possibly pilot the ship in its current condition, or her current size. He sat in the chair to her left. "I'll do my best to repair it. A friend of mine is coming back soon with tools and a computer."

She looked at him. "Tools?"

Linc smiled. "Yes, tools. Do you know what those are?"

"Nom aabe jaq forry tools."

His smile faded. "So you're back to alien, huh? Damn it."

"Damn it?"

He couldn't help chuckling. "If you're only going to pick up a few of the words I say, I'd better watch my mouth."

"Mouth?"

Linc touched his lips. "Made for talking, eating, drinking..." He looked at her mouth. "...kissing."

"Kissing," she whispered.

Dragging his attention away from her, Linc gestured at her ship. "Even if I can repair it, you won't be able to fit in it. Unless you can shrink yourself back to your original size."

She raised her feet to the chair, wrapped her arms around her legs, and rested her chin on her knees. At that moment, she looked like someone who had lost her best friend. That must be how she felt. She was on a strange planet, unable to speak the language. She had no idea if she'd ever be able to go back to her own world.

Her forlorn appearance touched his heart. He wished he could help her.

A loud growling sound came from her stomach. Eyes wide, she quickly dropped her feet to the floor and covered her stomach with her hands.

Linc laughed. "Hungry, huh? Me too. I promised Nyle a steak when he got back, and he should be here in about an hour. I'll fix one for all of us."

He stood and turned toward the refrigerator. The phone rang as he reached for the handle.

Few people knew he was here, and even fewer knew this phone number. Linc guess the caller was either his brother or Nyle. He picked up the receiver. "Hello?"

"My water pump went out," Nyle said. His voice sounded tinny, as if he were calling from his cellular phone. "I broke down outside of Auburn. I've called a tow truck, but I have no idea how long I'll be stuck. I have all your stuff. Can I bring it in the morning?"

"Sure."

"How's she doing?"

Linc glanced at her. "She's fine."

"I'll get up there as soon as I can tomorrow morning. I'm sorry, man."

"Hey, no problem. I appreciate everything you're doing."

"Like I said, I want to help. See ya tomorrow."

Linc slowly replaced the receiver. He'd planned to use Nyle as a buffer to help him stay away from her. Now that Nyle wouldn't be back until morning, his plan fizzled and died.

He glanced out the window. The snow had started falling again. That might be his solution. Walking in deep snow would help him cool off when his testosterone flared up, as he had no doubt it would. Right now, standing twenty feet from her, he wanted to kiss her more than he wanted his next breath.

"Guess I'll only be cooking for two. Nyle won't be back 'til tomorrow morning."

She looked up at him, her eyes once more puzzled.

"I know you can't understand me, but I feel like I should talk to you anyway. And if I talk to you, I won't be tempted to touch you."

"Juq nemhos aaba norf reesee."

Linc chuckled. "You keep on saying stuff like that. It helps me remember you're an alien and I should keep my hands off you."

Chapter 6

Chandra watched him move about the room, preparing...something. The scent was strange, but not unpleasant. It caused her stomach to make that unfamiliar, gurgling noise again.

Although she wanted to learn more about this planet's inhabitants, she paid more attention to *him* than to his actions. She admired his height, wide shoulders, long legs, and the way his covering fit him. Thinking of the way he'd touched her earlier made her chest feel heavy and the area between her legs throb.

She'd traveled to many worlds. Her journeys were fact-finding missions, rarely requiring her to interact with the inhabitants. When she did, her ability to transform made it easy for her to blend in with other beings and not be noticed. This mission was different. She'd never spent so much time with one of the world's inhabitants. She'd certainly never done with anyone what she'd done a short time ago with him. The feelings she'd experienced...she'd never felt anything like them. If she could communicate with him, she could find out if her feelings were normal for the beings of this world.

She wished she could communicate not only with him, but her Commander. Chandra looked at her smashed ship. That wouldn't be possible. Any chance she had of getting in touch with her leader had been destroyed.

Stranded. The word brought that strange moisture back to her eyes.

He set a glass half-filled with a deep ruby liquid in front of her. She looked at it, then back at him.

"Wine. I thought you might like it."

He took a sip of the liquid from his own glass. Hesitating a moment, Chandra picked up the glass and took a tiny sip. Fruity and bold, the flavor exploded on her tongue. She smiled and took another sip.

"Wine," she said.

"My little parrot. I only wish you really knew what I'm saying."

Chandra stopped in the process of taking another sip. She understood part of what he'd said. She didn't know what it meant, but the words were clear. Setting down her glass, she stood next to him. "Wine. Parrot. What I'm saying."

His eyes widened. "Do you understand me?"

Chandra shook her head. She didn't know how to make him realize that she could pick out only bits and pieces of what he said.

"Can you tell me your name?"

Name. Chandra frowned, trying to figure out what he wanted. He pointed to his chest.

"My name is Linc. Can you tell me your name?"

He wants to know my name! Chandra beamed. She understood him! "Chandra. My name Chandra."

Linc smiled. "Hi, Chandra."

"Hi, Linc."

"What happened? How can you understand me now?"

"I know…little bit. I no can know all."

He chuckled. "Then we'll take it nice and slow. Drink your wine and I'll finish dinner."

She returned to her chair, happier than she'd been since she awoke. Now she could talk to him, maybe explain how to repair her ship.

Her happiness faded as she looked at her body. Even if they managed to repair her ship, she couldn't fit in it.

One thing at a time. I have to be patient and take one thing at a time.

It wasn't in Chandra's nature to wait at the back of the line. She wanted to be first…first to experience things she'd never experienced, first to explore new worlds. She'd trained to be a Traveler the day she'd turned twenty lathas, the earliest she could begin her training. That had been six lathas ago, and she'd never regretted her decision.

Linc came to the table. "I'm going to move your ship while we eat."

Chandra didn't quite get everything he said. When he picked up her ship, she panicked and surged to her feet. "No!"

"Here, look, I'm just gonna set it on the floor." He moved it next to the large white box in the corner. Facing her, he held his hands up, palms toward her. "See? No harm done."

Her outburst shamed her. He had been nothing but kind to her. She should've known he wouldn't hurt her ship. "I am sorry I...overact."

"No problem. And it's over-*re*act."

"My words not so right yet."

"I think you're doing great, a whole lot better than me if I had to learn *your* language."

Sitting down again, Chandra watched him set items on the table. She leaned forward and peered into a deep, round, glass object of green and red things. She picked up a container of thick, white liquid. Curious, she removed the top and sniffed. She wrinkled her nose at the unfamiliar scent.

"Ranch dressing," Linc said as he set another round object holding something brown in front of her. "For the salad. Here's your steak."

Chandra stared at the brown item he had called steak. She had no idea what to do with it. Not wanting to appear stupid, she peered at Linc. He held the brown item with a pronged object, cut off a small piece with a knife, and popped the piece in his mouth. He watched her while he chewed and swallowed.

"Don't you like steak?"

"I no know."

"You've never eaten steak?"

"Eaten. Is consume?"

Linc nodded.

"I have no eaten. Liquid diet."

Linc took another bite of his steak and swallowed. "I don't think I'd be able to exist on a liquid diet. I like food too much." He gestured at her brown object. "Want to try it? If you don't like it, I can open a can of soup."

"I will try."

One bite of the tender steak had Chandra rolling her eyes in pleasure. Linc seemed pleased at her reaction.

"Want to try the salad now?"

"Yes, please."

✳ ✳ ✳ ✳ ✳

It didn't take Chandra long to decide she enjoyed food very much. She ate every bite of the small steak, salad, and roll on her plate. All through their meal, Linc pointed out various items and told her their name. Sometimes she got lost when he would lapse into a lengthy explanation about something. In those cases, she would shake her head and he'd start over again using different words.

Chandra appreciated all his efforts to help her, but she'd be happy to simply hear him talk. She liked his deep, rich voice. She liked the way he smiled, and how he'd push his cap of blond back from his forehead.

She especially liked the way his shoulders and chest filled out his covering.

He hadn't mentioned what had happened between them. He'd explained many things, but not the feeling she'd experienced when she'd touched him, when she'd touched herself.

She wanted to know more about those feelings.

"What is name when you inside me?"

Linc's gaze shot to her face. He'd had his wineglass at his lips as if he were about to take a sip. Slowly, he lowered the glass to the table without drinking. "It has more than one name. Some people call it sex, some say making love, some use other words that a man shouldn't use in front of a lady."

Chandra tilted her head. "What *you* call it?"

"Sometimes sex, sometimes making love." He grinned. "Sometimes one of those other words."

"They different? That why you use other words?"

Linc's grin faded. "Chandra, was that the first time you'd ever had sex?"

She nodded.

"So you weren't…protected?"

"What 'protected'?"

"Birth control."

"I no know birth control."

He pushed his blond cap back from his face again. "Well, I didn't expect to have this kind of talk until my son was about twelve."

"Tell me. I want know."

Linc gulped down the rest of his wine. He didn't know how to explain sex to her. He didn't understand *why* he'd have to explain it anyway. Chandra appeared to be in her mid-to-late twenties. Even if she were a virgin, she'd still know about sex.

Apparently, they did things differently on her planet.

"Where are you from, Chandra?"

"To'Ar."

He'd never heard of it, so it wasn't in Earth's solar system. She must've traveled... He couldn't even imagine how far she'd traveled to get to Earth. "Don't the..." He stopped, not sure if "people" was the right term. "Don't they have sex on To'Ar?"

She shook her head.

"Then how do you reproduce?"

"What 'reproduce'?"

"Make more To'Arians, or To'Arites, or whatever you call yourself."

Her eyebrows drew together. "I no know what you say. I want... What we did felt good. We do again?"

His cock said yes while his brain said no. This was one time when he definitely had to listen to his brain. "No, we don't do it again."

She frowned. "Why?"

"Because it isn't a good idea."

"You no like?"

"It doesn't matter whether I like it or not. It isn't a good idea for us to have sex again."

Chandra lowered her gaze and rubbed her forehead. "I no understand."

"I know you don't," Linc said softly. "I don't know how to explain it to you so you *will* understand. We're from two different worlds, Chandra. Literally. Making love again would feel good for a few minutes, but there's nowhere for us to go after that."

She remained silent. Linc didn't know what else to say since he had no idea how much she comprehended. Deciding it was best to change the subject, he stood. "I'd better get these dishes cleaned up."

"I help clean," Chandra said without looking at him.

The mundane chore of washing dishes would definitely push the sexual thoughts to the back of his mind. Linc picked up the salad bowl as Chandra stood. He quickly dropped it back to the table when he saw her sway. Reaching out, he grabbed her upper arms before she fell.

Chapter 7

Linc held her arms tightly and peered into her face. "Are you all right?"

"My head feel odd."

"Sounds like the wine made you woozy. I didn't think you'd drunk enough to bother you."

"What woozy?" She touched her forehead with one hand. "Room spinning."

"That's woozy, when it feels like the room is spinning. You'd better sit back down."

Chandra dropped her head forward until it rested on his chest. The top of her head almost touched his chin. Linc inclined his head and sniffed her hair. One whiff and he wanted her.

Taking advantage of Chandra when the wine had obviously gone to her head would not be very gentlemanly. His hands tightened on her arms. Linc didn't feel much like a gentleman right now.

She looked up at him. Lust flared in her eyes. She tilted her head slightly and licked her lips, as if begging for his kiss.

It would be even less gentlemanly of him to make her beg. Linc leaned closer and covered her mouth with his own.

Warm, liquid silk, Linc thought, angling his head to deepen the kiss. Her lips were velvety smooth and opened when he touched them with his tongue. He circled her lips, dove inside her mouth, then circled her lips again. He could taste wine on her breath, and desire. A soft moan came from her throat. She rose up on her toes and wrapped her arms around his neck.

Linc had never held a woman who felt so right in his arms...or responded so quickly to his kiss. Heat arced between them. It threatened to consume them if Linc didn't do something about it.

Unwise or not, he wanted her with a fierceness he'd never experienced.

Linc kissed his way down her chin to her throat. Cupping his hands under her buttocks, he lifted her. "Wrap your legs around me."

Chandra immediately encircled his hips with her legs. The juncture of her thighs cushioned his groin. Linc pulled her tighter to him and brushed his cock against her, using a side-to-side motion. Each brush made her eyes dilate a bit more, made her breathing more choppy.

Linc walked straight to the bedroom. Without releasing her, he lowered Chandra to the bed and lay on top of her. She grabbed the hair on both sides of his head and brought his lips to hers. The first time she'd kissed him had been uncertain, untutored. She'd learned quickly. Her kiss now was hot, wet.

Hungry.

She released his hair. Linc pulled back so he could see her face. Her skin was damp and flushed from arousal. Raising his torso a few inches, he looked at her breasts. Her hard nipples clearly showed through the sweatshirt. Linc cradled one breast in his hand and thumbed the nipple. She gasped.

"Linc, I feel..." She stopped.

"What do you feel? Is your head still spinning from the wine?"

"Not from wine." She pressed his hand more firmly to her breast. "Touch me."

Rising to his knees between her thighs, Linc pushed her shirt above her breasts and cupped both of them. Full and firm, they almost overflowed his hands. Linc had always been a breast man. He loved to fondle them, suck the nipples, lick the areolas. Large or small didn't matter to him. They were all beautiful.

Chandra's were flawless.

"Feels good," she whispered. "More."

Linc swiped his tongue across one nipple. He liked it so much, he repeated the action on the other one. First one nipple, then the other, received the attention of his teeth, lips, tongue. He could feel Chandra's heart pounding, could hear her uneven breathing. She appeared to be on the verge of a climax, but that couldn't be possible. Surely just sucking her nipples wouldn't be enough to —

A strangled sound, the arching of her back, the jerking of her body, proved him wrong.

"Incredible," Linc whispered.

Slowly, Chandra opened her eyes. A small smile touched her lips. "Nice."

"*Very* nice. I can't get over how responsive you are."

"Responsive. This good?"

"Oh, yeah." He shifted his hips against her, pressing his hard cock into the vee of her thighs. Chandra drew in a sharp breath. "Do you like that?"

"Yes."

If she'd come so quickly from having her nipples sucked, Linc wondered how fast she'd come if he licked her clit.

He planned to find out.

Rising to his knees, Linc unsnapped his flannel shirt and shrugged out of it. He tugged Chandra's shirt over her head, then scooted back a few inches so he had room to remove her pants and socks. She lay nude before him, arms by her head, legs spread wide. She had no modesty, no shame of her body.

Linc liked that.

"Put your feet on the bed and let your legs fall open."

Chandra did as he requested. Linc stared at the feminine delta. The curls between her legs were damp with her juices. Her lips were deep pink and swollen. Despite her having an orgasm a few moments ago, her clit peeked out from its hood, as if asking to be petted.

Linc stroked it with his thumb. Around and around, he drew circles over it, gathering moisture from her vagina to make his thumb slide easier. Her clit grew harder with his touch. He wanted to watch her face as she came again, but he wanted to taste her more.

Stretching out on his stomach, Linc covered her clit with his mouth.

Her musky scent surrounded him. Linc inhaled deeply as he wiggled his tongue over her clit and lips. Holding her lips open with one hand, he dipped his tongue inside her. She tasted…different. Not unpleasant, but different. A combination of woman and…

Grapes. Her pussy tasted like grapes.

"Mmmm," Linc mumbled as he drove his tongue farther inside her. God, she was delicious…not just her taste, but her freedom. He began fucking her with his tongue, wanting to send her over the edge again.

Chandra bucked her hips and grabbed his head in the middle of her second orgasm.

Linc couldn't wait any longer. Unfastening his jeans, he pushed his briefs down to free his cock. With one thrust, he plunged inside her.

She was so tight, so wet. Her pussy walls gripped his cock, milking him with the contractions of another orgasm. Linc had been with women who'd experienced more than one climax during sex, but never so close together.

He wondered how many she could have.

He remained still, his cock buried inside her, while the contractions slowed. Chandra looked into his eyes as the last one faded.

"What you say? Incredible?"

"Yeah," Linc said, his voice husky. "Incredible." He withdrew, thrust, then remained still again. "*You're* incredible."

"This feeling normal for female here?"

"How about if we talk later? Right now, I need to…" He withdrew and thrust again, this time harder.

Chandra wrapped her legs around his waist. "Yes."

✱ ✱ ✱ ✱ ✱

The sensation of fullness. The slide of skin against skin. The sound of heavy breathing. Chandra absorbed it all as Linc moved in and out of her body. She'd never imagined something could feel so good between a male and female.

He slipped his hands beneath her buttocks. Each time he thrust inside her felt better than the last. Each time he kissed her cheek or neck or shoulder felt better than the last.

She never wanted to leave his arms.

The feeling began to build inside her again. Chandra clasped Linc tighter as the wave washed over her.

"I can't believe how easy you come," he whispered into her ear. His warm breath sent a pleasant thrill through her. "I want you to come again. And again, and again, and…" He covered her lips with his and plunged his tongue into her mouth.

Chandra couldn't breathe. It had nothing to do with Linc's mouth covering hers, but the way he pounded into her. That glorious feeling built again, even stronger than all the previous times. It crested and flowed over her as Linc groaned and shuddered.

He didn't move, and Chandra couldn't since he lay on top of her. Not that she minded. His weight on top of her felt so good.

Linc propped up on his elbows. Chandra took a much-needed breath.

"I'm sorry," he said softly. "I didn't mean to cut off your air."

She smiled. "Worth it."

He kissed her tenderly. Chandra slid her hands over his back, enjoying his moist skin. She'd never felt moisture on anyone's skin.

All the differences in their bodies fascinated her.

"Yeah, I need a shower, and a shave." He touched a spot on her neck. "You have a whisker burn here."

"Whisker burn?"

"Your skin is red from where my beard scratched you. I haven't shaved since yesterday morning."

"What shave?"

"I guess since you didn't have any hair, you wouldn't know about shaving. I'll just have to show you. But first, we shower."

He pulled his now-soft piece of flesh from her body. Chandra groaned softly at the discomfort.

"Sore?" Linc asked as he removed the rest of his covering and dropped it to the floor.

"Some."

"You'll feel better after the shower." He held out his hand to her. "C'mon."

Chapter 8

Linc adjusted the water to a comfortable temperature and reached for Chandra's hand. She took a step back.

"What's wrong?"

She stared at the falling water as if she'd never seen anything like it. "What that?"

She didn't recognize a *shower*? "Water. We stand under it and use soap to clean our bodies."

Her puzzled look clearly said she didn't understand. Linc left his hand extended toward her. "Trust me."

Hesitating another moment, Chandra placed her hand in his. Linc stepped in the bathtub and tugged her behind him. He pulled the curtain, closing them inside a steamy cocoon.

Linc tilted his head back to wet his hair. Ah, heaven. He shook his head like a dog and wiped water from his eyes. Chandra stood at the end of the tub, watching him with trepidation in her eyes.

"C'mere. You'll like it, I promise." He pushed his hair back from his forehead. "You don't think I'd do anything to hurt you, do you?"

She shook her head. "No."

Chandra moved closer. Linc drew her into his arms and stepped under the spray with her. Her body tensed at first, but quickly relaxed as the water cascaded over her. She smiled.

"Feels good."

Linc returned her smile. "Told you so." He picked up a bottle of shampoo from the edge of the tub. "Hair first. Turn around."

Wanting to give Chandra as much pleasure as possible, he took his time with the shampoo. He massaged her head with his fingertips, then ran his fingers through her short hair. She leaned her head back until it almost touched his shoulder. Pure bliss covered her face.

"Like this?"

"Yes."

"Bend your head back so I can rinse it."

Linc took almost as much time rinsing her hair as he had washing it. Once every bit of shampoo had disappeared, he quickly washed and rinsed his own hair while Chandra watched. Picking up the bottle of liquid soap, he glanced around the tub for a washcloth, but didn't see one.

"Hmm, looks like I forgot the washcloth. Guess I'll have to use my hands."

A large puddle of liquid soap soon turned into lather in Linc's hands. Starting at Chandra's shoulders, he let his soapy hands slide over them and down her arms. When he reached her hands, he made the return trip up her arms to her shoulders.

By this time, her breathing had become deeper, slower.

Continuing his journey, Linc slid his hands over her breasts. Her nipples began to harden at the first brush of his thumbs.

So did his cock.

"Turn around," he said softly.

Linc added more soap to his hands and worked up a thick lather. He slipped his arms around Chandra's waist and cradled her breasts. Stepping closer to her, he positioned his rapidly-hardening cock in the cleft of her ass. She groaned and arched her back.

Those luscious breasts turned slippery with lather. Linc spread more soap over them so his hands would slide easier. Her nipples felt like hard little jewels in his palms. He loved the way her breath would hitch when he pinched them with his thumbs and forefingers. He plucked at them again and again while moving his cock up and down her cleft.

Linc tongued her ear and bit her earlobe. One hand coasted down her stomach until he reached her pubic hair. "Are you too sore for me to touch you?"

"No."

His hand skimmed between her thighs. She was incredibly creamy, her lips and clit swollen. She jerked when he pressed two fingers inside her.

"Am I hurting you?"

"No." Chandra tilted her head back to rest on his shoulder. She wrapped her arms around his neck, leaving her body open to him. "Please, more."

Reaching around her hip, Linc parted her lips with his other hand. He finger-fucked her while his thumb stroked her clit, increasing the speed and depth of his thrusts in time to the pumping of her hips. No more than a minute passed when the walls of her pussy pulsed around his fingers.

He couldn't believe her passionate response. "You really are incredible."

"I like your touch."

"I like touching you." He nudged her with his pelvis until she took a couple of steps forward. "Prop your hands on the wall and spread your legs."

She immediately did what he requested. Worried she might be sore, Linc held her hips and slowly slid his cock into her. When she didn't flinch or try to pull away from him, he quickened his thrusts until he was jamming into her as hard and fast as he could. Her cries of pleasure signaled her climax before he felt her walls pulse around him again. With a fierce growl, Linc pumped his seed inside her.

Not sure if his legs would support him yet, Linc wrapped his arms around Chandra's waist and held her tightly to him, his cock still nestled inside her. He wanted to stay there as long as possible.

The water turning cooler prompted Linc to pull out of her. He tugged her under the shower to rinse off the last of the soap and their sweat. Turning off the water, he slid back the curtain and helped her from the tub.

Linc handed her a thick towel and took one for himself. She watched him begin to dry his body before attending to herself. Once again, it reminded Linc that she came from another world and knew nothing about Earth's customs.

She draped her towel over the bar next to his. Linc gazed at her in the mirror above the sink as she stepped up next to him. "What now?"

"I'm going to shave." He grinned. "I don't want to give you any more whisker burns."

Chandra fingered her neck on the spot Linc had touched earlier. "Does not hurt."

"I don't want to hurt you *anywhere*. Besides, you'll like me better when I don't look so scruffy."

"Like you now," she said softly.

The tenderness in her eyes caused a tightening in his throat. She affected him as no other woman ever had. He'd never felt so drawn to another woman, so protective. He'd never been so turned on to where he wanted to be inside her constantly. Despite just having earth-shattering sex with her in the shower, he would be ready to fuck her again with nothing more than a touch from her.

To get his mind off that idea, he spread shaving cream over his face and picked up his razor.

* * * * *

Chandra studied Linc as he dragged the piece of metal over his face. First he'd put the white puffy stuff on his face, now he was removing it in strips. What a strange thing to do.

Enjoying the sight of him wasn't strange. The way she felt when he entered her wasn't strange. She experienced such pleasure when he touched her, kissed her.

The people of To'Ar were scientists, explorers. Physical pleasure had been eliminated many lathas ago in favor of advancing science.

Chandra wondered if that had been a mistake. The feelings a male and female shared were glorious.

She glanced around the small room while Linc rinsed the rest of the fluffy stuff from his face. She understood the use for the large white item where she and Linc had showered. Water also came out of a curved metal object atop the stand in front of him. The other white object in the room puzzled her. She lifted a lid and saw water inside. Perhaps it was another place to wash.

"What this?"

Linc paused while wiping the water from his face with the soft object he had called a towel. "It's a toilet bowl."

"What purpose is it?"

He dropped his towel on top of the stand. "You've never used a toilet bowl?"

She shook her head.

"You use it for… When you…" He waved a hand toward the object. "You know."

Chandra tilted her head and examined his face. His cheeks seemed to be a deeper pink than a moment ago. "No, I do not."

"I never expected to have to give an anatomy lesson," he muttered.

"What anatomy?"

He looked up at the ceiling, blew out a large gust of air, then looked back at her. "How about if we get dressed and talk while we clean up the kitchen? I think it'll be easier for me to explain...things if I'm busy."

Chapter 9

"Let's go, let's go," Cap said as he slipped on his jacket. "We have at least a ten-hour drive ahead of us and it's almost dawn."

His two morons traipsed out to the truck with the last load of equipment. If he didn't need their computer expertise so badly, he would've ditched them a long time ago.

Getting rid of them once they reached their destination would be his first priority.

Finally, everything was falling into place. As soon as he found that spaceship, he'd be set. Cap fingered the butt of his pistol. Only a few more hours to go…

* * * * *

Linc slowly edged out of bed so as not to awaken Chandra. After a trip to the bathroom, he added two more logs to the fire and started a pot of coffee. It would be a few minutes before the coffee was done, and even longer before the fire had a chance to warm the cabin. He'd neglected to bank the fire before going to bed last night and the cabin was cool this morning, even by his standards.

Going back to bed sounded like a really good idea.

He crawled under the covers as easily as he could, trying not to jostle the bed. Turning on his left side, he watched Chandra sleeping and thought about the previous evening. Neither of them had slept much last night. Between her insatiable curiosity about anything to do with Earth and her healthy sex drive, it had been well after midnight before they'd fallen asleep.

They'd gone to bed after cleaning up the kitchen. The touch of skin against skin set off their desire once again. After making love, Chandra had sat on her knees and explored his body. Starting at his head, she'd slowly traveled downward, asking questions along the way. Her questions were few until she reached his groin.

"*And these are where the fluid is stored. What is its name?*" she asked while cupping his balls.

"*Semen.*"

"*You eject it when you are inside me.*"

He swallowed hard, trying to ignore the softness of her touch. This was not sexual to her, but serious. "*Yes.*"

"*It gives you pleasure to eject the fluid?*"

"*Very much.*"

Her hands moved up to stroke his soft cock. "*And this is your...penis? Is that right?*"

"*Yes.*"

"*I like it when it is firm, but it is nice this way too. You put this inside a female to make more Earthlings?*"

"*At certain times of the month, yes.*"

"*So a female cannot reproduce at any time?*"

No matter how much he wanted to help her understand things, he drew the line at explaining a woman's cycle. "*Chandra, I'm not a woman. I don't know how to answer all your questions.*"

"*Oh.*" She continued to fondle his cock. He tried to fight it, but couldn't help responding to her touch. "*Things are very scientific on To'Ar. There is no pleasure in reproducing. A needle is inserted here.*" She pointed to a spot on her right side near her navel. "*A tiny bit of fluid is removed and mixed with the fluid from a male in a special dish. It is kept warm for five tentons while the To'Arian forms.*"

"*Do you choose whom to mate with?*"

She shook her head. "*It is all determined by our Council.*"

"*It sounds very...sterile.*"

"*It is efficient, but your way gives more pleasure.*" By now his cock was completely hard from her constant stroking. Linc had to bite his tongue to keep from groaning. "*I like having this inside me.*"

"*Me too,*" he rasped.

She bent forward and kissed the head. Linc jerked in surprise. "*Chandra.*"

"*You did not like that? I enjoy it when you put your mouth on me.*"

"*I would enjoy it, but I don't want you to do anything you aren't ready to do.*"

"*I am ready. Teach me.*"

He'd instructed her in oral sex, until he'd been out of his mind with lust. He'd pulled her on top of him and given her more instructions on how to ride a man.

She was an amazing student.

The memories ended when Chandra moved closer to him. She snuggled her leg between his and laid one hand on his chest. Linc lifted her hand, kissed the palm, and returned it to his chest.

She looked at him with sleepy eyes. "Good morning," she said, her voice raspy.

"Good morning. I'm sorry I woke you."

"It is fine. I like waking next to you."

That comment deserved a kiss. Linc rolled to his back and tugged her on top of him. Cradling her face in his hands, he gave her a tender kiss.

Chandra smiled at him. "Is nice to hold you and kiss you."

"I like it too."

She crossed her arms on his chest and propped her chin on them. "You do sex with many females?"

"I've…had sex with other females, yes."

"Many?"

"Chandra, that isn't the type of question you should ask."

"Did you not say last night to be honest is good?"

"Honesty is very good, up to a point. You have to learn when to be honest and when to…fudge a little."

She frowned. "What is fudge?"

"Sometimes being totally honest can hurt someone's feelings."

"I do not wish to do that."

"Neither do I."

"I can be honest with you?"

He linked his fingers at her waist. "Absolutely."

"And you will be honest with me?"

"I have so far."

She lowered her eyes a moment before gazing at him again. "There are many things I still do not understand."

"You've only been here for a day. You have to give yourself time to learn."

"I am not patient enough."

"Patience isn't my strongest trait either. Like right now…" He slid his hands down to her buttocks. "…I can't wait to kiss you."

Chandra smiled. "I do not want you to wait."

She covered his lips with hers. One kiss led to two, then three, until the kisses turned hungry and frantic. Linc pulled her legs up next to his hips so she straddled him. Her pussy, already hot and creamy, cushioned his cock.

Linc shifted, preparing to slip inside her, when he heard a noise. He lay still, listening.

"Why you stop?" Chandra asked.

"I thought I heard something."

He heard it again…a sound like a door closing. Someone was outside.

Nyle.

"Damn!" Linc scooted out from under Chandra and jumped out of bed. Grabbing the sweatpants he'd discarded last night, he managed to pull them on as the front door opened.

"Hey, man, how about some help with this stuff?" Nyle called.

"Stay here," Linc whispered to Chandra. He left the bedroom, closing the door behind him.

"There you are," Nyle said, leaning a folding card table against the bookcase. "You sleep in?"

Linc adjusted the pants over his deflating cock while Nyle faced the other way. "Uh, yeah."

"Coffee smells good. I could use some." He stepped closer and looked at Linc from head to toe, his expression puzzled. "You came out of the bedroom?"

He nodded.

"Isn't she in there?"

Linc heard a door open behind him. He whirled around to see Chandra come out of the room.

She was naked.

"Holy shit," Nyle muttered. His gaze snapped to Linc's face. "How...?"

"I'll explain later. Chandra, don't you want to get dressed?"

She didn't speak. Instead, she walked up to Nyle and kissed him.

Linc swore all the blood in his body dropped to his feet, then rushed back to his head. A red haze clouded his vision as he watched Chandra cradle Nyle's face in her hands and kiss him again. Nyle stood perfectly still, his eyes wide open. He didn't return the kiss, but he didn't pull away either.

Chandra ended the kiss. Still looking at Nyle's face, she laid her hand over his crotch.

Nyle inhaled sharply.

Linc really didn't want to kill his friend, but he'd have no choice if Nyle didn't stop letting Chandra touch him. He clenched his fists at his sides when she slid her hand under Nyle's balls and squeezed.

"Jesus," Nyle said with a catch in his voice.

Chandra released Nyle and faced Linc. "I do not feel for him what I feel for you."

Nyle's pale face and sweaty upper lip made him look as if he'd slump to the floor any moment.

Linc took Chandra's arm and led her back to the bedroom. "Slip on some clothes while I help Nyle unload his truck, okay? Then we'll talk."

"I do something wrong?"

You groped my best friend! "No, you did nothing wrong. We'll talk in a bit."

Linc shut the door, took a deep breath, and faced his friend. Nyle stood with his hands on his hips. "You want to explain what just happened?"

"She's...exploring."

"Obviously." Nyle tugged on the crotch of his jeans. "No offense, Carter, but I didn't expect to get a hard-on around you."

Linc ran his hand through his hair. It was either that or punch his friend for reacting to Chandra.

"Help yourself to coffee while I get dressed."

"I want an explanation more than coffee."

"I'll give you one, I promise. Just let me check on her."

Linc found Chandra sitting on the side of the bed, still naked, with tears rolling down her cheeks. His heart turned over in sympathy. He dropped to his knees before her. "Hey, there's no reason for you to cry."

"You are angry with me."

"No, I'm not angry. I'm...surprised at what you did to Nyle."

"He is a male. I wanted to see if I feel for him what I feel for you." She touched her chest, over her heart. "I feel something here when I kiss you and touch you. I did not feel that when I kissed him."

"I'm glad," he said softly.

Chandra swiped at the tears on her cheeks. "I do not understand all this moisture leaking from my eyes."

"They're called tears." Linc caught one on his thumb and gently wiped it away. "Don't ever be ashamed of them. They're a sign you're feeling something very deeply." He wiped away another tear. "I need to get dressed and help Nyle unload his SUV. You get dressed too, okay?"

Chandra nodded. She still looked so sad. Linc wanted nothing more than to take her in his arms and hold her. Instead, he dropped a soft kiss on her lips and rose to dress.

Chapter 10

Gentle flakes of snow were falling when Linc and Nyle stepped outside. There was already almost a foot on the ground. Linc grinned to himself. Maybe he'd show Chandra how to build a snowman later.

"Chandra, huh?" Nyle asked.

"Yeah."

"Interesting name." Nyle opened the back of his SUV. "You gonna tell me what's going on?"

"She grew and changed color."

"How?"

"I don't know, exactly. She's still learning how to speak English, so I haven't asked her a lot of questions yet."

"I guess you don't have to talk to her to fuck her."

Linc frowned. "Back off, Nyle."

"Well, hell, man, how stupid can you get?" Nyle picked up a box and tossed it to Linc. "You were in bed with her when I got here. Don't you think that's a bad idea?"

Unwilling to answer Nyle's question, Linc said nothing. Nyle picked up the tower of Linc's computer and led the way back into the cabin. Linc glanced around for Chandra, but didn't see her. The door to the bathroom was shut, so he assumed she was in there.

He hoped she took his advice and put on some clothes.

Linc set his box on the floor and followed Nyle back out to the SUV. Before he picked up anything else, he faced his friend. "It doesn't feel like just fucking, Nyle. The sex is great, *she's* great, but it's more than that. I feel... Hell, I'm not sure how I feel, but it's different than I've ever felt for a woman."

"But she's not a *woman*, Linc, she's an *alien*. She isn't going to stay here. As soon as you fix her ship, she's outta here."

"Maybe I won't be able to fix her ship."

Nyle froze in the act of picking up the computer monitor. "You wouldn't purposely keep from repairing her ship to keep her here."

"Of course not. I'll do everything I can to help her."

"Good."

Nyle's attitude made Linc see red again. "Why are you so against me being with her?"

"Because she isn't *real*! *None* of this is real, Linc. You seem to have forgotten that."

Nyle grabbed the monitor and stormed back to the cabin. Linc picked up the last box and slowly followed him. He knew Nyle was right, but he didn't want to accept that. He'd known Chandra for a day, yet it seemed longer. They couldn't have clicked so well in only a day.

Chandra was standing next to the kitchen table when Linc entered the cabin. He breathed a bit easier when he saw she wore a pair of his navy sweats. She looked his way. As soon as he gazed into her eyes, he knew. Despite their short time together, despite all the odds against them, he knew.

He was falling in love with her.

"Where do you want your PC?" Nyle asked.

Nyle's question jerked Linc's attention away from Chandra. "On the folding table."

"How about if I set that table next to the kitchen table? That'll give you more room to work."

"Good idea."

Nyle reached for the folding table, but stopped before touching it. "I have a better idea. I don't know about you two, but I'm starving. You set up your stuff and I'll whip up some breakfast."

"Sounds like a plan."

While Nyle checked out the refrigerator's contents, Linc set up the table for his computers. He sensed Chandra next to him before he saw her.

"I help you?" she asked.

"Sure. You can bring me my notebook from the bedroom."

"Note-book?

"It's a square black thing on top of the dresser, about this big." He indicated the approximate size with his hands. "I need the cord laying on top of it too."

Chandra nodded and headed for the bedroom.

Nyle set a mug of coffee on the kitchen table within Linc's reach. "Do you think you can fix the ship?"

"I'm gonna try." Linc dug through one of the boxes until he found the cable that connected the monitor to the tower. "Everything is small, but I'm used to working on small things."

"Rather you than me. I hate computers."

"You work on one to write your column."

"I don't work on the *inside* of one." He looked at Chandra as she came back in the room carrying Linc's notebook. "Would you like some coffee?"

"What is coffee?"

"Here, try mine." Linc took the notebook and handed her his mug. Chandra took a sip and grimaced. He chuckled. "You might like it better with milk."

Nyle turned toward the cabinet for another mug. "One coffee with milk coming up."

Linc connected his last cable and turned on the computer. While it was booting up, he plugged the power cord into the notebook and wall.

Chandra stepped closer and watched the images flash across the monitor. "You can correct my ship with this?"

"I'll try my best. I have to get it working first, then repair the outside so it'll travel."

"You are very intelligent."

"You'd better hold the compliments until I actually fix it."

"I have confidence in you."

Her words, and the adoring look in her eyes, warmed him. Linc ran one finger down her cheek. "Thanks."

"Here you go," Nyle said, handing Chandra a mug of coffee heavily laced with milk. "See if you like this one."

She took a tentative sip, and smiled. "Is good."

Nyle smiled. "Glad you like it."

He returned to the stove. Chandra pulled a chair close to Linc and sat down. "What I do now?"

"For now, just keep me company while I do some research."

* * * * *

Nyle stood and stretched his arms over his head. "I'm going blind looking at all these diagrams. How long have we been at this?"

"About four hours," Linc said.

"No wonder I can't think." He reached for his jacket draped over the end of the couch. "I'm gonna take a walk and clear my head."

"*You're* going to walk in the *snow*?" Linc asked, fighting a grin.

"Yeah, well, it's not my first choice, but I need some air. Be back in a few minutes."

Linc watched Nyle go out the front door, then returned his attention to Chandra's ship. Between peering at the tiny elements of the ship and the CAD diagrams on the computer, he figured he'd need bifocals before he got the ship repaired. Luckily, he'd remembered to tell Nyle to bring magnifying glasses.

A break sounded like a good idea. Linc also stood and walked to the refrigerator for a drink. Realizing he still held a pair of pliers in his hand, he laid them on top of the refrigerator before opening the door. He took out a can of Coke and popped the top. "Would you like a drink, Chandra?"

She shook her head. "I am fine."

Linc noticed the dejected note in her voice. She'd been right beside him the entire time he'd worked, although she couldn't understand what he was doing. Her limited English kept her from reading yet, and she had no knowledge of repairing her ship in its current size.

He wished he could do something to make her feel better.

"Hey, don't feel bad. We'll figure out how to fix your ship."

"I am no help."

Linc returned to his chair. He wrapped his hand around Chandra's nape and squeezed gently. "You're helping just by sitting next to me."

"I can repair most problems. There is back-up system. Travelers are trained to know every part of ship."

"That's when it isn't crushed. I doubt if anyone from To'Ar could repair it in this condition."

"You think you can?"

"I think I can get the computer working. After that, you'll have to tell me how to program it."

"I can do that."

Linc smiled. "Then let's get back to work." Releasing her neck, Linc reached for the pliers. He frowned when he didn't see them. "What did I do with those pliers?" he muttered.

"On the refrigerator. Is that what you want?"

"Yeah." He started to stand, but Chandra touched his arm.

"I will get them."

She held out her hand, palm up. Linc watched as the pliers floated from the top of the refrigerator and landed in Chandra's palm. Eyes wide, he swallowed hard.

"Holy shit."

Chapter 11

Chandra moved her hand closer to Linc, happy to be able to finally help him do something. "Here."

He hesitated before taking the pliers. "How did you do that?"

"Do what?"

"Move the pliers like that."

She shrugged. "Is easy. Can you not do it?"

Linc made a chuckling sound, but it didn't sound humorous to Chandra. "No, I can't do it. And I suggest you don't do it in front of anyone else."

"It is bad?"

"No, it isn't bad, it's just...different. People on Earth can't do anything like that."

"Can they do this?" Chandra tilted her head. Her ship rose six inches off the table. She glanced at Linc. His mouth hung open.

"Linc?"

Linc's mouth snapped shut. "No. No, we can't do that either." He cleared his throat. "What other...powers do you have?"

"I have no powers. I am no different from anyone on To'Ar."

"You're definitely different from anyone on Earth."

"So I should not move an object around anyone?"

"No."

"If that is what you wish."

* * * * *

Garry took a deep drag off his cigarette and blew the smoke toward the sky. Cap didn't allow anyone to smoke around him, so Garry had to sneak one in whenever he could. The last thing he wanted to do was piss off Cap. One look from those icy green eyes could freeze a man in his tracks.

After twenty years in the Marines, there wasn't much that scared Garry. Cap scared him.

Dwight rounded the side of the building and walked toward Garry. "That nasty habit will kill you."

"Better one of these than Cap."

Dwight stuffed his hands in the pockets of his heavy jacket. "Hey, he's okay. A little weird, but okay."

"You only think he's okay because of the money he's promised us. I've yet to see any evidence of that money."

"He's paying for stuff as we go along."

"Dwight, he promised us a hundred grand each. Whatever he's paid for hasn't amounted to anything *near* a hundred grand." Garry took a last drag, then dropped his cigarette and ground it out with his boot. "I *will* get my money at the end of this trip. I promise you that."

"What're you gonna do?"

"Whatever I have to. Cap carries that fancy pistol that he strokes like a woman, but that isn't the only way to kill a man."

Garry reached in his jacket pocket and took out his pack of cigarettes. Dwight frowned. "You don't have time for that. Cap sent me to find you. He's ready to go."

Releasing a heavy breath, Garry replaced the pack in his pocket. He followed Dwight back to where their vehicles were parked. The sight of Cap standing at the back of the large panel truck that he was driving made a chill skate down Garry's spine.

He and Dwight weren't allowed inside the truck, but Garry had caught a glimpse once when Cap had the door open and he wasn't aware of Garry's presence. The truck housed a large computer. It had more bells and whistles than any computer Garry had ever seen or worked on, and he'd worked on the best the government had.

Garry doubted there was anything he couldn't do with a computer, and knew Dwight wasn't far behind in that knowledge. Cap had given specific instructions on what they were supposed to build. Although confused by the strange components they were constructing, Garry did what he was told. The promise of a large payoff at the end of Cap's "mission" would make this worth it.

He'd started to wonder a few days ago if that payoff would ever materialize. Cap became more antsy and angry each day. Something was about to happen. Garry didn't know what, but this whole operation was about to come to a head.

He *would* get his money…one way or another.

* * * * *

Linc felt like throwing his arms up in the "touchdown" gesture when the lights flickered in Chandra's ship. "Yes!"

Nyle looked up from washing their dinner dishes. Despite Linc's protests, Nyle had done all the cooking and cleaning today so Linc could work on Chandra's ship. "What happened?"

"I have power."

Chandra leaned over and peered inside her ship. Her eyes brightened more than the colorful lights on the dash. "You repaired it!"

"Not yet, but I'm getting closer."

She threw her arms around Linc's neck. "I knew you were very intelligent."

The feel of her arms around him made Linc happy and sad at the same time. He wanted to help Chandra get back to her own world if that's what she desired, but he didn't want her to leave him.

His life would go back to building computers and designing games once she left. Doing something he'd once bounced out of bed every morning to get to no longer seemed so important. She'd brought love into his life. He didn't know how he'd be able to give that up.

He couldn't resist hugging her tightly before he released her. "None of that mushy stuff now, woman. I have work to do."

"What can I do?"

"I need to tinker a bit more, then I should be able to start programming it. See this wire?" He held up a thin black wire. "I've rigged it so my PC is hooked right into the main computer on your ship. I can program everything from my keyboard."

She clasped her hands together and beamed.

"Chandra, there's still the problem of your size."

"Size does not matter. I can contact my Commander for help."

A hollow feeling formed in his stomach. He wanted her to stay, and she couldn't wait to leave.

Linc understood why she wanted to leave. He loved to get in his truck and simply drive. When he visited his brother, he always took a side trip that was completely out of his way, just to see something different. Chandra saw more than a mountain range or a different view of the ocean in her travels; she saw new *worlds*, new *galaxies*. He couldn't imagine anyone turning down something like that.

Nyle turned a chair backward, straddled it, and rested his arms on the back. "Any idea how much more time you'll need?"

Linc shook his head. "Might be minutes, might be hours. I know you have to work on your column, so if you need to go—"

"I have this week's columns already written. I'm staying. Get busy on that keyboard."

* * * * *

The bright bleep on the notebook screen made Garry blink, certain he couldn't possibly have seen what he thought he saw. The bleep didn't disappear.

"I got it back."

Dwight swung his gaze toward Garry a moment before looking back at the road. "Are you sure?"

"I'm positive." Garry punched some keys to confirm his findings. "The signal is strong and steady."

"Do you have any idea what it is?"

"Not a clue. I'm following the coordinates Cap gave me. It could be anything."

Dwight rubbed his chin. "Are you scared?"

"Shitless. I want this whole thing to be over."

"Yeah, me too." He nodded toward the walkie-talkie on the dash. "Better tell Cap."

Garry picked up the walkie-talkie. "Cap, I've got the signal again."

"Where is it?"

"Close." He punched another series of keystrokes. "No more than fifty miles."

"Excellent. How are you on gas?"

Garry peered at the gas gauge. "We're good."

"Then there's no reason for us to stop until I find what I want."

226

Chapter 12

Chandra watched Linc rub his eyes. He'd worked all day on her ship, taking breaks only to eat and stretch his legs. He was trying so hard to repair her ship so she could return to To'Ar.

She wasn't sure she even *wanted* to return to To'Ar.

She'd been excited at first when she'd seen the lights flickering on the ship's console. The more progress Linc made, the sadder she had become. Each step forward for him meant getting closer to her time to leave.

Emotions, feelings, did not exist on her planet. Neither did physical love. What she shared with Linc was unlike anything she'd ever experienced. She enjoyed being in his arms, having him thrust into her body. She enjoyed the way she felt deep inside her body more.

The way he looked at her, the warmth in his eyes, had to mean he had feelings for her too. She wanted the chance to find out. She'd never get that chance if she went back to To'Ar.

Nyle rose from his chair. Chandra studied him as he started preparing coffee. His appearance pleased her, and so did his considerate actions. Looking at him, being close to him, didn't make her stomach flutter the way it did when she was close to Linc. Kissing him hadn't made the area between her thighs throb and moisten.

So much to learn. Chandra wanted the chance to learn it all.

"Okay," Linc said, "I think we're ready to try some tests."

Chandra didn't want to try any tests. She had no desire to establish communication with her Commander for help to leave here. A lump tightened her throat and tears flooded her eyes. She didn't wish to leave Linc.

Not wanting him to see her cry, she rose and headed for the bathroom to be alone.

* * * * *

Linc watched Chandra go into the bathroom and close the door. He almost followed her. He thought he'd seen the sheen of tears in her eyes before she walked away from him. That couldn't be possible. She had no reason to be sad. She was excited about having her ship repaired so she could leave Earth. All afternoon, she'd been beside him, offering her help, giving him suggestions about different formulas to try on the computer.

Her English skills had steadily improved all day, until she could read as well as he. Those improved skills showed Linc the high level of her intelligence. Once she'd learned the keyboard, her fingers had flown over it while she checked the damage of her ship's system.

She was amazing.

Nyle set a mug of coffee in front of Linc. "Chandra okay?"

"I think so. Why? Did she say something to you?"

"No, she didn't say anything specific. She seems... I don't know, she just doesn't seem as happy as she did earlier. The closer you get to fixing her ship, the sadder she becomes." Nyle sat in the chair opposite Linc. "I don't think she wants to leave any more than you want her to go."

"Am I that transparent?"

Nyle nodded.

"And you don't approve."

"Hey, it isn't up to me to approve or disapprove. It's your life."

"That's not what you said earlier."

"Yeah, I know. I was pretty harsh out there when we were unloading my SUV. I was only thinking of you, man. I didn't want you to fall for her when she was gonna take off. But I don't think she *wants* to take off." He grinned. "She looks at you with the same goo-goo eyes that you look at her."

Linc chuckled. "I never thought I'd hear you say 'goo-goo eyes'."

"Me either. But it fits. It's obvious you care a great deal for her. I think that's great, as long as—" Nyle stopped when Linc held up one hand. "What's wrong?"

"Shh. Listen." Linc heard it again—the unmistakable sound of a car door shutting. "Someone's here."

"Aw, shit!" Nyle jumped up from his chair. "Cover up the ship!"

A loud knock on the door made Linc scramble for the dishcloth hanging on the oven's handle and toss it to Nyle. "Grab some more out of that second drawer."

"Those little towels won't cover it up. Let me take it outside."

"I'll have to disconnect everything for you to do that and there isn't time." The knock sounded again, louder and longer. "Do the best you can."

Linc sauntered toward the front door, taking as long as he could to give Nyle the chance to cover the ship. Nyle leaned on the table, using his body as a barrier between the table and door.

Three men stood on the small porch when Linc opened the door. He didn't recognize any of them. A quick assessment of them showed one tall and slim, one tall and muscular, and one on the short side and husky, all in their late thirties to early forties. They all wore heavy jackets, jeans, and boots. Wanting to get rid of them as soon as possible, Linc smiled. "Hi. Can I help you?"

The tall, muscular one took a step forward. "I hope so. We're looking for a friend of ours and we must have taken a wrong turn. Do you know Tim Burton? He has a cabin somewhere up here."

"No, sorry, I don't know him."

He hunched his shoulders. "It's pretty cold out here. Could we come in and call him? I'd be happy to pay you for the use of the phone."

Linc's fear of them seeing Chandra's ship warred with his desire to help someone in trouble. Trying not to raise the three men's suspicions, he glanced over his shoulder at Nyle for help.

"Our phone's been out for the last couple of hours," Nyle said, "and a cell doesn't work up here."

"Yeah, I know. I tried to use mine to call Tim, but couldn't get a signal." He smiled. "Maybe we could — "

"Oh, for Christ's sake!" the short, husky man exclaimed before pushing Linc aside and entering the cabin.

"Fisher!" No longer pleasant, the muscular man's expression turned ferocious as he and his other cohort entered the cabin and shut the door. "Back off. I said I'd handle this."

The man called Fisher drew a small .22 from his jacket pocket and pointed it at Linc's chest. "Well, now *I'm* handling it. The signal led straight to this cabin. Find whatever the hell you're looking for."

The signal, Linc thought. *They know about the ship.*

"What are you doing with that gun, Fisher?"

"You aren't the only one who can carry a gun, Cap." He gestured with the pistol for Linc to move. "Over there with your buddy."

They might know about the ship, but he doubted they were from any legitimate government agency. He glanced from the pistol in Fisher's hand to the bathroom door, praying Chandra wouldn't hear the voices and come out to investigate. He moved to stand beside Nyle, using his body to help shield the ship. "What's going on, guys?"

"I believe you know *exactly* what's going on," Cap said. "I want the ship."

Linc saw Fisher and the other guy exchange a puzzled look. That look proved to Linc that they didn't know about the spaceship; they were simply musclemen following orders. He looked at the pistol in Fisher's hand again. Linc didn't doubt he could get the gun away from the guy, if he could get close enough. Right now, Fisher stood over ten feet away. Even if Linc lunged, Fisher could easily get off a shot before Linc reached him. He couldn't take the chance of Nyle being hurt, or Chandra.

"We're nowhere near the water," Nyle said with a chuckle. "No ships around here."

"I do not find that amusing," Cap said.

Nyle frowned fiercely. "Yeah, well, I don't find it amusing to have your thug pointing a gun at my friend."

Fisher raised his gun an inch. "Watch who you're calling a thug."

"If the name fits…"

"*Enough!*" Cap roared. He unzipped his jacket and pushed it back to expose a large .45 in a holster. "I don't want to hurt anyone, but I won't hesitate to do so if I don't get the ship. Hand it over *now*."

The bathroom door opened. Chandra took two steps into the room and stopped. Linc cringed. He didn't want her in the middle of this. "Chandra, go back in the bathroom."

Her eyes grew wide as she gazed at the three strangers. "Who are these males?"

"Chandra, go back!"

"Wait!" Cap said.

He moved closer to Chandra. He didn't care that he had a gun pointed at him. There was no way Linc would let Cap near her. He quickly stepped forward and jerked her behind him. "Back off, asshole."

Chandra gripped his shirt and pressed up against his back. "Linc?"

"It's all right, sweetheart. I won't let anyone hurt you."

"Aw, how sweet," Fisher snarled. "You won't be able to protect her from a bullet."

Cap whirled around to face Fisher. "I have had enough of your threats."

The pistol flew out of Fisher's hand and landed at Nyle's feet.

Fisher stared at his empty hand. "What the... How did that happen?"

"I told you I will take care of this." Cap faced Linc again. He took a step to the left and looked at Chandra. "Nom umbe mact pre jarv stak Darvell. Langly umqay eesh parday."

Linc's mouth dropped open. He sounded just like Chandra had before she learned to speak English. Surely this guy wasn't...

He heard Chandra gasp. Before Linc could stop her, she moved around him, dropped to one knee before Cap, and bowed her head.

Chapter 13

Cap reached down, took one of Chandra's hands, and gently pulled her to her feet. "Do not bow before me, child."

Still feeling the need to protect her, Linc moved to Chandra's side. "Do you know this guy?"

"Yes. He is Darvell. He was my Commander when I first became a Traveler."

Linc's gaze swung to Darvell. "He's from To'Ar?"

"Yes. Why are you here, sir?"

"Just a goddamn minute," Fisher said, stepping closer to Darvell. "This family reunion stuff is fine and dandy, but I want to know what's going on. What the hell kind of ship are you looking for, Cap?"

"It's none of your concern, Fisher."

"*I'll* decide whether it's my concern or not. I've spent months helping you build some kind of monster computer and track whatever you've been looking for while waiting for my payoff."

The tall, slim thug laid a hand on Fisher's shoulder. "Hey, cool it, Garry."

Garry shrugged off his hand. "Lay off, Dwight."

"Better listen to your friend, Garry," Nyle said, juggling the .22 in his palm. Garry glared at him and Nyle grinned. "You don't have your backup anymore."

"Oh, no?"

Linc suspected what would happen, but wasn't quick enough to stop Garry from jerking Darvell's gun from the holster. Garry backed up several steps, swinging the gun from one person to another.

"Now, who's in charge?"

"I've had enough of you, Fisher," Darvell growled. He clapped his hands once. Garry's eyes rolled back and he slumped to the floor.

"Jesus!" Dwight exclaimed. Eyes wide, he stumbled backward until he sat down hard on the arm of the couch. "You killed him!"

"I did not. I merely rendered him unconscious. He'll be fine when he wakes up. And I suggest you stay where you are until I've finished my business."

Dwight nodded, his eyes still wide and his face pale.

"So," Nyle said, laying the pistol on the table behind him, "the moral to this story is don't piss off the Commander."

Darvell glared at Nyle. "Chandra, is this man harmful to you?"

"No, sir. Nyle and Linc are good men."

"Very well." He faced Chandra again, and his face relaxed into a tender smile. "It is good to see you, child, even if you look different from the last time I saw you."

"You too, sir."

"May I speak to you in private?"

"Yes, of course."

She looked at Linc. He wasn't crazy about the idea of her being alone with this guy, even if she didn't seem to be afraid of him. Linc peered at Darvell through narrowed eyes. "Whatever you have to say to Chandra, you can say in front of me."

Chandra touched Linc's arm. "I will be fine. Please do not worry. The Commander would never harm me."

Despite his misgivings, Linc nodded. "Use the bedroom."

Chandra smiled and kissed his cheek. "Thank you."

After Chandra and Darvell entered the bedroom and closed the door, Linc gazed at the fallen man on the floor. His crumpled position would make him very uncomfortable when he awoke. Linc glanced at the shaken man sitting on the arm of the couch. "Hey... Dwight, is it?"

Dwight nodded.

"Help me get your friend to the couch, okay?"

"Yeah, sure." Dwight removed his jacket and tossed it to the armchair. He lifted Garry's feet while Linc lifted his shoulders. Together, they placed Garry on the couch.

Dwight stuffed his hands in the pockets of his jeans and stared down at Garry. Linc couldn't help the pang of sympathy. Dwight seemed more like a follower than a leader. "You okay, man?"

"No," Dwight said with a shaky laugh. "I don't understand what's going on."

"I think all of us are confused right now. You want a cup of coffee, or maybe something a little stronger?"

"A gallon of scotch would be good, but I'll settle for coffee. Thanks."

✷ ✷ ✷ ✷ ✷

Chandra waited until Darvell sat on the edge of the bed, then sat beside him. She had so many questions to ask him, but remained silent out of respect until he was ready to speak.

"You can speak first, Chandra. I'm no longer your Commander."

"I have many questions, sir."

"I'm sure you do, your first one being how I ended up on Earth. A meteor shower damaged my ship and I lost control."

"You left To'Ar almost four lathas ago. Have you been here all this time?"

"Most of it. I've learned to adapt to Earth's ways. I've made a bit of money, so I've lived comfortably. But the people here... They're easy to anger. They have a long way to go to find true peace." He shifted on the bed, placing one knee on it. "Anger and rudeness have more of an impact on Earthlings than happiness and kindness. They are also very greedy. To get the help I needed, I had to resort to bribery and viciousness, act and speak differently than I normally do. I don't want to live like that anymore. I long for the peaceful existence on To'Ar."

Chandra didn't know what to say. She'd been here such a short time and had met no one but Linc and Nyle. She didn't know about any angry people, other than the man lying on the floor in the living room.

"You kissed the tall blond man. Do you care for him?"

"I have...feelings for him. He's been very kind to me."

"Have you had sex with him, Chandra?"

Warmth flooded her cheeks and she lowered her head.

"Don't be embarrassed, child. Sex is a very natural thing here on Earth. I've experienced it many times since I've been here, and it's quite enjoyable." He touched her chin, and she raised her head. "But don't let a few moments of pleasure cloud your thinking. You're a Traveler. Your work is important, not only for To'Ar, but for many planets in our system. Do you really want to give that up?"

Put that way, Chandra wasn't sure what to do. She had an obligation to her people, an obligation that couldn't be ignored.

"What is the status of your ship?" Darvell asked.

"Linc has repaired the computer system. It still needs to be programmed. But having the system repaired will not help. My ship was ruined in the crash." She glanced down at herself. "And I no longer fit in it."

"That isn't a problem. I've built another one, much bigger than your old ship. It's in the panel truck outside."

Shocked, Chandra stared at him for a moment. "You built another ship?"

"With the help of those two goons out there. I've been working on it for a long time, just waiting for one of To'Ar's ships to come close enough to contact. I tracked you for three days before you crashed." He laid his hand on top of hers. "All I need is the main processor from your ship to complete it, then we can leave and go home."

✳ ✳ ✳ ✳ ✳

Linc looked at the bedroom door again, willing Chandra and Darvell to come out. The longer they stayed in there, the more nervous he became. The Commander was going to convince her to leave. Linc didn't know how they could leave in Chandra's tiny ship, but he had no doubt that's what they were discussing.

"Staring at that door won't make it open any faster," Nyle said.

Linc faced his friend again. "They've been in there a long time."

"They've been in there about ten minutes. Relax, Linc. Chandra is a strong lady. He won't talk her into doing something she doesn't want to do."

"Who is this guy, anyway?" Dwight asked.

Not sure how much to say, Linc looked to Nyle for assistance. Nyle gave a slight shrug. Since his friend was no help, Linc hesitated before speaking again. "We don't exactly know, Dwight. Chandra knows him, but we don't."

"Is she your girlfriend?"

"She's…a very special friend."

Nyle stood and retrieved the coffeepot. "How'd you get hooked up with him, Dwight?"

"Through Garry. Cap hired Garry first, and Garry recommended me. I couldn't pass up the money. An ex-wife and support for three kids means money's pretty tight." He held up his mug for Nyle to fill it.

"Thanks. Anyway, Cap had been tracking something and we helped him find it." He gestured at the ship, still covered by dishtowels. "I guess that's it, huh? Whatever he's been tracking?"

Linc didn't have to answer for the bedroom door opened. He quickly stood and faced Chandra. She gave him a small smile, but Linc didn't think she looked very happy.

Darvell was beaming.

"Gentlemen, in less than half an hour, my ship will be ready for travel. All I need from you is a little of your computer knowledge." He looked at Linc. "Chandra told me you repaired the system on her ship."

Linc nodded.

"Excellent. Then perhaps you could help me transfer the main processor from Chandra's ship to mine and we'll be on our way."

Linc's stomach dropped to his feet. "We?"

"Yes. Chandra and I are going back to To'Ar."

Chapter 14

He'd heard Darvell say it, but Linc couldn't believe Chandra would actually leave. She looked at him with such love in her eyes. She might not understand the emotion yet, but she still felt it.

Yet she was leaving.

Linc tightened a screw on Darvell's computer console. He had no right to complain or ask anything of Chandra. She'd known him for two days. She'd been a Traveler for years. He couldn't expect her to pick him over the universe.

"How's it going?" Nyle asked as he stepped inside the truck.

"Good. Dwight checked the entire system and everything's working the way Darvell said it's supposed to. Looks like they'll be on their way in a few minutes."

"So she's still going with him?"

"Yeah."

"How do you feel about that?"

"I hurt like hell."

"Tell *her* that."

Linc jiggled the panel to be sure it was tight. "She has to do what's right for her." Slipping the screwdriver in his rear pocket, he faced Nyle. "Why would she choose to stay here and live with a computer nerd instead of traveling to other worlds?"

"First, you're not a computer *nerd*, you're a computer *genius*. Second, she loves you, which is an excellent reason for her to stay."

"I can't compete with the life she'll have when she returns to To'Ar."

Linc jumped down from the truck and went back in the cabin. Chandra looked his way as soon as he walked in the door. He thought he saw longing in her eyes before she quickly turned her gaze back to Darvell.

"You two did a great job," Darvell said to Garry and Dwight. Linc noticed Garry was conscious and standing, even though his eyes looked a bit glazed. "Here's your payment." He handed each of them a thick manila envelope.

Dwight stuck his in his jacket pocket without a glance at the contents. Garry opened his and peered inside. He must have been satisfied with the contents for he nodded once and closed the envelope. "Pleasure doing business with you, Cap."

Linc watched the two men leave the cabin. He couldn't believe Darvell had let them leave, knowing what they knew about the spaceship. "How could you let them go? Aren't you worried they'll run right to some sleazy tabloid and spill the beans about you and Chandra?"

"Not at all. They won't tell anyone anything because they won't remember. As soon as they get half a mile from here, they will completely forget about the ship. All they'll remember is bringing me here to work on a new computer system."

"Well, that's handy," Nyle said. "You won't wipe out our memory too, will you?"

"No. Chandra trusts you, which means I trust you not to betray our confidence." He touched Chandra's shoulder. "Are you ready to leave?"

"Now?" Linc asked. He couldn't let her go, not yet. He had to think of some way to keep her here longer. "It's getting late. Wouldn't you rather get some sleep and leave in the morning?"

"We can sleep on the ship. Once we leave Earth's gravity, I will program the course and the ship will run by itself."

There was nothing else he could do, except stand back and watch Chandra fly off into the heavens...and out of his life forever.

"Will you help me remove the panels on the truck?" Darvell asked.

"Sure," Linc said past the lump in his throat. Chandra still hadn't looked at him, but stood before the fireplace, staring into the flames.

He couldn't let her go without one more kiss.

Linc shrugged out of his jacket, tossed it on the couch, and walked up to Chandra. She continued to stare into the fire. Needing to see those beautiful green eyes again, he placed his hand on her cheek and tried to turn her face toward him. She resisted at first, then he heard a soft sigh escape her lips before she looked at him.

Tears sparkled in her eyes.

"Why are you crying?" he asked softly.

"Be-because I do not want to leave you, and you do not want me to stay."

Her comment was such a shock, Linc couldn't speak for several seconds. "What made you think I don't want you to stay?"

"You helped my Commander complete his ship. You have done everything you can to help me leave. That must mean you do not want me."

"Chandra, I've done everything to help you leave because I thought that's what *you* wanted."

She shook her head. "No. I want to stay with you."

Unable to speak now for the lump in his throat had returned, Linc drew her close. She wrapped her arms around his neck and held on tightly. He could feel her tears against his cheek. "Hey, it's okay," he said, his voice husky. "Don't cry. I want you to stay with me too."

He kissed her tenderly, pouring all his love into the kiss. When he pulled back, there were still tears in Chandra's eyes, but she was smiling.

"Better tell your Commander you aren't going with him."

"I heard," Darvell said. Linc held Chandra's hand for support when they turned to face Darvell. "Are you sure, child? The whole universe waits for you."

"I have everything I want here."

"I can't promise someone could come for you if you change your mind."

"I won't change it. I want to be with Linc."

Darvell stepped closer. "You will become more human as time passes, but that does not mean you will ever be *completely* human." He looked at Linc. "I don't know if she'll ever carry a child. Do you still want her to stay, knowing you may never have children?"

"We'll work it out. If Chandra never gets pregnant and we decide we want children, we'll adopt."

Darvell studied his face, as if he were trying to see right inside Linc's brain. "You care for her that much?"

"I do."

239

His gaze passed between Chandra and Linc. "I believe you do." Darvell reached for her free hand. "I'm sorry you won't be accompanying me, but your happiness is all that matters."

"Thank you, sir."

Darvell kissed her cheek. "So, will you two gentlemen help me with the truck panels now?"

"Sure." Linc squeezed Chandra's hand. "Be right back."

Donning jackets, Linc and Nyle followed Darvell to the truck. They removed the truck's top panel while Darvell made a final check of his ship's system. By the time the side panels had been removed also, Darvell announced he was ready to go.

Linc and Nyle looked at the oval-shaped ship sitting on the bed of the truck. "Quite an idea," Nyle said, "to build a spaceship inside a truck like that. Just remove the panels and you're off to the wild blue yonder."

"Yeah." A movement caught Linc's eye. He watched Chandra step outside the cabin. Motioning for her to come to him, he opened his jacket and let her stand close, her back to his chest.

"Everything is set," Darvell said from the door to his ship. "This is your last chance to change your mind, Chandra."

She shook her head. "I'm happy right here."

"Then I will let your current Commander know you are well. Have a good life, child."

"You too, sir."

"Linc, all the papers to this truck are in the glove compartment. It is yours to do with as you wish. There is also an envelope with the rest of my money. I believe there's close to three hundred thousand. Consider it a dowry from Chandra."

Linc didn't have the chance to respond to that bombshell before the door to the ship closed. A moment later, a low hum came from the ship. Snow began to fall again as the ship slowly rose a few feet from the bed of the truck. The hum became louder. Linc tightened his arms around Chandra. In the blink of an eye, the ship zoomed off and disappeared in the clouds.

"Wow," Nyle whispered.

Chandra shivered. "Regrets?" Linc whispered in her ear.

"No. Just a bit cold."

"Let's go back inside."

"You two go inside," Nyle said. "I'm gonna take off."

"You don't have to leave now. You can sack out on the couch and leave in the morning."

Nyle shook his head. "Nah. I'd rather go home. I'm sure you two want to be alone." He headed toward his SUV. "Give me a holler when you're ready to head to Sac. I'll come back and help you move everything."

"Hey, man, thanks for all your help."

"That's what friends are for." He waved as he opened the door. "Take care of him, Chandra. He's one of the good guys."

"I know."

Linc stood with his arms around Chandra until Nyle's taillights disappeared. "Let's go inside."

As soon as Linc removed his jacket and hung it on the coat tree, he took Chandra into his arms. She held him as tightly as he held her. "I hope you don't regret staying instead of exploring the universe," he whispered into her ear.

"I could never regret staying with you."

Linc pulled back so he could see her face. "I don't have a very exciting life, Chandra, nothing like what you're used to."

"I don't need excitement as long as I have you."

Linc kissed her tenderly. "I love you, Chandra."

"This thing between us is love? It makes my stomach feel funny."

"I'll take that as a compliment." He laid his hand on her tummy. "Do you like the feeling?"

"Very much."

"Good, because I promise you at least fifty years of your tummy feeling funny."

The End

About the author:

Lynn welcomes mail from readers. You can write to her c/o Ellora's Cave Publishing at 1337 Commerce Drive, Suite 13, Stow OH 44224.

Coming Soon from Lynn LaFleur:

Two Men and a Lady

Why an electronic book?

We live in the Information Age—an exciting time in the history of human civilization in which technology rules supreme and continues to progress in leaps and bounds every minute of every hour of every day. For a multitude of reasons, more and more avid literary fans are opting to purchase e-books instead of paperbacks. The question to those not yet initiated to the world of electronic reading is simply: *why?*

1. *Price.* An electronic title at Ellora's Cave Publishing runs anywhere from 40-75% less than the cover price of the <u>exact same title</u> in paperback format. Why? Cold mathematics. It is less expensive to publish an e-book than it is to publish a paperback, so the savings are passed along to the consumer.

2. *Space.* Running out of room to house your paperback books? That is one worry you will never have with electronic novels. For a low one-time cost, you can purchase a handheld computer designed specifically for e-reading purposes. Many e-readers are larger than the average handheld, giving you plenty of screen room. Better yet, hundreds of titles can be stored within your new library—a single microchip. (Please note that Ellora's Cave does not endorse any specific brands. You can check our website at www.ellorascave.com for customer

recommendations we make available to new consumers.)

3. *Mobility.* Because your new library now consists of only a microchip, your entire cache of books can be taken with you wherever you go.

4. *Personal preferences are accounted for.* Are the words you are currently reading too small? Too large? Too...**ANNOYING**? Paperback books cannot be modified according to personal preferences, but e-books can.

5. *Innovation.* The way you read a book is not the only advancement the Information Age has gifted the literary community with. There is also the factor of what you can read. Ellora's Cave Publishing will be introducing a new line of interactive titles that are available in e-book format only.

6. *Instant gratification.* Is it the middle of the night and all the bookstores are closed? Are you tired of waiting days—sometimes weeks—for online and offline bookstores to ship the novels you bought? Ellora's Cave Publishing sells instantaneous downloads 24 hours a day, 7 days a week, 365 days a year. Our e-book delivery system is 100% automated, meaning your order is filled as soon as you pay for it.

Those are a few of the top reasons why electronic novels are displacing paperbacks for many an avid reader. As always, Ellora's Cave Publishing welcomes your questions and comments. We invite you to email us at service@ellorascave.com or write to us directly at: 1337 Commerce Drive, Suite 13, Stow OH 44224.

Printed in the United States
26318LVS00002B/100-111